ZANI

Feathers of a Lion, Book One

CHERIE KONYHA GREENE

For Chad, who once asked me to tell him a story
about a Harlequin. Sorry it took so long.

CONTENTS

1 *Silvio*

Silvio Speronelli slipped away from the tavern girl for the third time and thought about monasteries. Sadly, men of his trade made poor monks. Maìstro Zan Polo Liompardi, the Venetian bufon who had trained Silvio in the art of jesting, was convinced as a point of dogma that all clowns went to Hell.

If it weren't for the rain, they'd all be at Villa Lesse by now instead of shivering in the grubby common room of an inn at Ospetaletto. If it weren't for his patron Ser Carlo Pevari's obsession with Roman comedies, Silvio would be back in Venice, playing the fool for balls and entertainments at the city's great Houses, instead of dodging wenches deep in the Venetian terraferma.

"Don't be shy," said the girl, plumping up her bodice so her breasts seemed ready to burst out of her coarse linen camisa. She had damnably pretty breasts. "Your Venetian friend paid me in advance."

...A nice, quiet abbey on a mountaintop. Maybe a hermit's cave. "Which friend?" Silvio said, talking to keep his lips a moving target. It was probably Ser Antonio, Carlo's brother, who had paid her. Antonio was

1

still in the common room, while Carlo and his wife had already retired. Antonio had sent Silvio to the kitchen to see, he'd said, what was for supper.

Silvio took in a slow breath of heavy, aromatic cooking air. Marjoram, good for the lungs. Rosemary.

"The tall one," she said, hooking a finger through the front laces of Silvio's doublet, tickling his belly through his linen shirt as she closed the gap between their bodies, "Almost as handsome as you." With her other hand she stroked the two days' dark growth on his cheeks.

Silvio felt his pulse thumping like the thick bubbles in the polenta pot. His skin was hungry for the touch of a woman. One of these days he was going to meet one he couldn't say no to, and it would be a bad day for her.

He backed away, and the edge of the cook's work table pressed into his thighs. The girl stretched her face up toward his, blonde waves pouring down her back. It would be so easy not to pull away, to let his lips touch hers. They were so round and red. Maybe this time the breath wouldn't halt in her throat and he wouldn't be left gazing at a pair of bright eyes gone fixed and lifeless.

And maybe asses would fly.

Silvio gently disengaged her finger and retreated from the kitchen. He snatched an empty pitcher from the bar counter and pressed it into her arms. "I only came to say we need more wine." The words had to squeeze their way out of his throat.

He looked around the common room for help and found his brother Piero at the long table with his broad back to the fireplace. Piero's heavy wool cloak steamed as the fire worked to dry it. His mop of black curls hid his face, which was bent over the old rebec fiddle he was re-stringing.

Silvio grabbed Piero by the collar. "Help me," he whispered in their native Bergamàsch, "Antonio's sent another one."

"What do you want me to do about it? I'm married." said Piero, easily shaking off the smaller Silvio. He twisted a tuning peg and plucked the string, listened, twisted some more.

"I think, of all people, *your* wife would understand." It was a cheap laugh, Silvio knew, picking on the man who'd married a former *putana*. Smeraldina was a kind woman and was, by all accounts, completely reformed. Unfair, Silvio chided himself, and unprofessional. His alarm at the encounter with the girl had wiped away the fatigue of the journey and left him to fall back on his training.

Piero pulled a length of catgut from a bag at his side. "This one is your problem."

Across from Piero, the tall, "almost as handsome" Ser Antonio Pevari leaned back with his elbows on the table beside his elegant brown hat, stretching his long legs into the room. The man spoke up, in his native Vèneto. "The *ósto* said supper will be *fasan e farro*—pheasant and wheat polenta." He looked up at Silvio. "Is that right, Silvio?"

Their host spoke the local language, and Antonio's Bergamàsch was terrible. The "pheasant" would turn out to be bean soup, but Silvio wasn't in a mood to correct him.

"Get your own drink," Piero said. "Here's the girl with the pitcher."

She had come up behind Silvio, trapping him between Piero and the fire. Heart pounding, Silvio vaulted away over the table and landed in front of their other Venetian companion, Ser Pantalon Morèr. He was perched on a stool, wrapped in his loose zimara robe and resting an old-fashioned bowl of wine on one mud-spattered knee.

"Watch it!" said Piero, leaning protectively over the rebec.

Since all the other guests in the common room were now staring at him, Silvio bowed, twirling his large, soft hat around and around, letting its momentum drain a little of the panic from his arm. He switched his language to Vèneto.

"Messer Pan-ta-le-on-e Morèr!" he cried, spreading out each long syllable of Morèr's patron saint. *Pantaleone*, the old man was fond of reminding them, meant *all-merciful* in Greek. "Hail, grand high sovereign of worm spittle, most serene mothkeeper of the Most Serene Republic." The hat brushed Morèr's arm and nearly upset the wine bowl. A group of pilgrims at a corner table started clapping.

"Oh, for the love of God, Silvio," said Pantalon, holding his drink protectively above his head and, Silvio noted with professional pride, barely suppressing a smile.

4

Silvio leaned toward Antonio and said, "Remind me to beat you up later." He turned back to Pantalon and dropped to one knee on the gritty floor, playing to his growing audience. The rushes were thin and trampled and pricked him through his woolen hose. "Of your all-merciful heart," he said, "Give a poor Fool a drink." Silvio felt suddenly extremely thirsty. He snatched the bowl from Pantalon's hand and drank from it, then hopped up onto the bench beside Antonio.

"How about you, Siór?" Silvio said to Antonio as he stepped up onto the table, "Buy me a drink?" Antonio pulled his hat out of the way.

Piero said, "For the love of God, Silvio!" He gathered the half-strung instrument to his broad chest. A loose length of catgut whipped Silvio's ankles.

"I'll only buy your drink if you call me Toni," said Antonio.

"Not a chance, Siór." Silvio turned to face Pantalon, who was rounding the end of the table in pursuit of his wine. "Sorry, Pantalon, it will have to be you." He stepped down onto the bench beside Piero. "The *nobili* can't afford me." It was the one game Silvio could usually get Pantalon to play with him—reminding the high-born but less wealthy Patricians how much they needed investment from House Morèr.

Pantalon was up on the bench now, reaching for the bowl. "Get your own drink, mooncalf. The girl's right there."

"Only if you're paying for it." Silvio slid off Piero's bench and under the table. He resurfaced on the other side and raised the unspilled bowl to toast the cheering pilgrims. He could hear Pantalon laughing behind him from the top of the table.

Pantalon said, "All right, Silvio, I'll buy you a whole pitcher if you'll sit down."

Another group of wet travelers came through the door from the street. Silvio raised a toast to them, but then he realized Pantalon had stopped laughing.

Silvio turned. Pantalon's face had turned a flustered shade of red, like a child caught pilfering sweets, his dark eyes wide. He was staring at the newcomers the way one might stare at an angry viper. Silvio handed the bowl up to him, but Pantalon seemed to have forgotten both it and the table he was standing on.

A young lady in a fur-lined cloak led the trio. She took this off and shook it, showering the floor and revealing a rust-colored woolen riding gown of fine cloth but unfashionable cut. Her hair was mostly covered by a loose-fitting, embroidered snood, but a few honey-colored curls escaped to frame a pair of large, engaging gray-green eyes and a nose that was just a little too large for the delicate chin.

Her companions were dressed like prosperous farmers, a serious, gray-bearded man and a round-cheeked woman with smile wrinkles around her eyes. She stood with one hand resting protectively on the young lady's shoulder. None of them looked impressive enough to frighten a man like Morèr.

The farmer made a sign behind him, and two of the inn's porters brought in a modest-sized clothes trunk.

They set it down on the table beside Pantalon's feet.

The young lady looked up at Pantalon without blinking, as if tavern tabletops were perfectly ordinary places to find rich Venetians. Her chest rose and fell in several shallow breaths before she managed to say, "*Salve*, Siór."

Pantalon stepped down from the table, and Silvio had to admire how he managed to look dignified doing this. When he was safely on the floor, Pantalon spared only a brief glance for the young lady before turning to speak to the farmer. In a voice he might have used to address a Doge, he said, "*Bonaséra,* Giorgio. Francesca. To what do I owe this—unexpected pleasure?"

Silvio felt Antonio's sharp elbow prod his ankle, and he realized he was still standing up on the bench. He silently dropped to a seat. The tavern girl brushed his shoulder with her bosom as she placed a wine bowl in front of him. Piero quietly laid his rebec back down on the table and wound the loose string around the tuning peg.

The old farmer gave a stiff bow and said, "Siór, if you permit me to remind you, you said you would come to Moniga last June." Vèneto was clearly not the man's native tongue, but he spoke it well enough.

"A few months more or less could hardly have mattered," Pantalon said.

"*Last* June," the young lady said, stepping in front of Giorgio. "Fifteen hundred and *seventeen*." There was a tightly controlled tremor in her voice. She glanced briefly at the ground, then returned her gaze to Pantalon, who went on steadfastly not looking at her in exactly the way Silvio was not looking at the girl with the pitcher.

"What were you thinking, Giorgio?" Pantalon said, "Dragging a lady across the countryside like this?"

"In fact, Siór," Giorgio said, "She dragged us."

"I told you I'd come for her," said Pantalon.

The young lady said, "Siór, as it has never been convenient for you to visit your own villa, I've saved you the trip." Her green eyes flashed. Her Vèneto was fluent but practiced, with traces of a country accent.

Silvio was surprised to learn that Ser Pantalon had a villa at Moniga. They'd been only a few miles from there, not three days ago. Silvio looked questioningly at Antonio, who shrugged. Clearly Morèr was expected to know this girl. Had someone finally found him a new wife? Piero looked up from his rebec with a tiny smirk, gone before Silvio could be sure it had been there. He held the neck close to his ear and plucked the new string quietly.

"Francesca," said Pantalon, now to the old woman, "I expected better sense from you."

"Giorgio is right," said the young lady. "This was my idea." She turned to the farmer. "You may go now, Giorgio. That last hatching of my worms was about ready to spin. You'll know which moth to spare. Francesca..." She cleared her throat. "*Néna*," she said—*nurse* in Bergamàsch—and turned to face the old woman.

The nurse held her mouth taut and said, "Courage,

colonbin." *Pigeon* must have been a pet name between them. The lady's eyes grew watery, her cheeks flushed.

The farmer turned to leave. Silvio pretended to gaze at his wine bowl. Piero pretended to listen closely to the new string. Only Antonio was watching the exchange without pretending to mind his own business, but he was Venetian. Silvio had learned after six years in the city that Venetians considered everything their business.

The nurse embraced the lady, said, in Bergamàsch, "God be with you, Sciora," and pulled away with a small curtsy. That honorific—*my lady*—along with a formal *you,* produced a dramatic effect. The young woman straightened her back, took one deep, shuddering breath and turned to Pantalon with a face like stone, like the mask of a queen. Silvio saw the nurse blink hard as she turned away and followed Giorgio out the door.

Pantalon briefly looked the newcomer up and down and returned to his stool without a word. He drained what was left in his wine bowl and signaled the tavern girl for a refill, eyes fixed on the tabletop. No one said anything. Pantalon ought to speak first, since the lady had clearly been left in his charge. Silvio watched him gulp down another bowlful in silence while the lady stood with her arms crossed around her dripping cloak, now unconsciously chewing on her upper lip.

The innkeeper entered in a cloud of steam with the cook at his heels. They dished out the evening meal, which turned out to be barley (*far*) polenta with bean (*fasa*) soup, along with fried cheese and two more pitchers of extra strong wine.

The lady was still standing there waiting for Pantalon to look at her. Silvio passed a bowl of soup to Antonio and said, "Have some pheasant, Toni."

"You knew," said Antonio.

Silvio nodded.

Antonio said, "Is that how I get you to call me Toni, by failing at your language?"

"Maybe, *Siór.*" Silvio put a very slight emphasis on the honorific. Antonio kicked him under the table.

Pantalon still hadn't said anything. While he had Antonio's eye, Silvio cocked his head very slightly toward the young lady. If Pantalon wouldn't talk to her, it should at least it should be someone of her rank. But Antonio only shrugged and looked at Pantalon.

As the food was passed around and the guests at the other tables settled in to eat it, the poor girl looked absurdly forlorn. Even the pilgrims had lost interest. At last Silvio couldn't bear it. Someone had to say something to her.

"Dama," Silvio said, rising to his feet, "Have you eaten?" It was perhaps an idiotic way to start a conversation, but it was a start.

"No, we—*ehm*..." the lady stammered, her eyes darting between him and Pantalon. Evidently she also wondered why it was this unknown commoner who had spoken first.

"Have a seat, then," Piero said. "Piero Speronelli, fiddler, at your service, and this clown is my little brother,

Salvàn Mandragora, but his friends call him Silvio because that's his real name." He put a wedge of polenta on the trencher nearest to the lady and covered it with soup. She eyed Piero warily, as if he might be mad.

Silvio said, "Don't listen to him, Dama. I never do." He took away her wet cloak and motioned her to a spot on the bench, between himself and Pantalon. "I'm Silvio, he's Piero, this is el Siór Antonio Pevari."

Antonio rose halfway to his feet, said "Toni, please," and sat back down.

Silvio said, "Ser Antonio has a brother, but he's having a quiet dinner with his wife somewhere upstairs."

"Carlo and Betì," said Piero. "Our patrons. They like to disappear together after dragging us to inns in the middle of nowhere."

Silvio looked at Pantalon and said, "That quiet gentleman at the end of the table is Ser Pantalon Morèr, an eminent and respected silk dealer who has evidently mislaid either his manners or his tongue." Silvio spread la Dama's cloak over a barrel near the fireplace and sat down across from her. "What do they call you?"

"Oriela," she said with another glance toward Morèr. Silvio realized he had just forced a lady to introduce herself, and to a man below her station. Still, it was kinder than letting her stand there dripping until Pantalon retrieved his wits from whatever corner of the moon they'd flown off to.

Silvio pushed a bowl of wine toward her. "You'd better drink that," he said.

She raised it and took a long swallow, and then almost choked on it when Piero grinned and said, "You're going to need it." So he also thought the lady must be Pantalon's bride. Silvio bit his tongue to keep from laughing.

The innkeeper returned to ask if the lady would be needing a room. Not knowing *whose* lady she might be, he spoke to the whole table, rocking uneasily from one foot to the other.

"Put her in my room," Pantalon said quietly.

Their host raised his eyebrows for a moment, then masked his surprise and said, "As you wish, Siór." He moved away, whispering to the cook.

"Just like that?" Piero asked, "No procession? No banquet?"

Silvio said, "At least let us drink your healths."

"And tuck you in," said Piero.

"Filthy-minded cretins!" said Pantalon. Then he turned to Ser Antonio. "Siór, allow me to present la Dama Oriela Morèr. My daughter."

2 Pantalon

Pantalon Morèr took another look at this stranger who was his child, seated primly on the edge of the sagging bed she was probably expecting to have to share with him. Leaning a bit forward, her hands clasped tightly together on her knees, the girl studied him with eyes the color of the Lagoon. She certainly looked like a Morèr, with those high, unyielding eyebrows and—it must be admitted—that unfortunate nose. Poor girl, he thought. A pity she couldn't have resembled her *nobila* mother. At least she had the green eyes and deep, golden hair of a patrician, marks of a heritage older and more powerful than his own. The stray ringlets had fallen around Margarita's face in just that same way, like thin trails of honey drizzling from a spoon.

Pantalon turned quickly away from the sight and started pacing again, his loose zimara trailing behind him, velvet slippers scuffing a path through the floor rushes. Halfway across the small room, he turned to face her, still avoiding her eyes. "I suppose I'll have to drop everything and take you to Venice."

Oriela looked up and drew in a breath and said, "Sió̱r

—"

"Unless you'd rather go back to the lake," he said, "I'm sure you've got friends there."

"Not really—" she said.

He paced away toward the fireplace, talking over her. "You don't know anyone in Venice. You'll feel out of place."

"I've felt out of place all my life," Oriela said. He halted, stared. She said, "Siór, please don't abandon me again!" She was talking faster now, as if she had rehearsed this part. "For as long as I can remember, Francesca and Giorgio said that when I reached my sixteenth year, which I did last year, my father would come to fetch me and my exile would end—"

"Exile?" He cocked one eyebrow to show he thought it an overblown choice of words, although he knew it to be accurate.

"—But you didn't come, and then Giorgio told me you were at Desenzano, and he invited you to the villa but you still wouldn't come, not even to check on the worms."

Pantalon studied her face. Her eyes were reddening, growing moist. Could she have missed a father she'd never met? He said, "You must understand, there was the war. I was away on my galley. Did you know I commanded my own galley?"

"The war ended two years ago, Siór."

"It sank," he said. Talking about ships calmed his nerves. "At Agnadello. But the new one has already been launched from the Arsenale. You should see her! Three oars to a bench, masts as high as a church tower. The ramming prow is like a huge, bronze lance, and, well…" Enough. He was letting himself lose his point. He said, "Everyone is at least as busy after a war as they are during it." He advanced toward the bed again. She had to understand this. "There are new ships to build, oarsmen to hire, towns to restore, in fact that's what brought us all out to the terraferma at this time of year. The towns. We're going to fix Brescia."

"How?" she said. She was looking at him with less timidity and more interest.

"The Scòla di Santa Margarita, my confraternity —I'm the vice chancellor—asked the Conpàgna degli Alati—Carlo and Antonio's stocking club—to put together some entertainments to benefit Brescian foundlings. Next thing I know Carlo's talked me into a mask, his brother's brought along his pet clown, and, well…" He tried to interpret her blank look. "You see," he said, "Venice is very boring."

"No," she said. "It sounds fascinating."

"I would have come for you…soon…" He had to walk away to say this; he wasn't at all certain it was the truth.

"When?" she said. "Next summer? The one after that?" Her words came out low and sharp now, like small daggers at his back. "Maybe you were waiting until my mother was raised from the dead."

He whirled around and charged at her, the zimara's broad sleeves billowing out like sails. Oriela's head recoiled slightly, but he knew the sagging mattress would force her to hold her position or else tumble backward.

"*Mi dispiàse,*" *I'm sorry*, she whispered, "Pa--Siòr." Pantalon didn't move. She said, "I wouldn't have to be a bother. I'll stay out of the way. I'll even make myself useful. I can spin, and sew... I made this gown myself."

Pantalon stepped back, looked at the outmoded riding dress and repressed a snort of amusement. "You're not thinking clearly, Oriela," he said, her name falling clumsily from his lips after seventeen years unspoken. "You'll be bored, riding all day. There's the dust, the mud, no shelter but that teeth-rattling wagon, a different bed every night. We're still headed west, going all the way out to Bergamo before we turn back for home. You can't possibly have enough clothes in that little box, and it's not as though you're likely to meet any suitable gentlemen." He took a breath and forced himself to calm his voice, to find the arguments that would persuade a young woman. "Your horse can't come with us to the city. Why not wait by the lake, in peace and quiet, with Francesca and Giorgio and your own room, until I find you a good husband?"

He ventured a look at her face, to see if his cajoling had started to work. What he saw there instead was an uncanny mirror. Unmoved and immovable, she might have been stating her final offer for a bale of raw filament.

"I came this far without a wagon," she said coolly, "And it rained for three days."

"Go to bed," he said, turning toward the door, pretending he hadn't been defeated. "We'll discuss it in the morning." They wouldn't, of course. She had cleverly left him with no practical choice and so would have to come along at least as far as Villa Lesse. Pulling his zimara closed across his chest, he withdrew from the battlefield and shut the door behind him. He would sleep on a bench in the common room.

3 Oriela

Oriela found her father the next morning looking rumpled and weary, hunched over his porridge and beer with half-closed, puffy eyes. She wanted to thank him for giving her the bed, but his glance toward her looked so sour and bewildered that instead she sat far down the table from him and tried to be invisible.

She was distracted from this effort by the appearance a moment later of a lady so elegant that she seemed unreal in the rustic surroundings. The woman wore a blue gown of the latest cut, with generous sleeves and a velvet bodice, her thick auburn hair woven tidily into a ribbon-and-braid arrangement that would have taken Oriela all morning to produce. Realizing she hadn't even combed hers, Oriela tightened her kerchief and went back to trying not to be noticed.

Silvio Speronelli seemed to appear out of nowhere to sit beside Oriela and point to the lady. "La Dama Elisabeta," he whispered, "And that's Ser Carlo behind her."

The fair-haired man Silvio called his patron was

also unexpectedly well turned-out, in a green brocade doublet and a pair of pale blue hose completely and improbably devoid of mud. The pair were the only people in the common room who didn't look as though they'd woken up in a strange bed and stuffed themselves back into half-damp clothes. Oriela turned to say so to Silvio, but he had vanished as instantly and mysteriously as he had arrived. The next she saw him, he and his brother Piero were going out the courtyard door.

Out in the inn's courtyard, the rain had given way to steamy October sunlight. Oriela's little bay palfrey Stelina emerged from the stable looking fresher than she had since they left the villa. Three days of plodding with her head down, her hoofs making a sucking sound with each step along the muddy highroad, were erased by a single night in a warm stable. If only humans were so easily restored. Oriela was watching her father warily as he adjusted the saddle on his tall, black Spanish horse, muttering, "Stand still, Moro, you great savage."

She had noted the huge, canvas-topped wagon parked not-quite-inside the carriage house, but she was surprised when the stable boys rolled it out and attached it to a heavy team, one roan and one chestnut. She was even more surprised when the big fiddler Piero climbed up onto the driving box and took the reins. The tent-like canvas top was decorated with the image of some wild beast. Words in Vèneto were painted on the wooden sideboard: *Le Pene del Lión*.

Oriela had never seen a lion, but she was fairly sure they didn't usually have feathers. The creature on the wagon had a thick, catlike body but also sported a pair of splendid birds' wings.

Once the wagon had (only just) cleared the inn-yard gate, Silvio hopped up onto the box beside Piero. La Dama Elisabeta and Ser Antonio came out by the street door, La Dama saying, "*Andiam.* Mamma probably has the footmen standing at the gate already." Oriela was struck by the lilting sibilance of native Venetian voices. She had been too busy arguing with her father the night before to pay attention to the delicate, watery beauty of a language she only knew from her tutor.

Antonio helped Elisabeta into the wagon before climbing in himself. Ser Carlo, Oriela and her father followed on horseback, picking their way over still-slick cobblestones through the narrow streets of Ospitaletto. Oriela realized she hadn't asked anyone where they were going, but it mattered little so long as her father wasn't sending her back to Villa Morèr.

Once they were past the town gate and on the open road, the sun pressed down on Oriela's neck. She rode quietly between El Moro and Ser Carlo's fine sorrel Spanish mare. Stelina was the first of the two gifts her father had sent her during her exile. The other was enough Ca' Morèr silk for a single dress. She had sewn it with room to grow and had been letting it out year by year since she was twelve.

The dress was now folded carefully into the wooden box Giorgio had left on the table the night before and which had by the occult work of the inn's staff found its way into the wagon. Her everyday clothes, including this heavy riding dress, were made from whatever cloth Giorgio could buy in Desenzano out of his own salary.

The man on the black horse beside her was as silent as the portrait that hung in the central hall of the villa. Until last night, Pantalon had been to her no more than a painted face, a cipher on the wall in a Venetian gentleman's *tóga*. One couldn't tell from the plain black gown that he was only a Citizen. *Citadini,* she knew, wore the same public uniform as the ancient patrician families, giving the illusion that all men of means were equal in the Most Serene Republic—except, of course, that only the patrician *nobili* could vote.

Oriela took a sip from the warm water skin. The unseasonable warmth, combined with the sticky feeling of clothes that hadn't quite dried overnight, soured her stomach and dulled her wits. When they paused to rest, she tied Stelina's reins to the back of the wagon and tried sitting inside, but the cover blocked the breeze as thoroughly as it did the sun.

The only seat was a bench that ran along part of one of the inside walls, and there Dama Elisabeta sat with flawless poise while Ser Antonio and Silvio, who had now moved into the shade, made shift with trunks or with stacked rolls of curiously-painted canvas. She rearranged her skirt to make room for Oriela. After bumping along in silence for a few minutes, Oriela asked Ser Antonio what he was resting his feet on, he said, "My brother's house."

Giorgio had said something about Pantalon traveling with a band of players, that he had fled—that was Giorgio's word—in a mountebank's wagon after the farm manager met up with his *patró* in Desenzano a week ago. The conversation had reportedly gone something like this:

El Siór Pantalon said, "How is Francesca? How are the boys? And how are the worms?"

And Giorgio said, "All well, thank you, and la Dama Oriela is also well. She's seventeen now, by the way, and taller than my wife."

To which el Siór had replied, "*Sì sì,* and what of the new mulberry saplings?" And with that, he'd paid the wine merchant and left. Hearing that her father was so nearby and yet refused even to visit, Oriela had started packing her things within the hour.

Dama Elisabeta thrust one dainty foot forward and prodded Ser Antonio, who slapped himself on the head and said, "I'm sorry, I must have left my manners in my room. Dama Oriela Morèr, may I present Dama Elisabeta Lesse."

Oriela had the awkward sensation that she ought to stand up in order to curtsy, but La Dama turned a suddenly warm smile toward her and started to ask polite questions about making silk. Elisabeta had apparently learned a bit about Oriela already, to know that this was a topic they could discuss.

Oriela told how the women carried packets of moth eggs inside their bodices, the young worms tickling them through the cloth as they hatched. La Dama pitied the creatures that had to die in their cocoons, "never to fly." Oriela pointed out, hoping she sounded as pragmatic as Francesca, that the moths would destroy the thread if they broke free of the cocoons, and that silk moths' wings are too small for flying in any case.

"Have you ever seen a cocoon?" Oriela asked. Elisabeta shook her head. Oriela pulled on the silk cord around her neck and brought out a tiny purse from under her dress. It contained a single cocoon. She held it out for La Dama to examine, a fleecy white egg the size of a child's thumb.

"Is there a dead worm in there?" Elisabeta said, recoiling. "How can you carry such a dreadful thing?"

"It's not dreadful," said Oriela, thinking just the opposite, "It's perfect." It was perfect, a specimen really too fine not to be soaked and unreeled. Yet Giorgio had let her keep it because it was from her first hatching. She had warmed the tiny eggs between her then-small breasts, plucked the new mulberry leaves to feed and fatten the caterpillars, and brought in twigs for them when they began to fast and spin. She had wept when Giorgio put the cocoons in the oven.

The ladies lapsed into silence, and Silvio pulled a soprano *flauto dolse* from somewhere inside his clothes. He started piping a plaintive melody that wandered slowly up and down the scale, never quite deciding whether it was in Dorian mode or Hypodorian. Every time it sounded like the tune was approaching a cadence, it turned away, resolution always near but never reached. It was a song designed to go on all day if it had to, but at last it settled, more or less, on a sustained *ré.*

Oriela patted the cocoon under her camisa. Francesca had sewn the pouch for her, saying, "Soon you'll be a great lady and forget all about us. This will help you remember." Oriela doubted her nurse would be as lonely as she was pretending. Though Francesca's own sons were married, Mario brought the grandchildren around to the villa almost every day. Mario, who still called Oriela *la maledeta*, the accursed, like it was an old joke between them. It was also he who had told her, when she was six, that she wasn't his real sister but a high-born cuckoo, left there by her rich father to share their bread.

She would miss Francesca, but she had no nostalgia for the other children who called her *Dama* in mocking voices, who squealed and ran when she entered the cocoon shed, pretending to be afraid of the girl with the curse who never went to Mass. Nor would she miss the farmhands who fell silent when she entered a room, casting pitying glances and whispering when her back was turned. No one had ever explained to her why or how she had come to be *maledeta*, but they all made it clear that she was.

At their next pause, Ser Carlo pulled Silvio aside, called for Piero to get out his rebec, and had them start again with the tune Silvio had been playing in the wagon. Carlo struck a pose and began to declaim a flowery complaint about a lady whose face he couldn't see. He could as well have been reciting noun declensions. The hypnotic power of the scene was in that recorder melody.

When Carlo finished his speech and Silvio held the *ré*, Piero started playing a fifth above on the rebec and launched into a wild Saltarello dance. The beat was so infectious that Oriela found herself skipping, even though she didn't know the steps.

Oriela got back on her horse for the next leg of the trip. She was still humming Piero's Saltarello when they passed the southern tip of Lake Iseo and crossed the wide mouth of the Oglio at Sarnico with the setting sun in their eyes. Here they left the highroad and climbed a winding path to Villa Lesse where, according to Silvio, Dama Elisabeta's mother held court through the summer and fall. Beyond the high iron gate was a flight of stone steps that led up from a wide lawn to a garden terrace. The house must be even further uphill.

As soon as they were through the gate, a red-haired woman in green India silk, tall and stately as an elm tree, received cheek kisses from Ser Carlo, embraced Dama Elisabeta, and then said, "Betì, who's your friend?"

When Oriela's father introduced her to their hostess, la Dama Donata Mosto, Oriela realized this was the first she'd heard his voice all day, apart from when he spoke to his horse.

"Your daughter!" Dama Donata said, "Pantalon, my dear, *where* have you been—" She interrupted herself and called out, "Toni, have your *zani* take the wagon down to the south lawn." She nodded toward Piero and Silvio.

Elisabeta said, "Mamma, they're not *zani*." Her voice was tight with patience.

Dama Donata didn't seem to hear this, turning back to Oriela's father to finish, "—been hiding her?" She took his arm and marched him up the stairs to the house.

Dama Elisabeta led Oriela indoors and through the wide, central hall—a *portego* vast enough to house a Doge's ball—to an adjoining bedchamber, where she ordered a bath prepared and sent word to the kitchen to have their supper brought to the room.

The curtained bed was built into the wall like an elevated box or a cushioned cupboard. Over it was a small mezzanine with another mattress, which had probably served as the nurse's quarters when Elisabeta was a child. Wooden chests, some painted with country scenes, some with carpets on their lids, were ranged around the paneled walls, and a small table with a washbasin stood in one corner.

Two men brought in a deep, copper bathtub. They were followed by a procession of women with buckets. When the bath was filled, a maid helped the ladies undress. Another woman came in to collect the linen for washing; a third brought a tray with something fragrant steaming in two cups.

Oriela had never seen so many servants in one house before. They worked with such brisk efficiency that Oriela didn't have time to feel uncomfortable about standing naked in a room full of strangers. Soon she and Elisabeta were seated companionably in the water, and it felt delicious after four days on the road.

Dama Elisabeta said, "Mamma is terribly curious about you. She wants you to join us for dinner today, but you don't have to, since you're not feeling well."

"I feel fine now, Dama."

"You're wilted as a day-old petunia. We'll have a private table in here. And don't call me *Dama*. Meeting Mamma for the first time requires a good deal of strength as well as a fashionable dress, and you don't have either right now." Oriela started to protest, but Elisabeta said, "*Bemìo*, I'm not sure I have the strength." She dunked her head under the water, and said, when she came up, "Especially when you're the long-lost daughter of a man she dislikes. Besides, she's got Queen Truci here."

"Queen who?"

While a woman rubbed white olive oil soap on Elisabeta's head, la Dama told the history of Caterucia Canal, whose husband was sent to govern the island of Corfu. He'd told the Senate he'd only go if they gave him the title of king, so they did. When he was assassinated, his queen had to come home, where she retained her title and retired happily to her villa at Asolo. She was making the rounds of her friends' houses now, since the Emperor had taken Asolo in the long war that finally had ended the year before.

While Elisabeta talked, someone brought a board and rested it across the top of the tub, and they dined on poached whitefish with mushrooms and leeks while sitting in the bath.

Elisabeta said, "Mamma wants the Feathers to put on a play tomorrow."

Oriela had been wondering about the name on the wagon. She said, "Is that what Silvio and Piero call their act?"

Elisabeta said, "It's what Carlo calls all of us. He's obsessed with comedies." She said this with such near-giggling fondness that it was impossible to imagine she disapproved of her husband's obsession.

They soaked for a few minutes. Oriela thought of something else she'd been wondering about. "Why did Dama Donata call Piero and Silvio 'Zani'? Isn't their name Speronelli?"

"Because they're from Bergamo, and they're not *nobili*." Water swirled around Elisabeta's hand as it made a gesture of annoyance. "It's not just a name, it's also an epithet for vagabonds from the terraferma who come to Venice and do odd jobs."

"I'm not *nobila*, either," said Oriela. It was confusing being a *citadina*. A Citizen was in most ways equal to a Patrician, answering to the same titles and wearing the same *tóga*. Yet Oriela couldn't shake the feeling that she ought to address Elisabeta as her superior. She'd been avoiding second-person so as not to have to choose a formal or familiar *you.*

"No, you're not," said Elisabeta, using the familiar *te.* "And yet here you are in my bath while our friends get a room in the attic."

An hour later, their wet hair was combed and Elisabeta was braiding Oriela's. She said, "I can't believe you lived just across the lake all these years and never came over to Sirmione."

"What's at Sirmione?" Oriela said.

"Villa Pevari. Your father's closest friends." Elisabeta's voice hardened, and she pulled at the braid she was working on Oriela's head. "Ca' Morèr is practically a wing of Ca' Pevari."

Only a family's main headquarters in the city was called by the prefix *Ca'*—House. So la Dama and Oriela's father must be neighbors. "Uncle Pantalon dines with us more often than he does at home." Elisabeta tied off the braid at the back of Oriela's head while Oriela boggled at hearing this grand lady call her father *uncle*.

Elisabeta said, "I can't imagine what he was thinking. You're raised by peasants, you speak Vèneto like a *zani*, you've got no decent clothes—and him the very Doge of the silk trade!"

Oriela's mind hooked itself onto the one part of all this that she had an answer for. "I have a good dress in my trunk. He sent me a lovely bolt of brocade once."

"One dress." Elisabeta sniffed, "And you've let the hem down how many times?"

The hair finished, Elisabeta sent the maid to rifle one of the clothes chests and opened the other herself. Hoofbeats on the path below lured Oriela to the open window. Several armed men on horseback clattered through the front gate, followed by two carriages.

"That's Duke Bentivoglio," Elisabeta said, coming to stand beside her, "Formerly of Bologna. Mamma is fond of him. There will be a banquet tomorrow." A duke. What could Oriela Morèr, dressed in rags and talking like a *zani*, possibly have to say to a duke?

"This is a little long," Elisabeta said, "But the color will suit you." She turned and held up a rose-colored, side-laced organdy silk bodice with a matching skirt. A pair of slashed sleeves in gold-chased velvet completed the ensemble. "And that camisa has to go. Maria?"

The maid untied the neck of Oriela's shift while Elisabeta rummaged in the other chest and brought out a lace-trimmed wonder in the whitest, most translucent linen Oriela had ever seen.

The clothes were truly beautiful, and Oriela tried hard to smile when she thanked La Dama, but it would be hard to call her *tu* and *Betì* while wearing her ladyship's old gown.

4 *Tree*

S ilvio pulled his head out of the fountain in the upper terrace garden and let the water stream down his loose shirt. It dripped onto his bare feet and spattered the moonlit paving stones like sprinkled holy water.

No matter what Elisabeta said, Dama Donata seemed determined to look upon the Speronelli brothers as some species of servant. She had assigned them a stifling little room in the attic, about the size of the one they'd shared as boys. Piero coped by stripping down, lying on the cool terrazzo floor and snoring like a trombone. Silvio had abandoned the bed, wearing only his shirt, and escaped both noise and heat by climbing out the window, over the veranda roof and into the garden.

He dunked his head into the fountain again. This time when he came up he heard a woman's voice coming from the door to Dama Donata's airy sitting room. Two liveried youths emerged bearing lanterns.

"...*silly* of me to be so surprised," Donata was saying. "Of course she had to be *somewhere* all these years. But he *never* talked about her, and all his friends thought the child had simply *vanished* from the earth." Carlo and Antonio emerged in her wake. Morèr wasn't with them. A small, fluffy-looking old lady was arm in arm with Donata.

Silvio looked around for a hiding place. A twisted willow tree with wide branches stood between a pair of stone benches. Launching off one bench, Silvio took hold of the lowest limb and swung himself up as soundlessly as a cat—until his bare foot landed on a broken twig. Before he could bite back the curse, it was halfway out of his mouth, making a sound like a stifled goose. Donata looked toward Silvio's tree.

To turn her eyes away, Carlo pointed to the sky, saying, "There it goes."

"There what goes?" said la Dama.

"A great duck. It just flew away." Silvio swallowed back a laugh, grateful that la Dama's hearing was not as keen as Carlo's.

Antonio said, "She vanished? When?"

Donata said, "Right after the Christening, if you can call it that. Iacopo was to stand as her godfather. There were two godfathers, I think. The other was..." After carefully testing the branch with his naked toe, Silvio settled down near the trunk. Donata went on, "...who was related on his mother's side to my own great-uncle Claudio, or was it Oratio? Let's see, Claudio was Mario's father, who was second cousin to..."

The group had arrived at the stone benches, and Donata sat down, her tongue never slowing. Silvio wished he could disappear into the tree, the way his mother the *fata* would do. Some faerie talents could be useful.

The servants with the lanterns took up positions to illuminate the conversation. This came to a momentary halt when Donata, having talked herself into a dense corner of relatives, said, "Where was I?"

"The Christening," said the fluffy lady. She dusted the bench with her handkerchief before sitting down beside Donata.

"Of course you know she was *stolen*," Donata said. She paused to allow her audience to express proper astonishment. "You *don't*? I'd better go back a little. Poor Margarita was at the farm when she had her, with some *peasant* midwife, and she died. Margarita was *nobile*, you know. Ca' Condulmer, can you *imagine*?" Another pause while they imagined. "Well, you won't believe me, but Pantalon was actually *charming* back then, and Margarita was the fourth daughter of a rather *undistinguished* branch of the family. Her grandfather lost his fortune trying to keep the Turks off some little island, one of those Greek places with too many syllables—"

Silvio realized he'd been leaning forward to listen when a drop of water fell off his hair and landed on Donata's shoulder. La Dama looked up.

"What happened to Margarita?" Antonio recalled Donata's attention before she saw Silvio.

"I told you, she *died.* And the next day, the baby *disappeared*. Pantalon sent men out all over the countryside, and after a fortnight or so, they found her. Right out in an open field. At any rate," Donata patted Carlo's knee confidentially, "They found a *baby*, and Pantalon thought it was his. I'll admit I had my doubts at the time. A baby in the middle of a field might be *anyone's*. But now I see her, well—that's his nose, for certain."

"I'm sure a father can tell his own child from any number of random babies," Antonio said.

"Trust me," Carlo said, "They all look alike at that age." Carlo had three. "But Pantalon believed it?"

"He seemed to," la Dama said. "He sent for the godparents, and we all met at the Duomo in Desenzano. But Pantalon was terribly *nervous*."

"Nothing unusual about that," Antonio said.

"I don't mean the *regular* kind of nervous, that someone would drop the baby or it would spit up on the priest's vestments," Donata said. "Pantalon Morèr looked like a heretic facing the *Inquisition*." Silvio had time to feel the full, chilling effect of this image before she continued. "Iacopo was carrying her to the font, and she started fussing. Which they *do*, you know. No one was surprised but Pantalon. He looked like *he* might be the one to be sick on the vestments.

"When the priest touched her, she let out a howl that would curdle milk three farms away. Padre Marco has had dozens of babies scream at him. He scooped her up, noise and all, and held her over the water, and then he dipped his hand in, but he never got past '*In Nomine*'. All of a sudden Pantalon charged up the steps to the font, grabbed the baby, and practically *ran* out the door, like the devil was at his heels. The next day, he left her with the couple who manage the villa and took off for Venice, and that's the last any of us saw of her until now."

Her listeners sat in silence for a few minutes, contemplating the strange tale. A cricket started fiddling. Silvio recalled Morèr's stricken expression when Oriela had appeared at the inn. Was the man as frightened now as he had been back then? Frightened of what?

5 Basso

When Silvio and Piero went looking for breakfast, the kitchen was a scene of pandemonium. La Dama had changed the dinner menu several times before deciding on the most complicated of them all, and she wanted it served in the garden. Everyone who didn't have immediate duties was conscripted by the frantic cook to turn spits, stir pots and chop vegetables.

It was another two hours before they escaped, only to be pulled into a room full of music stands by a gray-haired man with a large bundle of papers tucked under one arm and a tenor *flauto dolse* in the other hand. He said, "Your master said you two are musicians. Why are you wasting time in the kitchen?"

Piero started to say, "We were wondering the same thing," and Silvio began, "He isn't actually our—" but the old *maìstro* took no notice of either.

"The treble and basso *flautisti* both have fevers. Can you learn these by tonight?" He pressed a stack of paper into each brother's hands. "Good," he said without waiting for an answer. "You can practice in here.

Maria will find you something to wear." He departed abruptly.

Silvio fingered the edges of his stack with a frown. He didn't mind playing his treble with a consort, but he wasn't fond of standing in one place for hours. "I don't suppose they'd let me juggle something instead."

Piero said, "You could always play from the top of the tree." Who had told him about the tree? Probably Antonio. It was always Antonio. Piero said, "I didn't have time to tell him I don't play the bass recorder."

The maìstro returned as suddenly as he had left, and said to Piero, "There's a viola da gamba behind the harpsichord," and then was gone again, *subito*.

Silvio said, "Dama Donata thinks we're *zani*."

"Aren't we?" Piero said. He pulled out the viola da gamba and dusted it off. It would need tuning. "We moved to Venice to find work, didn't we?"

Silvio said, "We moved to Venice because it was as far away from Clarissa's father as I could get without learning to row."

As servants in green Ca' Lesse livery lit garden lanterns, the two new recruits took their places among the musicians. Piero sat in the front row and gently adjusted the pegs of the neglected viola da gamba, struggling to bring it up to pitch without breaking one of the long strings.

Standing behind him, Silvio looked through the stack of sheet music. He pulled out a page, frowned, then leaned close to Piero and whispered, "Do you think you should play this one while they're eating?" It was a Pavana, a slow dance.

Piero glanced at it. "I have to play. I'm the *basso*." He went back to his tuning, trying as usual to pretend he had no idea what happened when he played. It was one thing in an open piazza, but guests dancing involuntarily at the dinner table were sure to be noticed. This was Piero's legacy from Mamma's side of the family, just like Silvio's lethal kiss. It had first appeared the year Piero had left the choir school, no longer a soprano but not yet reliably baritone.

Mamma hadn't remarked on it, as if this was something that happened to all fiddlers at that age. Maybe she thought it was. It was a common enough power among her people. It was only when Silvio's difficulty arose around the same age that la Fata Viola had been sufficiently surprised to reveal her heritage to her boys.

Fortunately the consort played the Pavana as the diners filed in two by two, so no one minded that they entered more or less in step. They arrived in order of rank: queen, duke, *nobili*, and finally the *citadini* of Ca' Morèr.

A narrow, ribboned braid circled Oriela's head like a crown, knotted in the back with a blue and amber comb. Dama Elisabeta had been busy. From the comb, Oriela's hair flowed like waves of wild honey around her bare shoulders and across the golden lace border of her rose-colored bodice.

Silvio could hardly believe this elegant creature was the road-weary country waif who had joined them at Ospitaletto. The man on tenor kicked his ankle, and Silvio realized he had not been playing for several bars.

6 Forcheta

As her father arranged her chair, Oriela studied the table, feeling less elegant and more uncouth than she had ever felt in her life. A duke next to Papà, a queen across the table. She was surrounded on every side by splendid people in splendid clothes not borrowed from their hostesses. Even the servants seemed more refined than she felt.

A recorder consort was playing discreetly under the feathery larch tree—a location that might have been chosen to perfectly match their identical green velvet doublets. It seemed the Speronelli brothers had been enlisted into the ensemble. Elisabeta was far down the table with Carlo, looking effortlessly perfect with her sky-blue sleeves and gracious nods. To Oriela's right, the Duke of Bologna was discussing popes with her father.

"What Julius did to Venice was rotten, but what he did to France was worse." Duke Bentivoglio was speaking Vèneto, not his own language. Oriela wasn't sure whether this was a sign of respect or condescension.

All she had seen of the war was the inside of the small

Moniga fortress, the whole town crowded together, with Giorgio and the other men watching along the top of the wall.

"What he did to France?" Papà said, "He handed them Milan on a serving trencher!"

Bentivoglio said, "First his Holiness asks King Francis and Emperor Maximilian to help teach the Venetians a lesson, lets them conquer everything from Florence to the Alps, and then one morning he wakes up and says, '*Mater Dei*! There are Frenchmen and Austrians all over the *cazzato* peninsula,' and begs Venice to help get rid of them. Was he an idiot or a devil?" The man was getting excited, waving his hands around.

"Both," Papà said calmly. "A clever devil could have snagged Ravenna and Bologna without dragging any foreigners into it. No offense."

"I'd have liked to see him try!" said the Duke. "So what kind of devil is your Republic? You dragged the French in when Aragon came knocking."

Papà said, "What would you have done? There were Spanish cannonballs splashing into the Lagoon."

With this startling picture in her mind, Oriela felt quite lost when someone on her left asked her a question in Bolognese. She turned to see a gentleman with a flawless beard, looking expectantly at her over his soup. "*Scuxa?*" she said, in Vèneto.

"I hear Venice gets very warm in the summer," the man repeated slowly in Vèneto, as if he thought she was simple.

"Does it?" she said. From her right, she heard Bent-ivoglio say, "Lucky for you the *idioti* Spaniards didn't bring any boats."

"Of course, there must be a breeze from the sea sometimes," said the man with the beard. "Does it help?"

"What?" Oriela glanced over at Silvio and Piero, envying the musicians. They had only to stand there, blend into the tree, and play the notes in front of them.

"The breeze," said the gentleman.

"Probably." Why couldn't he ask her about some-place she'd actually been? If only there were a musical score for dinner conversations. She wondered if Papà would speak to her at all during dinner.

She also wondered what this object was that she had absent-mindedly picked up off the table. It looked like someone had attached a pair of thick pins to a spoon handle. With her other hand, she reached for a mor-sel of fish from the nearest platter and found herself stabbed by an identical implement. The white-headed little queen apologized while Oriela sucked her finger and blushed.

So the meal went on. With some practice, and only minimal damage to the tablecloth, Oriela figured out the use of the *forcheta*. If only learning to talk to Bolo-gnese aristocrats were as easy. As the last course was served, she managed to make eye contact with Queen Caterucia and said something inane about the beauty of the garden.

This turned out to be a perfect subject, and her Highness was soon happily complaining about the damage Imperial cannons had done to her knot garden, when a sudden gust of wind off the lake put out several candles and tipped over three of the music stands.

The sky over the water was split by a *forcheta* of lightning, and the music dissolved into dissonant chaos as the players dashed off to retrieve their scattered pages. The last few, brave notes scraped out of Piero's viola da gamba were supplanted by a long roll of thunder. Oriela had never before been so thankful for a storm.

7 Lamento

While the guests fled indoors, Silvio and the other musicians had no sooner secured their instruments than they found themselves assigned to move furniture. Dama Donata had called for the *spinetta* harpsichord to be brought into her sitting room along with enough chairs for the company and declared that the guests were now to entertain one another with songs and poetry. Silvio had just set down the last music stand in the curve of the spinetta and was on his way out of the room when Dama Elisabeta sat down at the instrument and started to sing a terribly pretty song about shepherds.

Antonio was out in the hall, tuning his lute. Silvio would have liked to stay and hear the performances, but a senior manservant sent him back out into the storm to bring in candlesticks. Passing by Donata's room some time later, his arms full of silver candelabras, Silvio found himself absent-mindedly humming along with the tune coming through the door. The next moment, he realized what tune it was he was humming and nearly walked into a chair.

Lamento di Tristano, that bit of incidental music he'd composed in the wagon. Moving with care to prevent the candlesticks from making noise, he eased nearer to the door and nudged it a toe's width further open.

Oriela was playing a soprano *flauto dolse*, and in the chair behind her, surely without Dama Donata's approval, sat Piero with his viol. How had he managed to get in there with while Silvio was getting drenched saving the table linens? He wanted to be irritated, but the music quickly drove all other thoughts from his head.

In the candles' glow, Oriela looked like a painting of a saint in ecstasy, her eyes focused upward, her face serene in contemplation. Not only had she memorized the tune in one hearing, she played it with the exact longing and frustration Silvio had intended. Her audience was sitting up a little straighter, taking in new breaths.

After playing the theme through once, as she turned the mode for the inversion, Oriela lowered her gaze. She was now looking at her father, and the spirit of the lament, infinitely deeper than anything Carlo might recite in a play, was as plain on her face as it was in the shifting modes. Morèr stirred uncomfortably in his seat, no doubt sensing the curious scrutiny of the other guests.

Silvio felt something inside him twist as he was drawn into Oriela's interpretation of his own melody. He knew in that moment what it was to grow up unwanted and feared.

Someone tapped Silvio's shoulder. He shook them off without looking. He watched Oriela and Piero make the transition to the up-tempo Saltarello section. Oriela kept to the melody, letting Piero follow with bits of canon and counterpoint. Silvio was surprised to see that most of the guests were able to keep still, only a few feet tapping restlessly. He was going to give Piero credit for extra self-control until he started watching Oriela more closely.

While her fingers flew with surprising skill through the difficult runs, she was taking the playful dance-chase in an unexpected and alarming direction, so that it wasn't a dance at all. At the half-cadences, where Silvio normally took a breath, the two-beat crotchet was lengthened with a harsh trill like an irate song-sparrow. It accentuated the dissonance and increased the tension, burnishing the wild caper with a spark of frenzy, even of rage.

It was miraculous and unbearable to watch. Poor Pantalon looked like he wanted to fly from the room. His abandoned child was standing up there in front of queens and dukes, pouring the full contents of her broken heart right into her father's lap. Furthermore— the realization left Silvio stunned—the mad innocent was using his little tune to do it.

There was that tap on his shoulder again. "Are you going to stand there and hold those all night?" The *maiordomo* whispered, closing the door to the sitting room.

Silvio looked dumbly at the man for a moment, then at the candlesticks still cradled in his arms. "Sorry," he said. "Where do these go?"

"The attic, remember?"

Silvio apologized again and went up the stairs. After

stowing the candlesticks in a storeroom at the other end of the top floor, he went to his room and took off each wet piece of his borrowed suit, hanging sleeves and stockings from pegs and bedposts to dry. He pulled on a dry shirt and lay down, closing his eyes to immerse himself in the memory of the music.

The creak of the bed ropes told him when his brother joined him. Still not wanting to break the spell, Silvio pretended to be asleep, but Piero either wasn't fooled or didn't care.

"Once." Piero said. "She only heard it once."

"*Sì*," was all Silvio managed to say.

"Only once," Piero said again. "You should have seen Donata's face. She isn't going to let Morèr forget this any time soon."

"*Il Lamento d'Oriela*." Silvio said. He rolled over to face his brother. "Did you notice what she did with the Saltarello?"

"Oh, yes," said Piero, "Poor old Pantalon looked like someone was rocking his gondola."

"Serves him right," Silvio said. He told Piero what he'd heard while up in the willow tree.

Piero was quiet for a long time. Then he said, "Mamma's people?"

"She's no changeling," said Silvio.

"They couldn't fake that nose," said Piero.

"And why would they want to?"

After another long silence, Piero said, "It looks better on her, though."

Silvio rolled toward the wall, reminded unwillingly of Oriela's face. The pain in her eyes. He said, "Morèr's an idiot. If I had a daughter like her..."

"Well, you won't," said Piero. As if Silvio needed reminding.

8 Comedies

Tired though he was, sleep fled Pantalon's company like a mouse from a terrier. What sort of creature was this that Giorgio had dropped in his lap? Playing Silvio's silly tune with the most vulgar display, and with that uncanny fiddler Piero. It was at last beginning to dawn on Pantalon that he had been hanging a great many hopes on the behavior of someone he had never met.

Over the years, if he had imagined the girl at all, it was in only the vaguest possible terms. He had assumed that Oriela would turn out pretty much like the other young ladies one met in great Houses, as if daughters more or less raised themselves.

Since her arrival, he was discovering with growing concern that she hadn't turned out much like any lady he'd ever met anywhere. Maybe he shouldn't have left her at the villa for so long. What had she done to fill the days? Feed the silkworms? Climb trees? Muck out Stelina's stall? Or maybe dance with the Aivani.

Maybe she never would have been like other girls, no matter what Pantalon did. When Giorgio and the farm hands had found the stolen child, she was on the edge of a circle of midnight dancers, being suckled by a woman with three breasts. *Giorgio* had said that. Sensible, reliable Giorgio. Three breasts. And when they approached, everyone vanished except the child, and she was lying in a ring of mushrooms in an empty field under a full moon.

It wasn't hard to deduce what sort of people those were, what Francesca called *spèrt* and *foleti*, but in Vèneto it was *Aivàn*, feral forest demons who would kill a mother to take a girl-child from her home, away to the forest, and turn her into a witch or sacrifice her to Hell, and maybe swap it for one of their own.

Margarita's death had been nearly bloodless, the midwife saying she'd died by elf-stroke. Padre Marco had dismissed Pantalon's concerns, yet the infant couldn't abide the holy man's touch when Pantalon took her to be christened. Wasn't that clear evidence that something was wrong with her? Didn't it suggest she had been changed, might not even be the same child?

Still, as long as he'd been saddled with her upbringing, he probably ought to have done a better job of it. If he couldn't bear to live with her, he might at least have sent her more clothes so she wouldn't have to come to dinner in Dama Elisabeta's cast-offs. He should have sent a proper governess to teach her about dinner conversation and forks. He should have sent her a dancing master. The gouty old pedant Gregorio, hired to teach the girl her letters, had not been selected for his agility or his sense of rhythm. Oriela might have learned from the farm workers any number of dance steps and gestures that would serve well enough for a village fair but would cause a scandal among her peers and betters in the city.

His daughter's future, the future of his House, would depend upon her deportment at the many gatherings of Venice's Winter social season. A triumph could draw the attention of a *nobile* suitor and place the name Morèr alongside families who'd been listed in the Golden Book of patricians since the arrival of St. Mark's bones. It would go some small way toward repaying his unpayable debt to Margarita if he could set her grandsons back up in the Great Council where they belonged. Conversely, if the girl danced like a peasant, he'd be lucky just to find a respectable *citadìn* willing to take her, at any dowry.

Thank the Virgin, Dama Elisabeta was taking an interest in her. If anyone could turn the young savage into a lady, it would be Elisabeta Lesse. But even she was no dancing master, and the first of the winter balls would be just days after their return to Venice.

In the blackness behind his bed curtains, Pantalon watched dueling comedies of his own future upstaging one another in the empty air around his head. By the time he finally dropped off, light was beginning to penetrate the cracks between the shutters, and servants were clattering water pitchers outside his door.

Someone knocked; Pantalon mumbled "*'vanti*," and moments later he had a steaming ewer on the washstand and a steaming tray on the side table. He pulled back the bed curtain on one side with a groan and shoved his arms into the sleeves of his zimara. The fragrances of spiced wine and warm toast started his stomach gnawing and propelled him to his feet.

On the tray, a roll of paper was tucked between the bread-sop bowl and a small plate of anchovies. He shook the paper open with his left hand, his right having already stuffed a fish into his mouth and holding another in readiness. When he started to read, however, his appetite vanished as suddenly as it had appeared. He mopped at his face with the tray cloth and stormed into Carlo's room next door. He strode to the desk where Carlo was sitting half-dressed, ribbons dangling loose from the shoulders of his jerkin, awaiting sleeves.

"*The Toe of San Pazzio*?" Pantalon slapped himself on the forehead. "Here?"

"Don't worry," said Elisabeta. She was curled up at the foot of the bed, wrapped in something lacy. "None of Mamma's guests are fond of the Pope these days."

"Who is?" Pantalon said, "But at least the Republic is not, for the moment, excommunicated!" He was thinking of Duke Bentivoglio, chased out of Bologna by Papal troops. Surely there would be spies in his retinue. That Queen of Corfu, on the other hand, was always a pro-Pope Guelph and wasn't likely to have turned Ghibelline after the Emperor's men destroyed her prized peonies.

This play, which raised the subjects of relics and indulgences, could start them all quarreling, might draw unwanted Vatican attention, and wasn't likely to open the guests' purses.

Carlo said, "We're doing your play, *barba*. I thought

you'd be pleased." Calling him *uncle*.

Pantalon said, "Bentivoglio will be afraid to donate." Had Carlo forgotten the war widows, the Brescian foundlings?

Elisabeta said, "With Mamma asking, he'll be afraid not to."

"All you think about is the money," said Carlo.

Pantalon said, "Someone has to. All you think about is having fun."

Ser Antonio eased himself between them. "I like *The Toe*," he said. "You wrote some wonderful lines for my Capitàn, and Silvio gets to walk on his hands."

"You like anything where Silvio turns upside-down," Pantalon dismissed Antonio with a wave. "Carlo, why today?"

Elisabeta said, "Mamma asked for a satire."

Pantalon felt his shoulders sag. There would be no changing their minds, then. Whatever the consequences, they would perform the razor-toothed satire Pantalon had penned while more than half drunk, back when all of Venice was furious at being excommunicated over a land dispute.

Carlo had been too timid to mount the performance then, when there was a ready audience for it, but now that Pope Julius was dead, the interdict lifted and the war over, now, this afternoon, they would perform *The Toe of San Pazzio* for a pack of foreigners because Dama Donata Mosto had asked for a satire, and Ser Carlo's fear of his mother in-law was greater than his fear of either

Pope or Emperor.

9 The Toe

Oriela watched with great curiosity as Piero and Silvio, along with Donata's men and under her father's direction, transformed the wagon into a stage on the lower lawn. They set it up in front of the stone wall that slanted down the hill toward the lake, blocked the wheels in place, and opened out the sides. These they set to rest on trestles to form a playing area. They stuck poles with forked tops into slots in the floor and hung a plain curtain around the sides and back.

Piero and Silvio were carrying a big piece of painted canvas that was wrapped around a long pole, maneuvering it into position between a pair of the upright poles. Oriela's father was on the stage, inspecting the base of one of these as the brothers nested the scenery into the forks. They had both turned to take smaller rolls that the men were passing up to them from under the floor, when her father gave a cry of annoyance. The whole arrangement had started to sag and tilt perilously toward his head.

"Papà!" In an instant Oriela had gathered up her long, borrowed skirt and leapt onto the stage. The post gave way just as she was reaching for the end of the backdrop pole. She caught it in both arms.

Her father ducked as the post clattered to the stage. After a moment, when nothing had landed on him, he looked up. Only then did Oriela realize she had called him *Papà*, not *Siór,* out loud. When he saw her standing over him, panting, with the half-fallen scenery in her arms, his face looked both astonished and annoyed.

"What...are you...doing...out here?" The words burst out of him in little pops like so many corks.

"Saving you from a bump on the head, I thought," Oriela said, using *tu* to see how he would take it.

He rose up straight and took the backdrop from her. "Why aren't you with Dama Elisabeta?"

"I wanted to watch you, Siór." she smiled and brushed a few bits of dry grass off the fine velvet of his jacket. She'd gone back to the formal *vu*.

"Go inside," he said. "All the *ladies* are in Dama Donata's sitting room." He turned from her and called to Piero.

Oriela sighed and started to walk away. At the edge of the stage, she almost stepped on Silvio's head. He was bent over, attaching a short flight of steps to the front with iron latches. She thought they must be hot because he was handling them with a rag.

"Those steps would have been helpful a minute ago," she said.

Silvio looked up at her, black curls falling sideways across his forehead. He said, "That was a gallant feat, Dama." When she was on the ground, Silvio said quietly, "If someone had just stopped a large object from falling on my head, I think the first word out of my mouth would be *thanks*."

She hadn't noticed the color of his eyes before, an unusually bright amber, clear and startling. He looked so earnest that she had to turn away. She hoisted her skirt to climb the stone stairs back up to the house.

Passing along the portego, fully intending to join the ladies in Donata's room, she noticed a row of paste-hardened canvas half-masks laid out on a table. She stopped to look at them. One was painted dark red and had a large, sneering nose under a heavily lined brow. It gave her an uncomfortable feeling, so she examined the others. There was a brown one with a very long nose and elegantly curled moustaches made of waxed horse hair, and two identical, black ravens' beaks with slightly sad, quizzically wrinkled brows.

As she was speculating which of these belonged to which players, Antonio came out of his chamber across the hall, dressed in a garish, red and yellow striped costume that seemed to light up the shadowy hall with its own fire. The ornate scabbard on his belt nearly reached the ground. Antonio came to the table and picked up the mask with the moustaches. When he saw her watching, he buckled the mask over his face, and at once his posture changed. He stood up very straight and walked with more emphasis, as if his feet were suddenly plated with lead. Striking a menacing pose, he pulled out a jewel-hilted sword—about a quarter the length of the scabbard. Oriela giggled, and Antonio took the mask off and showed it to her.

"I call him the Captain," he said. On closer inspection, she could see that the paint was chipping off several cracks at the base of the nose. The rag-paste construction was probably not meant to survive more than a few performances. "Carlo had them made last year for Carnevale. He'd gotten a copy of an old Roman play about a soldier and had the Alati do it at Ca' Corner. I played the soldier."

"The *alati*? The wings? Who are they?"

Antonio said, "Sorry, I forgot you didn't know," then gave a quick, apologetic head bow, "The *conpagna delle calze* Carlo and I belong to."

This hardly clarified matters. Why would men belong to a club for stockings? Oriela left the subject and asked, "Do you always wear the same mask?"

"So far we have." He held up the mask and looked at it from the front. "Carlo keeps writing the same sort of play, so we keep playing the same sorts of parts."

"Whose are these?" She motioned to the table.

"Silvio and Piero usually wear the black ones," he said, then pointed to the red face that had alarmed her, "And that's your father's. We call it Magnifico."

A respectful title for a Venetian gentleman. It seemed at odds with the leering mask. "Is he *nobile* or *citadìn*?" she said.

"Depends on whether you're asking your father or my brother. Not that it matters."

She thought it probably mattered a good deal to Papà. She changed the subject. "Do the other two have names?"

"Sometimes. When they do, they're Zani."

"Both of them?" It was an epithet, then. Yet Antonio didn't strike her as a snob.

He looked amused as he said, "Today Piero is playing a priest. And an astrologer. He should have a different mask for at least one of them, but these are all we have."

"What about your brother? Where's his mask?"

"He and Elisabeta usually play without masks. They're always the Lovers."

"Elisabeta?" Oriela realized she had shouted in her surprise. "La Dama is in the play?"

Antonio said, "Betì didn't like the idea of her husband making cow eyes at some boy in a dress." He tucked his mask under his arm and went out the door to the lawn.

Oriela wandered into Donata's room and listened to the other ladies talking about the Duke of Bologna's men, but gossip is dull when you don't know any of the people. Elisabeta wasn't there. Oriela thought of saying something about the man with the beard from dinner, but what would she say? That she had utterly failed at discussing the weather? A few of the women were spinning, but no one had an extra spindle, and she'd left hers in her trunk. Even asking Queen Truci about flowers didn't seem to work a second time.

She decided to go to her room for the spindle and was in the hall when Carlo's oversized, foppishly beribboned hat passed by and vanished out the garden door. The players must be dressed. Here was Elisabeta, her auburn hair loose like a maid's, draped in elegant gold satin. Her face looked unusually pale, her lips more red than was natural. Had she painted them?

Next came Silvio, lithe and agile in the plain linen tunic and leggings of a farm laborer. He had a split paddle tucked into his belt, a *batochio*, which would make a loud clap when a herdsman used it to slap a cow. While Oriela was wondering how it would be used in the play, Piero came out wearing a priest's alb that was too short and clung awkwardly to his wide shoulders.

Last to appear was her father, and his costume was as disconcerting as the mask. Tight red hose were tied to a scandalously short red jacket, a *zupon* like young men wore to parties, which left his codpiece plainly visible and let his linen show between the laces. Completely failing to cover this was his old black zimara, a garment never meant to be worn out of doors. Oriela thought she might have laughed had she seen any other mature gentlemen dressed like that, but it was hard to find it funny on her own father.

She was still staring at the doorway he'd vanished through when Donata led the ladies like a flock of hens through the portego. Her eyes lit on Oriela, and she exclaimed as if she hadn't seen her in years.

"My dear," said Donata, taking possession of Oriela's elbow, "You *must* come sit with Truci and me." They started down the stone steps to the lawn, Oriela struggling to keep her skirt from tripping her while one arm was attached to la Dama.

"Since my daughter *insists* on making an *exhibition* of herself up there with the men, we *venessiane* are all alone in this crowd of foreigners." Thus complaining (but not without a note of pride, Oriela noticed), she led Oriela to a seat right in the middle of the front row of folding chairs, near where the white-haired Queen of Corfu was already enthroned, her small, wrinkled hands lost in a mountainous froth of pale yellow taffeta.

Oriela curtseyed and sat down. Donata kissed her Highness' papery cheeks, then lowered herself slowly into her own chair, carefully, so as to ensure that her crimson velvet surcoat draped into perfect folds on either side. Oriela wondered whether she ought to have done something more with her excessive fabric than simply tuck it under the chair.

"This should be *very* amusing," Dama Donata said. "Carlo promised me a satire. He said it might even cause a small *scandal*. I do *love* a scandal, don't you? " She patted Oriela's knee. "So, tell me all about Villa Morèr," Dama Donata rested a ring-crusted hand confidentially on Oriela's forearm. "Do you know, I've *never* seen it! For some reason, your father doesn't invite his friends to his estate. As if we would *care* if it's small and rustic." Donata angled her head to catch Oriela's eyes. "Is it?"

"Is it what?" Oriela said.

"Small and rustic."

Oriela suspected that her father was being insulted, but the lady said it so sweetly that she couldn't be sure. "Well, it's not as large as yours," she said. "And we grow silk instead of wine."

"Yes, Betì tells me you helped look after the *worms*!"

Donata wrinkled her nose delicately.

Fortunately for Oriela, who had no ready reply to this, Carlo mounted the stage and bared his fair head to give a prologue. While Carlo was talking, Silvio crawled out from beneath the wagon. With his mask on, the paid clown was transformed into a kind of feral acrobat. He crept around the lawn, yawning, and trying out various locations to take a nap: the stage steps, two rocks, Queen Truci's lap, finally settling down on the grass in front of Oriela's feet. She almost didn't notice when the play started.

Piero the priest came and scolded Papà—Magnifico, Oriela reminded herself—for not giving money to the Church. Magnifico made excuses, but Piero said, "According to my calculations, you now owe Holy Mother Church enough to keep you in Purgatory for five hundred years."

At the word Purgatory, a low, tremulous murmur passed through the audience. Oriela had heard the name before but didn't know where it was. Why did it cause Magnifico to grab at his chest and gulp for air? He called for Zani, and his voice sounded oddly nasal and seemed to resonate from up inside the mask.

Silvio (Zani) sprang from his napping spot and onto the stage. He spent some time trying to revive his master by pumping his arms up and down, until Antonio's fiery striped Captain strutted out from behind the backdrop. Magnifico's fit passed when he saw the small, golden box in the Captain's hand.

"I have just had the most wonderful adventure," said the Captain, "Permit me to tell you of my herculean conquest!" Antonio's voice came out from below his mask sounding like a trumpet.

"Oh yes, please, Capitàn, What have you conquered this week?"

"Patrikerypsili," said the Capitàn, bouncing his empty hand in time to the dactylic syllables. Magnifico and Zani repeated the word with the hand motion several times until they could all pronounce it successfully and got some of the audience to say it with them. Whatever had been bothering the crowd seemed to have passed.

However, when the Captain started to list the prizes he had looted from the conquered island, Oriela thought the conversation was taking a very odd turn. He seemed to have been collecting parts of someone's body.

"From the Chiesa delle Sante Mani, I gathered the holy man's hands. His forearms were only a block away, at the Chiesa delle Sante Bracchie. Church by church," here he began taking large, slow steps. Zani followed in step just behind him. "Reliquary by reliquary, we gathered every bone," he enumerated on his fingers, "Every limb, every hair from the beard of the blessed martyr Pazzio!"

"*Töt* of him, *sciòr*?" said Zani. These first words from Silvio were a barely intelligible mixture of Vèneto and Bergamasco, further garbled by the resonance from the mask's huge nose. "You can put him back together! His *pé* to his *gàmber*," he drew his batochio and used it to tap, in turn, his foot and his leg, with a loud crack at each stroke. "His *gàmber* to his *còssa*," (leg and thigh)

"His *còssa* to his—" Before the paddle could reach and possibly damage the next part in the sequence, the Captain snatched the paddle away and cracked it over Zani's head.

The Captain said the golden box contained a toe from this Pazzio, and he kissed the box three times, crossed himself, and opened it. Oriela understood very little of what followed, some of which was in Latin, but by the end it was clear that Magnifico had decided the Captain should marry his daughter. The toe, it seemed, could pay the priest what he owed and save him five hundred years in Purgatory, wherever that was. Again the crowd behind Oriela grew quiet, and the silence only thickened when the priest returned and began haggling with the Captain—so many years for one of Pazzio's fingers, so many for an ear.

The Queen's nervous giggle pierced the silence that had settled over the crowd like a roosting hen. Dama Donata seemed to be the only one thoroughly enjoying herself, clutching her sides with laughter. Oriela could feel the people behind them holding their breath.

The next scene was Carlo talking about the wonderful lady he'd seen in church, who was Magnifico's daughter. Oriela noticed that Elisabeta's painted lips didn't seem as garish in the sunlight. Indeed, without the paint, she might have appeared to have no mouth at all.

Carlo was giving the speech he'd practiced on their way from Ospitaletto, with Silvio's melody behind it. When Piero struck up his viol, the Captain came out, drew his undersized sword and a confused chase ensued, everyone after everyone else.

Magnifico was looking for a place to hide the box with the toe and leapt up onto the table. He froze for a moment with his mask facing Oriela, and she felt like her chair had tilted. Magnifico looked as terrified as Papà had when she first saw him. Standing on a table.

She lost track of the plot after this. There was an astrologer (also Piero) who predicted Magnifico's imminent death. At one point, Zani was hiding under the table, and Magnifico chased him away from the curtain that represented his house, saying, "May the devil drag you bodily into Hell if you ever set foot on my street again!"

When Zani entered next, he was walking on his hands. Silvio did this as lightly as if it were all one to him, right-side-up or upside-down. He said to the audience, "Magnifico says, 'don't set foot' on this street or I go to Hell." A wave of quiet, guilty chuckles ruffled through the tense air around the audience.

Soon the Captain had joined him and was delighted to learn he could avoid damnation by keeping his feet off the street, and then Magnifico was trying to save his soul by the same method, and at last the laughter was flowing freely even among the Bolognese. Oriela was clapping, shouting *bravo*. Her father trying and failing to walk on his hands was the funniest thing she had ever seen.

Magnifico cried, "If someone will hold up my feet, I will give him anything he might ask."

Carlo came out of the other painted house and picked up Magnifico's feet, for which assistance he was awarded Elisabeta's hand. This might have been the end of the comedy, but upon hearing that Elisabeta was not to be his, the Captain demanded the toe back. Magnifico began to weep. He no longer had it, he had given it to the church because he was about to die. He collapsed at Carlo's feet, grabbing his chest. "Oh, I am dying!" he cried. Hearing this, Elisabeta called for the priest. The lovers cradled the dying man, the priest (Piero) knelt beside them, and Zani cried like a baby.

They created what might have been a tender tableau, had Piero not stood up and waved a cross at the lovers, told them they were married, and then pulled off the alb to reveal a set of work clothes like Zani's. He said Magnifico had owed him a year's wages and only this deception had induced the man to pay up. But he knew, he said to the audience, that none of their worships were as tight-fisted as Magnifico, and they would all donate generously to the support of the poor orphans of Brescia.

Papà then performed a dramatic and eerily convincing death scene as Piero walked off the stage and started playing a popular tune on his viol. Silvio approached the front row of chairs with his big hat upturned. One by one the other actors stood up and sang along with the viol. They came to the front of the stage, removed their masks and bowed.

Dama Donata was on her feet before the second note, shouting "*Bravi!*" She was alone in this action, however. Oriela stood with her but timidly resumed her seat when she looked over her shoulder and saw no one else had moved. There was a scattering of polite applause, and people started walking away, muttering curious words like *heresy* and *interdict,* before the song was over. None of them put anything into Silvio's hat.

10 Vultures

Pantalon pulled his mask off by the nose. He knew this would hasten its destruction, but just now he thought Magnifico deserved it. Every joke that had fallen flat, every satirical jab that had been greeted by stunned silence, had left his face a little redder behind his red mask, his brain a little hotter under his close-fitted cap. Now his skull felt like it was packed into a too-small battle helmet.

He watched Donata fluttering and clucking among her dazed guests, herding them toward the stairs and the upper garden. They would all be discussing the play they'd just seen, and the play was the very last thing Pantalon felt like talking about. He hurried up the steps, intending to make a quick and unobtrusive retreat into the house, when his daughter caught up with him.

"I thought you were very funny, Siór," Oriela said, slipping a hand around his arm.

If so, she was the only one. "*Grassie*," he mumbled, patting her hand by way of dismissal.

But she took it as an invitation. She dropped her voice to a whisper and leaned her head closer to his.

"There was one thing I was wondering about."

Pantalon suppressed a groan. "Yes?"

"Where's Purgatory?"

"*Cáca!*" He'd been wrong, he realized. The play was only the next-to-last thing he felt like talking about. He pulled away from Oriela and took the remaining stairs two at a time, his overstuffed brain now plagued with yet another worry. The invisible helmet tightened around his head.

After Oriela's botched Christening, before he'd returned to Venice, Pantalon had told Giorgio and Francesca to keep the strange infant away from the Church. It had been a hasty decision, made in a blind panic, and over the years he had been too embarrassed to openly rescind it.

For years he'd been telling himself that sooner or later Giorgio would decide he hadn't meant it, that he would raise her more or less as a Christian because it would be too awkward to do otherwise. He had clearly underestimated Giorgio's obedience.

Now the girl was going to sound downright feeble-minded whenever a suitor made some remark about going to Mass, or about the Feast of the Ascension, or even about St. Mark. Of course she would ask questions. She'd be constantly asking questions, constantly reminding Pantalon of his own short-sightedness. He supposed he would have to baptize her sooner or later anyway, which was sure to stir gossip. She couldn't very well marry a Christian until she was one herself. And to think he'd been up all night worrying about whether she could dance.

Pantalon made it as far as the bench under the willow tree before his legs decided to stop working. He ventured a glance across the garden and saw that Oriela was now talking to Silvio, which only increased his panic.

Naturally, the silly girl wouldn't think to be discreet with her curiosity. She would try her question on the next fool who came along, and naturally, for Pantalon's sins, it would be that particular Fool. Pantalon groaned aloud, imagining the jokes a professional *bufon* like Silvio could make about crazy, old Morèr, who not only wrote blasphemous plays but had raised a child who didn't even know what Purgatory was.

He looked across the lawn toward where Dama Donata was talking to the scowling Duke of Bologna and his stiff, nervously shuffling companions. That one, Pantalon was sure, was a Roman. Donata flapped her hands in the air and turned her back on them. She strutted away to swoop across the pavement toward Pantalon. There would be no help for the Brescian foundlings from His Grace of Bologna, then.

Donata came to roost beside him like an elegant vulture, folding her velvet wings in her lap. "Now, *now*, Pantalon, don't blame yourself," she cooed. "It's not *your* fault if all Bolognese are born without a sense of humor." Vultures, he thought, should never try to coo.

At Donata's signal, someone in green livery brought Pantalon a glass. He wondered when Ca' Lesse had acquired so many servants for the villa. Was Donata trying to impress Duke Bentivoglio by emulating the excesses of such aristocratic despots? He drained the glass hopefully, but it only made his headache worse.

Donata nudged his shoulder, causing him to follow her gaze. His Grace returned a cool glare, at which Donata lifted her pointy little nose and turned her attention even more enthusiastically toward Pantalon.

"I thought it was *brilliant*, dear, *really!*" she said. "I'm sure Publius Terentius *himself* couldn't have done better." Her smile glowed with the illusory warmth of a midwinter sun as she referred to the ancient Roman playwright who had been wildly popular a few years ago, and Pantalon suppressed the urge to snort. If the harpy was showing this unsettling friendliness toward him, she must be up to something. Probably flirting with the Duke and using him as a foil.

"Dama," he said, turning his most innocent face toward her, "I imagine you must miss Ser Iacopo greatly." It seemed like a good time to mention her ladyship's husband. "We must find a way to get him out of Venice next season, don't you think?"

Snow clouds blew over Donata's face and blotted out the smile. "Some *nobleman* would have to convince His Serenity to do without him," she said.

Pantalon almost admired the layers of irony in her voice, the way she pretended that her stressing the word *nobleman* implied nothing about Pantalon's own access to the Doge's ear. He had succeeded in returning Donata to her accustomed hostility, and the ground now felt more solid beneath him.

Maybe he should be grateful to Dama Medusa for

taking his mind off Oriela's Purgatory question. But returning his thoughts to *The Toe of San Pazzio* was little improvement. The Duke's Roman friend gave him sidelong glances, whispered with the Duke. A Papal spy, for sure. Pantalon shook his head sadly, waves of pain sloshing back and forth across the inside of his skull. Getting his House excommunicated for penning an anticlerical satire would make it difficult to christen his daughter. At some point, he realized that Donata was still talking.

"I'm sorry, Dama," he cut into whatever she was saying, "I'm afraid I'm not feeling well. Please excuse me."

This disclosure only caused the velvet vulture to follow him most of the way into the shade of the house, asking about his symptoms and recommending completely unrelated cures.

To his momentary relief, Carlo caught up with him at the door. Pantalon's headache had evidently become a general pestilence, because he and Carlo were followed into the house by a dozen other grumbling people. Carlo pulled him to a chair near the silver-laden credenza in the hall.

"Betì and I have been talking," he said.

"Mh?" Pantalon sat down with a sigh. A conversation that started this way could only end by giving him another headache on top of the one he already had. He rested his elbow on the credenza and used the hand to hold up his head. That helmet was now three sizes too small.

Carlo said, "This morning, my wife wasn't feeling

well. Had she been unable to perform in the afternoon, the play would have had to be canceled."

"And that would have been bad?" said Pantalon.

Carlo said, "But if there were another lady who knew the lines..."

The Bolognese were scattering by twos and threes into various rooms. Donata was rushing from one of them to the next with pleading gestures. Pantalon lifted his head to look Carlo in the eye. "You mean my daughter."

"Only until we're back in town. Then Betì's brother can take over her parts."

"No."

"There's only Brescia and Verona left, and really, I don't think it's likely we'll need to call on her. It would just make Betì feel better, knowing she could stay in bed in the morning if she has to."

Across the hall, Donata was clinging to the arm of a Bolognese lady, saying "...just got here."

Pantalon said, "When will the baby come?"

"Probably after Ascension Day," said Carlo.

Pantalon rubbed his face with both hands. "Fine. But only in houses. I won't have her performing in the public square. Have la Dama show her the scripts." The pain was almost blinding now. He would have promised Carlo half his fortune just to be left alone.

Carlo sat silently beside him for a long moment. Then he said, "It's a good play, Pantalon."

"It was a good play five years ago. It was a bad play today."

"The Alati want us to do it at Ca' Foscari for the San Martino ball."

A ball. Yes, that was the other thing he didn't want to think about. That feast day was only a few weeks away. Pantalon took a breath, then lowered his voice, as if the gold filigreed soup tureen at his elbow might carry the tale to Donata if it overheard him. "Speaking of balls," he said, "Oriela needs a dancing master."

"Is that all that's bothering you?"

"Siór, it's one of a dozen things that are bothering me, but it's the one I can think about right now without feeling that my head has been squeezed like an olive."

"Well, don't worry. There's time," Carlo said, patting Pantalon's shoulder (the gesture jarred his neck and shot an arrow through the back of the unseen helmet), "Especially since we happen to have one of the finest dancers in all Italy with us right now."

"What?" Pantalon was confused for a moment, but then he realized who Carlo meant. "No. Not him."

"Why not?"

Where could he begin to list the reasons why not? "Siór," said Pantalon with what he felt was heroic restraint, "I'll admit Silvio can dance, but that doesn't mean he can teach it, not to someone of her station. Imagine the dreadful manners she might pick up!"

"Betì can teach her the manners."

"He's too young," Pantalon said, "Dancing masters are usually old for a reason."

"You'll keep an eye on him," said Carlo. "Do you have a better plan?"

The fact was, Pantalon didn't trust the Speronelli brothers, with their eccentric herbalist mother and strangely compelling music. He was sure they were Ai-vani, but Carlo would call him an old woman if he said so. "No," he groaned, "I really don't."

"Good," Carlo said, "Soon we'll be back in Venice, and you can hire the knock-kneed old cretin who teaches my children." Getting up (finally!) to leave, Carlo said, "It's a good play."

11 Swans

Silvio took a minute to inspect his mask while Donata's guests filed up to the garden. He'd had to adjust the buckle several times during the performance, and he now saw that the strap was starting to tear away from the right temple. All the edges were frayed, and the nose was sagging. The whole lot would have to be replaced soon if Carlo meant the Feathers to continue past this season.

He put Zani away in the storage box and started up the stairs, thinking about the competing virtues of wood and leather as alternatives to pasted cloth. He nearly ran into Oriela, who had halted on the top step with her skirt bundled up in her arms like a load of washing.

"Papà? Wait, Siòr! Papà!"

"What's wrong?" Silvio said.

"I asked my father a question," she said, throwing the heap of skirt at her feet, "I guess I shouldn't do that."

Silvio started walking past the fountain toward the patio, and she followed. They reached the terrace that overlooked the lake. Silvio leaned against the stone railing and looked at her. "What was the question?"

She didn't answer. Silvio turned to look out across the water. "It must have been a hard one," he said. "It's not easy to scare Ser Pantalon away from a chance to talk."

"And yet he is so often struck dumb by my presence." Oriela crossed her arms as if she were cold, which was unlikely. Silvio had just been thinking it would be nice to stick his head in the fountain again.

He bent forward and rested his elbows on the railing. "Why don't you try it out on me, and if I can answer it, we'll know it was easy." She rewarded him with a modest upturn at the edges of her lips.

"You're going to think I'm silly," said Oriela.

"I like it when people are silly," he said with a mad grin that had no effect on her at all. Strange. That particular grin always made girls laugh. Had his muse wandered off?

She said, "During the play, whenever you mentioned a place called Purgatory, everyone seemed to get nervous. So where's Purgatory?"

Silvio turned his face away quickly and gazed out over the lake, so she wouldn't see his surprise. How could someone live sixteen years in Christendom and not hear about Heaven and its alternatives? Half a dozen swans dabbled in slow circles on the water below.

"Swans," he said, nodding toward the distant birds, to distract her, to stall for time.

Oriela glanced briefly at them before turning her back on the rather splendid vista. "You think I'm stupid," she said.

Silvio could feel the heat of her humiliation on the back of his neck. He studied the swans. "There's a brown one," he said. "I didn't know swans came in that color."

"It's young," Oriela said without looking. "The flight feathers are new. If Giorgio were here, he'd get his crossbow and shoot it for supper." She tossed him a brief scowl. "And you're not answering my question, either."

"Purgatory," Silvio said, "Is one of the places people go when they die." His words sounded to him like he was talking to a child of four.

"Oh." She was quiet for several breaths and then asked, "Where else do they go?"

"The other two options are Heaven, where everything is wonderful forever, and Hell, where everything is terrible forever." He couldn't think of a serious way to say it. Most people didn't ask him serious questions. "And Purgatory is in between."

"In between doesn't sound that bad," said Oriela. "Isn't that pretty much like being alive? Why would people walk around on their hands to avoid that?"

Silvio looked at her more attentively. It was a valid point. "Well, from what the priests say," he said, "Purgatory is where you get rid of all your leftover sins." He thought of one of Mamma's nastier medicines. "Like a taking a purgative."

Oriela said, "So people in Purgatory are always vomiting?"

A picture of Dante's mountain popped into Silvio's head, a great spiral staircase full of people throwing up on each other, gobbets of pride washed downhill on putrid waves of envy. He couldn't stop the first laugh from bursting out of his throat, but the second was choked off by the furious look on Oriela's face.

"You do think I'm stupid."

"Not at all," said Silvio, "That's the cleverest description I've ever heard. Better than Dante."

He watched her face change slowly from sour to curious. "And the other two places?"

"Well, after you're done—" he paused for effect, "Purging," and now, finally, her eyes started to smile, "You get to go to Heaven."

She watched the swans for a minute before saying, "What about Hell? Who goes there?"

"Oh, usually only people who aren't b—*mh*, that is," Silvio managed to shut his mouth before saying *Who aren't baptized*. "People who are very wicked."

Oriela was quiet for a while, and Silvio was afraid she was figuring out what he'd been about to say. But then she said, "So—giving money and bits of dead people to the Church..." She scowled. "Does that work?"

Silvio said, "*That* is a hard question." He shook his head. "Between you and me, Dama, you probably shouldn't ask people about it." She blushed, and he was sorry for her, but she should be warned. "Your father was right. We shouldn't have done his play today."

Oriela's eyes widened. "His play? Papà came up with all that wonderful nonsense?"

Elisabeta walked up to them and caught the end of this. "You didn't know?" she said. "Carlo's been telling everyone." La Dama took Oriela's hand and pulled her away toward the house, saying, "Mamma is in a terrible state. The Bolognese are leaving."

12 Fata

While he helped Piero load up the wagon the next day, Silvio tried yet again to convince himself that he was glad to be going home to *Bèrghem*. It was, after all, an exceptionally pretty town, perched there on her hilltop with the farming villages around the hem of her skirt, surrounded by snow-capped admirers. He listened in his mind for the great, bronze voice of the Campanone and felt how his bones still vibrated to the big bell's note.

The bell naturally drew his thoughts into the eclectic beauty of Santa Maria Maggiore, only to drive them out the opposite door to the tombs in the old porch. Since his mind was unwilling to linger in the *Cànposanto* with the dead, it ran off home to the Piazza Mercato del Fieno, where it was obliged to go into the apothecary shop and kiss his mother, Viola dei Fiori. This was always the point at which he gave up trying to be glad.

Viola was probably the one person in the world whom Silvio could safely kiss, and he was still too angry with her to want to. She should have told her sons from the beginning that she was a *fata*, instead of letting the fact drop onto their heads the way it had, at the worst moment of Silvio's young life.

He was fourteen, and it was Carnevale. He was dancing with Clarissa, the girl next door, his playmate since they could both walk, and—being a boy of fourteen, masked and a little drunk—he kissed her. A moment later his friend was dead and Piero was dragging him away, dodging revelers, tripping over cobblestones while behind them the music gave way to screams.

That night, blundering through the shop door in a panic, Silvio and Piero had seen Viola in her true form. It turned out that their mother's familiar face was a carefully constructed illusion. That was also when she told them, by way of explaining Silvio's predicament, that some members of her side of the family had traits that were dangerous to humans.

She should have given them some warning. Piero had already been making people dance for four years and didn't know why. She could have explained it all when they were younger. It wouldn't have surprised anyone in their ancient hometown to learn that the apothecary Enrico Speronèl, their *babbo*, had caught and married one of the immortal Aivani from the mountains. Had Silvio known, he could have avoided killing Clarissa.

Accepting that the day's journey would be as unavoidably depressing as every other visit for the past six years, Silvio loaded the last basket into the wagon. He turned and saw Pantalon Morèr approaching him, wearing a broad smile that filled Silvio with misgiving. When Morèr took off his hat and said "*Bon dì,* maìstro," Silvio became seriously nervous.

"Is there something you need, Sióre?"

"In fact, there is." Pantalon replaced his hat and faked a cough. "I've decided—that is, I want to ask you..." He paused, looked at the ground, and began again. "My daughter is in need of a few dancing lessons, and Ser Carlo suggested—well, as we are currently traveling in company, and as I had observed that you possess some skill in this area..."

Silvio nodded, not at all liking where this was going.

"In short," said Morèr, "I wish to engage your services as her dancing master."

"I am honored, Sióre," Silvio said cautiously, "But I'm sure you can find someone better qualified in Venice."

"Of course I can," Morèr said, "And I certainly will. But, you see, by the time we get there, it will be almost winter."

"Yes." *Of course* was a bit harsh, Silvio thought.

Pantalon said, "And you know the first ball of the season is always at Ca' Corner, right before Advent."

That explained why Morèr was desperate enough to hire him. Silvio had never given formal dancing lessons before, although he was sure he could do it. What kind of wage could he get away with asking? Maybe a soldo a week?

Morèr said, "We have two more weeks on the road. Shall we say—ten soldi?"

Silvio was staggered. Half a lira for less than a month's work was much more than he had any right to expect. An image flashed through his mind of Oriela's hand in his, her green eyes gazing up at him for instructions. The idea was alarmingly agreeable.

"*Siorsì*,"—yessir—he heard himself say, thinking he was probably digging his own grave, "When would you like me to begin?"

13 Viola

Oriela found the ride from Iseo to Bergamo a delight. Rows of yellow poplars glowed like small suns under a crisp, blue sky, and cyclamen the color of early sunrise nodded along the roadside over their round, dappled leaves. Stelina's neck was like velvet after three days of pampering in the Villa Lesse stables, and Oriela felt regal on her back, even in borrowed clothes.

As the road widened and began to creep uphill toward the San Giacomo gate, the houses grew larger and closer together. Then, all at once, they left the roofs of the houses behind, and the world opened wide. The patched and terraced valley spread dizzyingly far below them. Further uphill, city walls rose out of a deep, green trench, over which the road hovered on an impossibly tall causeway, and beyond the wall, the town kept climbing up and up, as if the houses had been stacked on top of each other.

They rounded the last curve toward a dazzling, white gate, and Oriela was startled by a loud whoop.

"*Mé fiöi!* My boys!" A small woman in a plum-colored dress and clashing red kerchief ran towards them out of the gate, flapping her arms as if to launch herself off the causeway and into the air.

"Mamma!" Piero stopped the horses and reached a hand down to pull the woman up onto the box between him and Silvio, where she unleashed a rushing torrent of Bergamasco so dense even Oriela could barely make out more than one word in five. She wondered why Papà prodded El Moro and rode on ahead with his face averted, like he was afraid to look at her.

The wagon was inside the big gate. "You are all welcome to stay at my house for as long as you are in the city," said the woman. Her Vèneto, now that she was speaking to all of them, was oddly archaic—though no slower. "You can't trust the innkeepers. They might put *anything* into their food. And the beds—"

"Mamma," Piero said, in a low voice that nevertheless echoed from the brick vaults overhead, "You've only got two beds." Oriela heard Antonio laugh as they all emerged into the street.

"Well, at least say you will come for dinner," the woman said, "I have got a lovely lamb stew in the pot, more than enough to go around, and fine spelt meal for the polenta, and—"

Antonio said, "I would be delighted, Madóna. What about you, Carlo?"

"You know the Podestà is expecting us all to dine with him this evening."

"Make my apologies to Governor Barbarigo, will you?" said Antonio with a broad grin. He turned to Oriela. "Will you and Ser Pantalon accompany me to her house?"

The small woman looked directly at Oriela for the first time and said, "Silvio, did you leave your manners in Venice? Tell me who your new friend is."

Silvio sighed as he said, "May I present la Sciora Oriela, daughter of Pantalon Morèr," and Oriela realized that until that moment he hadn't spoken to this woman who was clearly his mother. "Dama Oriela, Viola dei Fiori."

"*Piassu*," Oriela said in Bergamasco, "Papà and I would be happy to dine with you, Madóna Viola."

"Really?" Viola seemed astonished by this. "Oh, how wonderful! Sciòr Morèr? You too?" She used the familiar *tu*.

Papà, three horse-lengths ahead of the group, tossed a *No, thank you!* over his shoulder as Madóna Viola hopped off the wagon and hurried away up a cobbled street to their right.

They followed El Moro around a corner into the Piazza Vecchia, where an enormous clock tower tolled the half-hour, a deep, throbbing note that would carry for miles.

What looked like a small army in livery poured out of the tower's base and took charge of the horses, the wagon, and the *nobili*. While the others went into the Palazzo del Podestà, the Venetian governor's house, Papà pulled Oriela aside. Her heart dropped into her boots when she saw the almost feral look on his face.

He said, his voice deadly quiet, "Why did you tell

that woman we'd dine with her, without even asking me?"

Oriela realized she wasn't sure why. She said, "She was so excited, it was hard to say no." What was that emotion that was flashing from Papà's dark eyes? Anger? Fear? Not exactly... "Ser Antonio is going," Oriela said. "Why not come along?"

"I wouldn't take so much as a pomegranate seed from that female's hand," Papà's words came out through his teeth, snarling, "And neither should you. She's not like us."

Then Oriela realized what she was seeing on his face. Hate. Active, focused hate.

"Or maybe you know what she is," he said. "I daresay you'd still be fond of her kind."

"Her kind?" Oriela tried to think of a group Silvio's mother might belong to that would call forth such a reaction. Widows? Lombards? Maybe apothecaries? "Oh!" she said, picturing Madóna Viola in a room full of mortars, bottles and bundled herbs. "Are you saying she's a witch?"

"No, I'd much sooner trust a witch," Papà said. He seemed to be studying her. "Are you still determined to go?"

She thought it would be rude to cancel after having already accepted the invitation, and Antonio probably wouldn't want to go alone. On the other hand, Oriela was tired of upsetting her father, something she seemed to do almost daily without even trying.

"Are you going to forbid me?" she said at last.

"What would be the point?" Papà said, fiercely and bitterly, without further explanation. "Go ahead. Keep Toni company. Just take one piece of advice, will you? Before you decide whether to eat that creature's cooking, take a good look at her eyes." Oriela was left to ponder that enigma for the rest of the afternoon.

14 La Mandragora

Viola's apothecary shop was on the ground floor of a narrow house with a walled garden. It sat on the hay market square, a busy neighborhood of artisans and shopkeepers. A wooden sign in the shape of an uprooted mandrake hung over the open door of a tunnel-like workshop. Antonio had to duck to avoid getting poked in the eye by a dangling bundle of rosemary that contributed its fragrance to the olfactory assault of hundreds of different plants drying, simmering and being soaked in grappa.

Oriela and Antonio followed Silvio past the workbench with its big mortar and pestle, between shelves full of bottles and up a flight of stone stairs in the back.

Madóna Viola met them at the door and kissed them all on both cheeks, even Ser Antonio. As Papà had requested, Oriela made a point of looking at her eyes. One blue and one green. That was unusual, but Oriela couldn't imagine how it might affect her cooking.

More interesting to her mind was the sword Antonio unhooked from his belt and hung from a peg by the door. It was neither a stage prop nor a ceremonial adornment but a serious weapon.

The central room of the apartment was an old-fashioned *sala* with a round fireplace in the middle. Three smaller chambers opened off the sala on the wall opposite the stairs. In spite of the open, unglazed windows, the room was warm and a bit smoky. Viola's stew competed with the firewood for the attention of Oriela's nose. Shelves on the cracked plaster walls were laden with bottles, stacked dishes, and dented copper cooking pots.

A table was set up near the windows with chairs at either end and benches on the sides. Piero offered the two chairs to Antonio and Oriela while Viola swung the pot hook out of the fire with one hand and pulled out a pan of polenta with the other. Silvio was pouring out the wine, and then he and Piero sat down on the bench by the window.

Viola didn't sit down on her bench but kept circling the table, filling and refilling bowls and platters and wooden trenchers. She talked as volubly as she dished out the food, filling their ears with news while she filled their stomachs. The abbey across the square was getting a new roof, the blacksmith had taken an apprentice, the glassblower's son had a new baby, and...

"I'm going to be a godmother again."

A hush dropped on the room like a log into a fire. Silvio had frozen with his spoon halfway to his mouth.

Piero said, "Really? Whose?" Oriela thought he looked uncomfortable, but Viola didn't seem to notice.

"Francesco Vedesta's baby. You know, Clarissa's brother? He seemed to think it would be good luck. I don't know why. I didn't bring Clarissa much lu—"

"I remember when they baptized Silvio," Piero broke in, a little too loudly. "I was only four, you understand. I had helped Mamma pour the baby's bath that morning, and she taught me to test it with my elbow." He stuck his out, dominating the table with the gesture. "So when the priest dunked Silvio in the old font and he let out a howl, I thought the water must be too hot, because, of course, the priest only blessed it with his fingertips, not his elbow."

"Oh, no!" Antonio said, "You didn't!"

Piero grinned. "I climbed up on the rim and stuck my elbow in the water. It was as cold as melting snow! Babbo tried to grab me, I fell in, and they carried me dripping wet out of the baptistery, and I was yelling at the priest, '*Pàder*! The bath is too cold!' "

"I remember Clarissa shrieked like a scalded cat when the priest dunked her," Viola said. "What a set of pipes on that girl! Louder than a consort of shawm players when she got going. Remember, Silvio, how she'd beg you to chase her around the piazza? But then if you ever caught her, how she'd yell! I could hear her from three streets away."

Oriela glanced at Piero while Viola chattered and noticed that he had gone still as a statue. Silvio looked pale, his eyes fixed on some point just beyond his bowl, one fist pressed in front of his mouth. Oriela thought he might be sick.

"Madóna," said Antonio, "I know it is part of a mother's duty to embarrass her sons, but it is my duty as their friend to stop you before you reveal which one was Clarissa's sweetheart."

With a mumbled, "*Permèss*," Silvio slid from his end of the bench and vanished into one of the adjoining rooms. There was a sudden jolt of the table, followed by a small gasp from Viola. It appeared, though Oriela refused to believe it, as if Piero had just given his dear, old widowed mother a kick.

Everyone was looking down at the table or out the window. When the quiet got intolerably thick, Oriela said, "I was wondering what these aromatic seeds are. I can't quite place the flavor."

La madóna instantly recovered and said, "Oh, that must be the fennel, *car' mia.* An excellent carminative. You like it?"

Piero said, "Mamma chooses seasonings for their medicinal properties."

"It's quite unique," said Oriela, smiling graciously and making a note to herself never to add fennel seeds to a gravy for lamb.

The talk turned to trade. The fields of the lower town had not yet recovered from all the trampling soldiers, and crops were only a little improved from last season. Those medicines Viola couldn't gather for herself had gone up in price, few of the cash-poor locals could afford them, and the apothecary shop was not doing as well as before the war.

A few minutes after this, Antonio thanked Viola and collected his sword, and Oriela followed him down into the dark shop. As they neared the bottom of the stairs, Oriela was startled by the sudden appearance of a face in a crested helmet. The man in the helmet held a lamp in one hand, and its glow illuminated the uniform of one of the guards at the governor's palace.

"Paolo Da Brixia!" Antonio cried, leaping over the last step. "What in the name of San Marco are you doing here?"

For a moment, Oriela's ears felt disoriented, until she realized that Antonio was speaking Bergamasco. She hadn't heard him do this before, not even with Viola.

The man in the helmet snapped to attention. "Capitàn Pevari! I am to—at—your service," he said in badly-phrased Vèneto.

"None of that!" Antonio said in Bergamasco, gripping the man by both shoulders and kissing his cheeks. "No one has the permissions to call me Captain now unless I am wear a mask." His syntax was execrable and his Venetian accent was thicker than day-old polenta, yet he kept trying. Antonio must have felt an unusual level of respect for this man.

"If you say it, Siór," answered the soldier, who continued to reciprocate the respect with his awkward Vèneto, "The Podestà sent me for to bring you and your friend to his house in safetiness."

"*Sciori*, please," Oriela said in Bergamasco, "Choose one language." As the third member of the conversation, she figured she had the deciding vote, and Antonio probably needed more practice. Da Brixia looked at her with some surprise and removed his helmet. His round-cheeked face was much friendlier without it.

Da Brixia said, "I have orders, Capitàn."

"The Podestà is an old woman," said Antonio, "We don't need a guard to walk from here to Piazza Vecchia."

Oriela looked at Antonio. "Then why did you bring your real sword?"

" 'Real sword'?" Da Brixia said, lips quirking with amusement.

Antonio said to Oriela, "There's a reason the *zani* come to Venice." He led the way out the door and through the dark alley behind the shop, then the trio started up the steep cobblestones toward the governor's house.

While they walked, Antonio and his friend talked about the war. Although they spared her the worst details, Oriela's mind was soon filled with bits of the terrible knowledge these men carried. Cavalry horses that trampled crops, leaving whole villages to starve. Women and children roasted alive in a cave, in the hills outside Brescia. When Antonio asked his friend why he hadn't gone home to his farm after the treaty, the man had only said, "What farm?"

When Da Brixia reached the top of the stairs into the Palazzo's atrium, he nearly tripped over Papà, who had evidently been waiting just behind the door.

"It's about time!" Papà snapped. Then he put on a more relaxed, almost jovial face—Oriela could see him changing it—and asked, "Well, how did you find our *beverindièra?*" A disparaging name for Viola's trade, *potion-maker.*

"She never stopped talking, hardly stopped moving," Antonio said. "Drove her sons to distraction, I believe. Absolutely delightful. You should have been there."

Papà waved this away and looked at Oriela. "We all know Toni finds her amusing. I'm asking you." He drew closer and took hold of both her upper arms, examining her face. "What did you learn?"

Oriela, still under the spell of the soldiers' tales, met her father's gaze levelly and said, "Fennel doesn't go with lamb."

She noted his bewilderment with cold satisfaction. What had she learned? She had learned, for one thing, that her own behavior at her unfinished christening had not been unusual—which meant that her father's had been. She had also learned why the cities of the terraferma needed repairing, and that the easygoing Antonio was ready and able to use his real sword against human flesh—had, in fact, done so.

The eccentricities of one widow were a very minor ingredient in the vast stew of things Oriela had learned, and her father's fixation on the woman was as discordant as the fennel seed in the gravy. Surely Madóna Viola wasn't the only person around here who'd gone a bit peculiar in the last several years. It was frankly a wonder the whole countryside wasn't raving.

Antonio said, "You know what I'd like to see? A chattering contest between Viola dei Fiori and Donata Mosto. It's even money which one would run out of breath first. What do you think, Paolo?"

Papà ignored Antonio and kept looking at Oriela as if she might sprout asses' ears. She smiled as sweetly as she could and said, "*Bona note*, Papà." She was relieved that he didn't flinch at the word. Instead he just released her arms with a sigh.

15 Clarissa

Silvio was slumped on the edge of his old bed with his elbows on his knees, his head resting in his hands, but he wasn't really there. He was once more feeling Clarissa drop lifeless from his arms like an empty sack. Piero had gone out back for water and was washing the dishes.

When la Fata Viola appeared in the bedroom doorway, Silvio glared at her, his stomach tight with the effort not to get up and toss her bodily across the room. He didn't want to see her, didn't want to think about her and her feral ancestors.

Mamma sat down beside him, pinched his cheek, and said, "What's curdled your cream?" As if Silvio were a pouting toddler.

Silvio said, "Why do you always have to talk about Clarissa?"

Mamma waved a hand dismissively. "I was talking about her family. They live next door."

"I'm amazed they're still speaking to you," he said, folding his arms, trying to avoid touching her with even an elbow, "Much less letting you help christen their children."

"I told Francesco that Clarissa's death was an accident."

"You lied," Silvio said. "I didn't kiss her by accident."

He watched her try on an affronted look, just to see where it got her. Or maybe he really had wounded her. It was so hard to tell.

"For the love of Pan, Silvio," she said, pulling off her kerchief. "It was Carnevale! No one remembers anything the next morning, much less five years later. Stop worrying." She shook out her hair, letting the illusory gray fade to its natural purplish-black. "As far as anyone knows," said Viola, "You were just the unlucky boy who happened to be dancing with her when she stumbled and hit her head."

Was that what she thought was bothering him, that he might still be accused? "Mamma," he said, "She didn't stumble, and she didn't hit her head. I killed her."

He pulled his feet up onto the bed and retreated toward the back wall, wanting to vanish into the plaster like a faded fresco, thinking someone else's mother might have taken this moment to say something kind, or would perhaps have had the sense to leave him alone, but Silvio didn't have someone else's mother. He had Viola.

Mamma's eyes flared petulantly, one grass-green and one indigo. "I didn't expect you'd take after Zio Herlakin."

Silvio dropped back against the pillows and shut his

eyes. Had Mamma been actively trying to find a way to make him feel worse, she couldn't have done better than to remind him of the lethal kinsman from whom Silvio had inherited his curse.

An Aivàn of incalculable antiquity and many names, Herlakin was able to transport souls to the next life by way of a kiss. Of course, Silvio thought, raw anger coiling at the base of his spine, Herlakin could decide when and whether to use the power. That was one trait the old devil hadn't passed to his grand-nephew. That and the antlers.

Pondering this, Silvio was startled when Mamma slapped both her knees and said, "I just figured out why that girl smells so familiar."

Silvio reluctantly opened his eyes. "Smells?"

"Yes, *smells.* Bacchus' Beard, Silvio! Humans only have five senses as it is; why should they be ashamed to use one of them? Anyway, I remember now. There was a baby at Tumolo Magasa for Vestalia that year. Gulfara brought her from a mulberry orchard near Benacu."

It took Silvio a minute to translate all this. A *tumolo* was a cave, Vestalia must be some sort of festival, and *Benacu* was the Aivàn name for...Lake Garda. He looked at his mother. "Dama Oriela?"

"I'm sure of it. The child had lost its mother, and its father didn't have the least idea what to do, trying to quiet it with a rag soaked in gruel. When Mèda Gulfara got there, your friend was wasting away. I don't think she would have survived if la Materluna hadn't grabbed her."

"Wait—Mamma," Silvio sat up with a jolt as her words formed a pattern in his head. "You *knew* the stolen baby was Pantalon Morèr's daughter?"

"Yes, that's what Gulfara said: 'A stupid lagooner who calls himself Mulberry'. And she didn't steal the baby, she rescued it."

"No rowan branches on the cradle to ward her off?" Silvio said, to annoy her, chagrined even as he did it. Why did he always feel like he was fourteen again whenever he came home?

"Gulfara's not that superstitious," Mamma said. "She gave the child to my cousin Althea to nurse, and everything was going well until Vestalia at Midsummer, when some very rude men burst into the dancing ring and scared everyone off. Poor Althea panicked and took plant form before she remembered the baby couldn't do it too, and so the men took it away."

Silvio sat up straight on the bed, turned to face his mother, and locked her odd-colored eyes in his gaze. "Mamma," he said, "They put humans in prison for child-stealing."

"Humans," Mamma dismissed the entire species with a brush of her chin. "You know how Gulfara is about babies. I always told her it's just as well she was late getting to Bethlehem."

Bethlehem? Silvio blinked a few times before returning to his point. "Listen, Mamma. Do you know what happened to Oriela, after your people stole her?" Silvio felt his jaw tighten with the effort to keep his voice cool.

"Rescued," Viola raised a finger to correct him. "No. Should I?"

"*Should you?*" Silvio swallowed the sudden rage that was creeping up his throat. He gripped her shoulders, "She lived like an orphan. Ser Pantalon left her at the lake and never went back. She met her own father for the first time a week ago."

Mamma wriggled free of his grip. "Considering who her father is, that's no great loss." She stood up and faced him. "If an idiot human leaves his child behind after going to all that trouble to take her back from us, I don't see how that's our fault."

"What's our fault?" asked Piero, appearing in the doorway with a damp rag in one hand.

"Oh, there you are," said Mamma, and the clouds of their quarrel had already cleared from her voice. "Dishes done already?"

Piero waved the rag by way of reply. Silvio turned his back on her and took his brother's arm, dragging him across the *sala* toward the back stairs.

"They're all clean, I swear," Piero said. He whisked a bottle off one of the shelves as they passed. They took the stairs to the courtyard without a light, each hopping over the broken step in turn, veered around the horse trough, slid through the alley between Viola's garden wall and the bakery, and emerged into the small piazza by the fountain.

A few lights still shone from the windows of the Golden Lamb Inn and reflected on the water. Silvio sat down on the cobbles, leaned his back against the damp stone of the fountain, and realized he was shaking.

Piero pulled the cork from the bottle he was carrying, took a swig, and audibly sucked in his breath as he passed it to Silvio.

"What's this?" said Silvio.

"Really terrible grappa." said Piero. "The stuff Mamma uses for tinctures."

Silvio peered dubiously at the bottle, thought again about Clarissa, Herlakin, Gulfara, and raised it to his lips. "*Ostia!*" he coughed, "What did they do, boil the whole vine?"

"Probably tossed it into the still, roots and all, with the dirt still on," Piero said. "Tastes like pickled sweat, I know, but it'll sort out your humors."

"How? By obliterating them?" Silvio passed the bottle back to his brother and leaned his head on the edge of the fountain. He said, "So you were wondering whether Oriela's kidnappers were Aivani."

"I was right?" Piero took a swig and pressed the grappa bottle back into his hand.

Silvio tried a larger swallow than the first and grimaced only a little. "Auntie Gulfara." Silvio washed the name down with another vile mouthful.

"Sweet Jesus," groaned Piero, reaching for the bottle. He drank, then asked, "Do you think Pantalon knows?"

"That it was Gulfara? Probably not," said Silvio, "But he must suspect something of the kind."

"I mean about Mamma," said Piero, "And us. Do you think he knows we're—"

Silvio swore and grabbed the bottle back. "You're as bad as she is."

"What?"

"Steal a baby, kill a girl—who cares, as long as we don't get caught?"

Piero raised his hands in surrender. "I'm only asking."

"If you're so worried, you could stop making people dance." Silvio knew he was provoking his brother, and that Piero probably didn't deserve it, but he couldn't find the will to stop himself. "I mean, one day someone's bound to notice half the audience doing the Coranto in the middle of a play."

"I've told you before, I can't help it!"

"So you say."

"I've tried," Piero said, taking his turn with the bottle, "And I'm getting better, you know. It used to be the whole audience."

"No one forced a rebec into your hands and made you haul it to Venice looking for patrons. You know what I think? I think you *can* help it. I think it amuses you."

"So what if it does?" Piero pulled himself upright. "It's harmless enough, unlike *some* family traits I could mention." He made a kissing noise into the air.

Silvio spun toward his brother with his fist flying.

Piero caught the arm and started to twist it, but Silvio grabbed Piero's ear with his other hand. As Piero fell sideways, Silvio snatched the bottle to prevent it from tipping over. Piero grabbed him around the waist and hoisted him into the air.

Had they still been boys, had Silvio not spent the past six years learning to turn cartwheels on balcony rails and walk up vertical walls, Piero's maneuver would have ended with Silvio in the fountain. Instead, Silvio pushed off hard from the ground, using his brother's momentum to knock him off balance. Piero landed on his ass while Silvio sailed over his head and rolled away in a diving somersault. When he righted himself, the bottle was still upright in his hand, not a drop spilled.

Silvio resumed his seat by the well. "Go to the devil," he said cordially, taking another drink. He passed the bottle to his brother, who was uninjured, having spent the better part of two years learning how to fall.

Piero raised the bottle in a salute. "Right behind you, demon-spawn."

Silvio tossed back the last swallow and lapsed into silence. *Demon-spawn.* Stupid Lagooner Mulberry treated his daughter like demon-spawn because she'd acted like an ordinary baby. Yet it seemed Aivani could get away with any amount of mischief and still be mistaken for appropriate godparents, standing in a fateful ring of dubious luck around the pool of the baptistery, throwing blessings at children, who screamed. *And if you'd catch her, how she'd scream!*

Except for that one afternoon, right here by the

fountain, when he'd caught Clarissa and she hadn't screamed. The winter sun revealed veins of topaz in her loose, black curls, and Silvio noticed for the first time that she was pretty, and then it was night, and those same curls were spread across the cobblestones of the Piazza Vecchia, Clarissa's face breathless and still, his pretty friend gone forever.

Silvio drew his knees to his chest and coiled himself into the darkness. Too tired to quarrel with the sorrow or wrestle with the regret, he surrendered to that terrible image, knowing now that some part of his soul would always be there, in that moment, the Campanone tolling above him, forever staring down at the wreckage of whatever beauty he touched. As he stared, the black curls turned the color of honey. *No, wait, that's* her *hair,* he thought, just before he passed out.

16 Cuckoo

O riela dropped her spindle into the basket with the roving and looked out the window of her room in the governor's palace. The church into which her friends had vanished that morning was, from the outside, the most interesting she had ever seen. It looked as though a gigantic infant had collected bits of several completely different buildings and assembled them according to his whim. There were stacked layers of flat, conical domes and octagonal spires, high-arched porches, colorful columns like twisted marzipan pastry, bas-reliefs, frescoes, doors in unexpected places, even statues stuck randomly high up on the walls. Most amazing, the higgledy-piggledy arrangement created an effect of stunning beauty.

Bells were ringing. Would Papà be coming out yet? Oriela was supposed to be feeling ill, to explain her staying in while the others went to Mass. There wasn't much pretense required. Her father had been watching her so closely all that morning, since her visit to Viola's house, that she thought he must be expecting her to sprout horns.

She looked down into the piazza but only saw one figure moving. It was Silvio, sneaking—yes, that was the right word—around from the *Cànposanto* toward the fancy porch. He stooped to pat one of the stone lions, put his hand on the door handle, and then turned away and sat down on the chessboard steps. So Oriela wasn't the only one who wasn't at Mass.

Oriela had always wondered about the insides of churches. The exterior of Moniga's San Martino was solid, square and unadorned. She'd assumed it was as dull on the inside, but one day she slipped away from Francesca at the market and found the heavy, wooden door ajar. She found herself in a dim, fragrant room with lofty ceilings and was amazed to see every surface covered with pictures. There were painted pictures on the ceiling, colored glass pictures in the windows, even tile pictures on the floor. Churches, it seemed, kept their wonders for those who could enter. If they were all like San Martino, fancier inside than out, what marvels must be hidden behind the fabulous outer walls of Santa Maria Maggiore?

More bells. A crowd started pouring out through the porch. Oriela climbed back onto the bed and tossed a blanket over her feet. Presently a Bergamasco servant brought her some dinner on a small table. She sat on the edge of the bed to eat it and had just finished when there was a knock at her door, and Papà came in.

He sat a little further down the bed and gazed at her with a face that was probably meant to be friendly.

"When we get to Venice," Papà said, "You're going to be busy."

Oriela pushed the table away from the bedside. "Doing what, Siór?"

"You'll be invited to balls at all the great houses, both *citadini* and *nobili*. You'll need to learn how to dance properly. You can't fling yourself around like a peasant girl at the Ca' Corner ball. So I have engaged a temporary dancing master for you."

"Why temporary?"

"Because it's Silvio." His eyes bored into her, gauging her reaction, so she kept it blank. He said, "When we get home I'll find someone more suitable."

"Very well, Siór." She decided not to ask what was unsuitable about Silvio. Another question was heavier on her mind. She pulled her feet up beside her. "Siór," she said, and her limbs froze up with the tension of saying this out loud, "Last night you asked me what I learned at Madóna Viola's house."

"Besides not liking her recipe?" Papà cocked an eyebrow, like he was trying for humor.

Oriela said, "She was a godmother for one of the neighbors' children."

"Really." What was that look on his face now? A smirk?

"She said..." Oriela felt her cheeks burning, "She said babies often cry when they're baptized. They don't like the cold water, the strangers..."

"They killed her," he said. He turned his profile to her, his head dropping a little. "The people who took you away, people like Viola, they killed your mother." His voice was quiet the way ice is quiet. "And when my men found you, you were..." His eyes flashed in her direction, suddenly bright with pain. "... happy."

"Papà," Oriela raised a hand to touch his.

He shrank back against the far bedpost. "Whoever you were."

She felt her hand turn to dust and fall back to her lap.

He said, "You looked the same, but something was different. You cried all the time. And then you couldn't bear to be touched by a priest. It seemed that Margarita's child, my child, was gone. I didn't know who or what came back from the forest."

Oriela tried to swallow the cold mass gathering in her throat. Even if she had lived with him, then, she would still be a cuckoo. "Do you know now?"

He shrugged. "I live in a world of masks." He turned and examined her. Oriela blinked, and drops started down her cheeks. After a few moments, Papà shook his head. "No I don't. Not yet."

He rose and brushed his sleeves, as if Oriela's presence had left dirt on them. "Silvio should be down in the atrium in an hour or so for your first lesson," he said, then turned in the doorway with a face like stone. "In Venice, you know," he said, "There are even masks that can weep."

17 Pavana

"*Allora*, the Pavana," said Silvio. He looked up at the wide landing above the atrium. The door was open to the study where Ser Pantalon was talking with Carlo and the Podestà about money. Silvio was not in a mood for dancing.

He had had another nightmare about Gianna, the scullery maid at Smeraldina's brothel, where Piero had brought him when they fled Bèrghem, because by then Silvio had a fever and couldn't keep traveling. Homely, harmless little Gianna, sent to the sick boy's bed to keep him warm, had kissed Silvio while he was asleep. The girl had survived, but she had never walked or spoken in the six years since the incident.

Whenever Silvio dreamed again of her staring up at him, her useless legs tangled on the floor, her mouth working to form words that never emerged, he invariably woke up with a crashing headache.

Instead of attending Mass with Mamma and Piero, Silvio had been to visit Clarissa at the churchyard. As this failed to offer any feeling of absolution, he went to the tavern. There he managed to replace the headache with a deep fatigue and the sensation that someone had removed his vital organs and replaced them out of order. And now, here was Dama Oriela, just as he'd imagined, waiting attentively for him to teach her something he was completely unprepared to teach.

"I should probably tell you," he said quietly, "I've never been anyone's dancing master before."

Oriela said, "I've never been anyone's dancing pupil, so I won't know the difference. What do we do?"

"We start with your feet and work our way up," said Silvio. He heard what he'd just said at the same moment that Oriela pressed a hand to her mouth to stop a giggle. *Casco!* He'd be dismissed before he'd even started.

From overhead he could hear Ser Pantalon saying, "... five thousand ducats isn't much. I wish we could have done more." No one came out to yell at Silvio.

He cleared his throat and tried again. "The Pavana is a processional dance. It often opens a ball, and it's always used to introduce a young lady into society. It will display your grace and breeding to your father's guests."

He demonstrated the basic step, speaking more loudly now, so the people upstairs could hear. "Watch me first. Step forward with your inside foot—" he took a step with his right, "And bring the other one forward to join it. Stop. Then step with that foot and bring the first up to meet it, and another stop. You try it."

She stepped as he counted. "*U-no, do. U-no, do.* Right. That's the feet. Now the ankles." He took a step, gliding the toe of the leading foot a finger's width from the floor while his ankle did a little, spiraling twist. When

Oriela tried to imitate this, first she kept catching her toe on the floor and nearly tripping, and then when her foot cleared the floor, she teetered and almost tipped over. He watched four or five failures before he figured out the problem.

He pointed at left side of her skirt, "You lifted your knee a little too high."

"How can you tell what my knees are doing?"

"Your shoulders tell me that your hips have tilted, therefore your knee was too high." This could be a useful way to think about girls, Silvio thought, as collections of mechanical parts. But it wasn't helping her dance. He prodded his head in search of a metaphor. "Think of a swan, its feet paddling underwater."

Oriela closed her eyes for a moment, and then began to glide forward, swimming over the marble floor. It was time to do it together. Oriela stood at attention on his right and reached for his hand, which he almost took before he remembered, "Wait. First you have to reverence your fingers. Like this," he brought his fingertips toward his mouth and kissed the air just above them. "Every time you join hands or drop them. It shows respect for your partner's hand."

She gave him an incredulous look. "Respect?" She looked at her fingertips for a moment, like they might be attached to someone else. "Doesn't it look silly?"

It looked ridiculous, but Silvio couldn't say that. "It's considered good manners."

A complete pass from one side of the atrium to the other went smoothly, so he decided to work on her posture. "Your feet are right, your hands are right," he said, "So now, you need to carry your upper body like this," he stretched his spine and tried to look haughty, "Like a peacock."

She cocked her head and said, "I thought I was a swan."

"Feet like a swan, head like a peacock," he realized he was talking faster. Dancing with Oriela was starting to be fun, which was making him nervous. He said, "Imagine you've got wings."

"Wings?" Her brows arched with a charming confusion.

"No, not wings," he said. "You might flap them. What I mean is...feathers?"

She stared for a moment, then shrugged. "Very well, maìstro. I've got feathers."

"Feathers," he said again, "On your head, and they don't flap, they sort of..." he waved his hand above his head, trying to get the motion, "Bob, or wave, or...*basta!* Now I'm picturing a rooster." He had tangled himself in a web of his own whimsy, like he usually did when he was starting to enjoy a girl's company. He said, "Forget the birds."

"The birds are forgotten, maìstro," Oriela said, smiling.

He searched his foggy brain for a better image, flexed his neck muscles, and realized what the motion reminded him of. "Eyes in a mask. Wait here." He dashed up to his room and back with his Zani mask. She hadn't moved, but she was looking at him as if she were worried for his health. But this would work, he knew it.

"When you're wearing a mask, you can't see anything on the periphery. Your eyes have to lead your head. The audience can tell what you're looking at from a hundred paces away because your nose is always pointed where your eyes are."

"So the dance is like a play."

"Exactly. A play called *Here I Am, World, What Do You Think of Me?* You'll look at your partner, but only briefly, and then you'll look away to the people who are watching. Now and then you make eye contact with another dancer, someone you've chosen carefully. And —here's the most important part—everyone needs to see you looking. They have to see whom you're looking at and how long you look. If your eyes meet your partner's and stay there too long, you'll be seen as forward, as overly attached to one man. Look too much at other gentlemen, and you're either an unschooled infant or a whore. Conversely, if your glances at your partner are too short, or if you spend too much time looking away at nothing, they'll say you're cold and haughty. The Pavana," Silvio realized this as he said it, "Might be the most dangerous dance you ever perform. Here," he handed her the Zani mask. "Try it with this on."

She said, "That's the first time I've ever heard anyone describe a dance as dangerous." She started to pull the mask over her head, but suddenly something bright blue and shining appeared at the top of the back stairs. It was Antonio in a suit of armor, with golden fleur-de-lis scattered over the skirt and overlay of the blue cloth *bases.*

"Ser Antonio," Silvio said, "If I ask what you've been up to, am I likely to regret it?"

Antonio strode into the center of the atrium and drew his sword, striking a pose. "When we perform at Brescia, *le Capitaine* will be French."

Silvio said, "You've developed a taste for rotten fruit?"

Carlo came out of the library, looked down over the balustrade at his brother and let out a cry. "Toni, are you mad?"

The governor appeared on the landing. "I don't recall giving anyone permission to take uniforms from the armory."

Carlo said, "The whole third act is based on your Captain being Venetian. You're asking us to rewrite the play!"

"No, we just have to change a few words," said Antonio. "I'll do it tonight."

Pantalon emerged next. He gave a short, explosive laugh and said, "They're going to tear you limb from limb and toss you in the polenta pot. You know that, don't you?"

"That's what I'm hoping," said Antonio. "I think a nicely boiled Frenchman will be just the cure for that city's melancholy." He turned to head for the stairs up to his room.

The men on the landing and the dancers in the

atrium stared at each other in silence for a moment. Then Pantalon said, "How go the lessons?"

"Pavana already mastered, Siór," said Silvio. He bowed to Oriela and turned to follow Antonio, thinking to help with the rewrites.

In spite of the bold entrance Antonio made in that French uniform, Silvio had noticed how his friend turned pale when he mentioned Brescia. Silvio spent an hour or so walking around the writing table in Antonio's room, tossing out suggestions that were ignored. Antonio sent Silvio for wine, and they shared the first bottle. The quill fluttered like an alarmed thrush between Antonio's fingers. By the time the Campanone rang curfew, a third wine bottle sat empty beside the inkwell. At that point, Silvio bid him goodnight and went back to Mamma's house.

He stopped in the apothecary shop to collect a few small brown bottles of a special tincture: valerian, holy basil and wood betony. Viola had given it to Silvio the night Clarissa died, and Piero had kept it on hand for two years afterward to give to Silvio when he woke up screaming. More recently, Mamma had been selling it to veterans of certain very nasty battles, to women raped by the foreign soldiers, to anyone with memories likely to take them for rides on the night mare. Then he paused a moment, listening to make sure Mamma was still upstairs, before slipping behind the counter to a dusty cupboard for a box of a much less popular potion for himself.

Antonio had coined the name *mal del castèl*, castle fever, for the distemper that struck his humors whenever he was near the castle at Brescia. It was, *ol Sciòr* said, a wickedly clever fortress. Its layers of walls shifted and twisted like the tumblers of a lock so that attackers would be pressed inexorably into a maze of blind alleys, there forced to fight one-to-one with the equally terrified defenders.

One rainy day in 1512, some twenty of those defenders—mostly Venetians, accustomed to fighting on the open sea—had been led by el Capitàn Antonio Pevari. Of those, only Pevari and his corporal Da Brixio had survived to surrender to the French. The destruction which the exhausted and enraged enemy had visited on the city afterward was common knowledge among even the children of the surrounding towns, who acted out the news in their games.

Even though Bèrghem had been spared the wholesale slaughter by emptying the city's coffers and paying the French to stay away, fathers like Enrico Speronèl had gone out to defend nearby villages and had not returned. Silvio and Clarissa had once surrendered Mamma's garden to Piero and another boy by handing them a large pile of mint leaves, begging not to be burned alive.

18 Castle

The view of the mountains from the San Giacomo gate almost made Silvio regret leaving Bèrghem for Brescia. He leaned over the wagon's tailgate for a last look at the newly carved *Liù di San March* that gazed out over the valley from the rebuilt Venetian gate, gleaming white against an overcast sky. The sculptor had evidently been instructed to convince the Bergamaschi of the Serene Republic's deep, genuine affection for them. Maybe they meant it, maybe not, but Silvio couldn't help liking the beast with its tender, sympathetic gaze. It was so unlike every other St. Mark lion he'd ever seen.

Carlo and Elisabeta were riding together behind the wagon, she sidesaddle in his arms, he talking inaudibly with Pantalon. Antonio, having been up all night changing the script, was asleep on the other side of the wagon. Silvio settled in between Elisabeta's clothes trunk and the stack of scenery scrolls. He rolled up the flap to look out the window and found Oriela's face there. She had ridden up alongside the wagon, just high enough on her palfrey to peer inside.

"Silvio, can I ask you another silly question?"

"If you dare." Was she going to make a habit of bringing her difficult questions to him?

She nodded over her shoulder at the gate. "Do lions have feathers?"

He blinked at her.

She said, "The ones outside the church didn't. The ones you patted."

Silvio needed a moment to put the images together, jarred to realize he'd been seen skipping Mass.

"But the name on the wagon says..." she said.

"The lion's feathers," he said. The Venetian Lion of St. Mark had wings, and the wings had feathers, and feathers can tickle you and make you laugh. Carlo thought it was clever, but Silvio thought it was just as likely to confuse people, even those who knew all about saints. "Most lions don't," he said. "Just that one. It's St. Mark."

"St. Mark is a lion?" Oriela leaned closer to the window.

"No, he wrote a Gospel." That got him a frown. She probably thought he was mocking her. Maybe he was, a little. "The lion is just..." What was it, anyway?

"Why is he on the gate?"

"Mark is the patron saint of Venice." *Madóna*! Had she been raised in a cave?

Oriela said, "Why? Did he live there?"

"No, he's just buried there. He died in Egypt."

"Then how did he get to Venice? No, wait. Don't tell me. Someone stole him, like San Pazzio."

That's what Silvio would have said if he were in front of an audience, speaking as his *bufon* alter ego Salvàn Mandragora. Instead, since Antonio was nearby, he suppressed a laugh and said what a good Venetian would say: "They rescued him. From the Saracens."

Looking at Oriela as he said this gave him a moment of vertigo. *Stolen...rescued...?* He was back in his room over the apothecary shop, arguing with Mamma. Was he talking to a girl who had been rescued or stolen?

Oriela let her horse fall back, and Silvio watched the countryside rattling by. Between the road and the mountains, all the fields were in cultivation this year, but you could still see the scorched walls of the farmhouses under their new roofs. Barns and corrals still stood empty. Stumps from burnt orchards poked up through the fast-growing beans and buckwheat. One abandoned house was surrounded by rows of some crop Silvio hadn't seen before. Stalks as tall as a man waved and hissed in the wind that bore down from the heaving clouds.

When the gray outer walls of Brescia appeared on the even grayer horizon, Ser Antonio opened the box of provisions and pulled out a mostly-full bottle of wine. He yanked out the cork and tossed it into the corner. He didn't offer to share it.

Silvio fished the cork out from behind the mask box, then pulled out the brown medicine vial. "Ten drops," he said to Antonio, "Wash it down, and then give me the wine bottle."

But Antonio didn't give it to him. After watching his friend drink morosely for some time, Silvio closed the window flaps to spare Antonio the sight of the approaching castle and storm. Rain would make Capitàn Pevari's malady worse. Silvio crawled out front to sit by Piero on the driving box.

The air grew sodden. The wind turned colder and sent the first few drops of rain like flecks of spittle into Silvio's face. He peered up through the rain at the castle gate. It was also new, but this lion's mouth was open wide, the teeth bared. Not at all like the one at Bèrghem. "Piero, look at their lion."

Piero spared a glance for the gate before returning his attention to the road. He chuckled grimly. "He's roaring. I would, too."

Beyond the castle gate, the leering circle of covered battlements crouched in ambush against the sky. Still higher up, a trackless spire of mud rose beyond the tower to the chained coffin-lid of the drawbridge. Silvio could almost pity the French, clawing their breathless way up that slope toward the unattainable keep, the sky overhead dropping iron bolts, raindrops, hail and cannon shot in equal quantities. Did the French also suffer from *mal del castèl*, or had their post-battle orgy of pillage and demolition cured them of their terror?

They turned a corner toward the center of town, and the wind hit the wagon broadside. The light rain became a pounding deluge. The riders drew their hoods down over their faces. When Silvio slid back inside the wagon, Antonio's now-empty wine bottle whirled toward his head. It wouldn't have missed, either, had it been aimed at anyone but Silvio, whose practiced reflexes saved him from a cracked skull.

"Where'd he go?" Antonio said.

Silvio knew better than to ask who he meant. "Siór, it's just me."

"*Ou êtes-vous?*" Antonio raised the bottle again, his eyes flitting over the shadowy objects in the wagon's bed. "Thrice-damned *francéxe!*" He stumbled as he swung the bottle again, and Silvio was able to get past him and put his head out the back.

"Ser Carlo!" he called through the pelting rain, "We're going to need some help."

19 Barbarians

"**D**on't look at me like that," Pantalon said to his horse. El Moro was dancing at the end of his bridle, water flying off his black mane. "Go with this nice groom and have a rub-down. What?" The tall black Spanish horse had blown steam at him. "It's October. It rains." Pantalon stroked El Moro's withers. "No cavalry around here." As far as Pantalon knew, his horse hadn't been in battle. Yet something about the air of the place was making him skittish.

Oriela's hand touched his, appearing from the other side of El Moro's neck, patting the horse and saying, "See, Stelina's going inside. She'll be warm and dry with her nose in a bucket of oats while you're out here in the rain." Pantalon couldn't see her face, only a hand and a voice, and his horse slowly quieting. "Shh. Go on, Moro. *Alón.*" And El Moro went. Well. Maybe more *citadina* ladies should grow up on farms.

He offered Oriela his arm to go into the house, which belonged to Pantalon's friend Trivisàn, one of the merchants whose post-war success was rebuilding Brescia. Like Pantalon, he was a citizen with more money and wits than any ten *nobili*. The patricians came to his house for important conversations and sumptuous dinners. They were to be joined that evening by Francesco Diedo the Podestà, a lady poet from Canoggio, and the famous *condottiere* general Orsini. Soon the bustling city would be its old self, thanks to men like Trivisàn. Thanks to *citadini*.

With El Moro tucked away in the ground-floor stable, Pantalon climbed the grand staircase into his friend's house. In the portego, its walls dazzling with new frescoes, a table had been laid. Silver and gold platters and Murano goblets sparkled in a shimmer of candlelight.

General Orsini was already seated and delivering an oration. "...No business getting those Gallici barbarians involved in Italia." Even after ten years in the pay of Venice, the hired *condottiere* retained his Tuscan habit of adding unnecessary syllables to Vèneto words. "They have no idea how to conduct a civilized war! When you lose a battle, you ought to be able to surrender like a sensible *persona* and wait to be ransomed. *Perbacco*! Even the Turchi understand this!"

Pantalon caught sight of a disturbance in the corner of his eye and looked across the portego toward one of the adjoining doors. Why were Silvio and Piero dragging Antonio through the side rooms?

"But it's no use surrendering to the *francese*," said Orsini, "They only say they've got no place to put you, and run you through right there on the spot. Absolute savages! Oh, *bu-ona sera*," he said, having only then noticed the newcomers.

Trivisàn hurried forward and embraced Pantalon,

called servants to take them to their rooms to dry off, and then said, "But Ser Carlo, I thought your brother was with you."

Carlo reddened a little and said, "Antonio sends his apologies. He was feeling unwell and went directly to his room. I'm sure he'll join us later."

"I'm sorry to hear it." Trivisàn turned to Pantalon and assumed a sly grin. "And what about your *zani*?" His friend was waiting for a laugh, Pantalon knew, so for the sake of friendship he gave one. But Carlo glared. Trivisàn said, "I mean Mandragora and his brother. I heard they were with you."

Pantalon said, "They're here. But you mustn't call them *zani* around Ser Carlo. He's more sensitive than they are."

An hour later when Pantalon returned to the portego, dry and dressed in an indigo brocade doublet, he wasn't surprised to find Piero and Silvio seated with the other guests. Trivisàn wouldn't have called them *zani* if he really meant to treat them like vagabond laborers. The Venetian governor Diedo had also arrived in the meantime.

Orsini was still on the same subject. "...and then, one stroke of a *penna*, and the borders are back where they started. Complete waste of time." As if he'd been talking the entire time, which seemed likely.

"Except," said Pantalon, "That our towns are now in ruins."

"We're putting ourselves back together," said Trivisàn.

Orsini drained his glass. It was instantly refilled by a servant who was standing behind his chair. Pantalon wondered whether Trivisàn wasn't perhaps showing off just a bit with that many servants. Trivisan used to have a sensible staff, back when he was well off. Now that he was nearly ruined, there was a footman at every chair. It was ostentatious, impractical, and frankly un-Venetian. On the other hand, it may have been an act of charity. Jobs in the ruined city would be hard to find, which is why Venice was currently being flooded with unemployed Brescians.

"Maybe that is what Papa Giulio was up to," Orsini said, downing half the wine in one gulp. "La Serenissima can't threaten the neighbors while she's crippled by repair bills."

Pantalon laughed politely at this. He was doing a lot of polite laughing tonight. He noticed, however, that Governor Diedo wasn't amused.

Silvio said, "Did you hear the story about Pope Julius and the boy bishop?" He must have thought he'd been invited as a jester. As no one answered, he went back to eating his pheasant.

Trivisàn said, "The walls alone need thousands of ducats' worth of work." From there, the conversation turned to the price of stone at this or that quarry and went on to even duller topics. When Pantalon ran out of wine, the footman behind his chair was there with a silver pitcher. The clear, golden liquid flashed through the intricate patterns on the glass. It was good wine. If only Orsini would stop talking, the dinner might prove enjoyable.

At last Carlo brought them around to the subject of the play. The governor had thought they would perform inside his palazzo, but Carlo wanted to do it out in the square. Trivisàn objected to the palazzo idea as elitist, but Diedo was nervous about the crowd. And Carlo hadn't even told them yet about Antonio's new costume. Pantalon decided that he, at least, would not be the first one to mention the *fleur-de-lis* insignia in Brescia.

Pantalon said to Diedo, "We had an idea we thought you might like. At the very end, you could come up on the stage, and we would present you with a purse. Just a token amount, of course."

"You'd hand the purse to Silvio," said Carlo, "And he rides around the piazza on Piero's shoulders, tossing out the coins."

Elisabeta said, "Like a new Doge."

Pantalon was amused to see the look on Piero's face. Apparently no one had told him the plan yet.

Silvio said, "I always knew my brother was an ass."

20 Toni

After dinner, Silvio followed Carlo to Antonio's room. They found him on the floor in a corner opposite the fireplace, barricaded behind a long, carved chest that he'd dragged over from beside the bed. On the wall above him hung a display of a dozen swords, sticking out from behind a shield like hedgehog quills.

Antonio had his outer garments unlaced, sleeves dangling, his rumpled shirt sticking out everywhere. A plate of pheasant—actual pheasant, not beans—sat untouched on the chest, but the wine glass was empty. An empty bottle rested on the floor by his left elbow. He looked up for a moment when Silvio came in and then resumed staring in the general direction of a thick bedpost that was draped in blood-red velvet.

"Siór?" Silvio said.

No response. Silvio looked at Carlo, who nodded wearily and sat on the edge of the bed.

Silvio sighed and said, "Toni?"

"That's better," Antonio said, "Nobody here you need to be calling *siór*. Come. Join me in my trench."

Silvio slid down behind the chest next to Antonio. He said, "You haven't eaten your beans."

Antonio's lips quirked—it wasn't quite a smile. "Got you to call me Toni."

The chest had a battle scene painted on the lid. Trivisàn had probably thought the décor would honor el Capitàn. Silvio wondered what Orsini's room looked like. He said, "You took your medicine?"

Antonio picked up the vial from somewhere on the floor. Firelight refracting through the brown glass showed it was about half empty.

"Still afraid to sleep," Antonio said. His voice reminded Silvio of his little nephew Rico, asking Smeraldina for a song, a story, another kiss. It was amazing the man could still sit up after half a bottle of Valerian, not to mention another whole bottle of wine.

Carlo crossed his arms and said, "The problem will be getting you up tomorrow in time for the play. Which, I might add, was your stupid idea."

Antonio pulled further into the corner, hugging his knees. They came to his chin. "I know. I'm a terrible coward."

"I'll do it," said Silvio.

"I ought to be hanged between the columns," said Antonio. The punishment for treason.

"I'll do it," Silvio said again. "If you're not better by tomorrow, I'll do your French captain." Carlo tossed up his hands and walked away across the room.

Silvio realized with a shock that Carlo agreed with Antonio. He thought his brother a coward. Yet by all accounts Antonio was ferocious in battle—which was most likely why he got sick when he thought about it.

Carlo should understand this, that there's no shame in looking horror in the face and calling it horror, that it's one way to be sure you have a soul. It was a belief Silvio clung to like a rope over his own abyss.

Carlo said, "If this causes a riot, I'll hang you both between the columns myself."

Antonio's head dropped to his chest. Carlo sighed as he crossed the room and bent to hoist his brother onto one shoulder. He nodded toward the bed, and Silvio turned down the coverlet. Carlo said, "If anyone asks…"

"An ague brought on by too much yellow bile," said Silvio.

Once they'd managed to stuff the unconscious Antonio between the sheets, Carlo gave Silvio a disgruntled look. "I thought it was supposed to cure him, not knock him out."

"I told him ten drops," Silvio said, "Not half the bottle."

It wasn't until he was out the door and halfway up the stairs to his own room that Silvio remembered how the Mask called Captain had become French: the purloined armor. Armor made of cold iron.

Silvio, the son of la Fata Viola, the boy who broke out in hives when he ventured into the smithy across the square, who couldn't so much as pick up a horseshoe nail without feeling as though a knife had been plunged through his hand, had for the sake of friendship promised to pack himself into a suit of that poison like a crab in its shell.

21 Understudy

Oriela's first duty as Elisabeta's second was to sit backstage, on the prop box, listen, and follow along with the script. This third task turned out to be more difficult than it sounded.

The script, such as it was, had been written in two different hands. Lines of dialogue in a shaky cursive that grew less legible with each page alternated with cursory references to entrances and exits. These were written clearly and must be Carlo's, since they would have been added after Antonio fell ill. By the last page, only Carlo's notes remained, with no spoken lines and only the barest clues to the intended action.

Oriela slipped behind the backdrop while Piero and Carlo were hanging up the other scene pieces. There was a bench back here, next to the box of props. Oriela sat down to read. Elisabeta was still getting dressed, and there was no sign of Silvio. It was probably taking him a while to get into that uniform.

Piero had added another set of stairs onto the back of the stage, to allow the players to come and go out of sight of the audience in case the crowd grew hostile. Papà climbed up these steps and joined Oriela on the bench. He was in the same costume he had worn at Villa Lesse and held his mask in one hand. He gazed at it for a moment and shook his head. "It's going to be a diplomatic disaster," he said quietly, "Worse than *The Toe*." He sighed. "Well, Carlo always did let his little brother do as he pleased. And Elisabeta indulges Carlo, so there you are."

Piero had started singing a popular madrigal to signal the market crowd it was time to come and see something. Papà got up and started pacing, back and forth along the length of the backdrop panel.

A jingling and scraping announced Silvio's arrival. Oriela raised the hem of the plain outer curtain to see what he looked like. The armor was still bare metal. He had the cloth overlay and French plume stuffed inside the helmet, which he passed up to her, looking over his shoulder. The Captain's mask was stuck into the helmet nose-first.

Silvio hauled himself up the steps with a visible effort. He held out his hand. "*Bases*," he said. He sounded out of breath.

"What?"

"Cloth thing."

She pulled the skirted garment out of the helmet, shook it and passed it to Silvio. After he got the blue and yellow cloth tied on over the breastplate, moving a little stiffly, he sat down heavily on the bench and sighed.

Oriela said, "You're not getting sick now, too, are you?"

Instead of answering, Silvio picked up the script she'd set down, looked it over and said, "I've got till the second scene. How long has Piero been playing?"

"Two songs now."

Elisabeta came backstage from the front steps, having no need to sneak across the piazza like Silvio. Carlo followed her. He said to Silvio, "Don't let anyone see you before your scene. You're a surprise."

Oriela couldn't blame Silvio for rolling his eyes as he affixed the plume to the top of the helmet. Then Papà and Elisabeta went on stage as Piero ended his song and came backstage to set his rebec on the table. Oriela rose to stand near one end of the backdrop and watch.

The first scene proceeded as written, but Silvio's first entrance in the French uniform brought the action to a halt. The crowd booed and shouted insults, and there was a small commotion near the well as a woman fainted and had to be carried away.

Silvio as the arrogant soldier made quite an alarming villain, standing a hands-breadth too close to Elisabeta and punctuating his orders to Piero with an insult or a kick. By the time Papà's Magnifico was greeting *le Capitaine*, air-kissing the cheeks of the long-nosed mask and calling him *mon cher ami*, the men who had carried the fainting woman away had returned with friends and made their way toward the front of the crowd. Some of them carried baskets.

Following along with the script, Oriela heard Magnifico ask the Capitaine, "What have you brought for my niece today?"

The Capitaine said, in flowery language with many extra pronouns, that he had only brought her the *honneur* of being asked to marry him.

Someone called out, "Don't trust him, *venessià!*" A moldy orange burst against the metal ridge on Silvio's left shoulder. Bits of fetid pulp splattered on Papà's mask. "You kiss the *fransés*," shouted the heckler, "He'll make you his whore!" Sour juice dripped down the backdrop. Oriela pulled her head back behind the panel.

"*Mais* no," Silvio said. He was off the script, talking to the orange thrower. "I kiss Mademoiselle, a whore *plus jolie*, take her money home to *la belle* France, where the whores are the prettiest." Oriela was surprised Silvio knew that much French.

Magnifico told *le Capitaine* to come back later for his answer, bid him *au revoir*, and Papà exited from the far side of the stage. He grabbed a rag from the prop box to wipe his mask.

Silvio came off on Oriela's side. He pushed his mask up onto his helmet almost before he was out of sight of the audience, and he was wheezing. Piero handed him a rag to wipe the sweat off a face that looked, Oriela thought, pale to the point of being almost blue. Piero whispered something, and Silvio nodded, the kind of overly emphatic nod people use when they aren't at all sure they really mean yes.

Papà held out his hand to Oriela, and she passed him the script. He paced the narrow aisle behind the backdrop, mouthing lines. Out on the stage, Elisabeta and

Carlo had started talking, though it might have been better described as panting.

Carlo exclaimed, "Dearest lady!"

Elisabeta breathed, "Yes!"

Carlo: I beg you, tell me your name!

Elisabeta: Flaminia!

Carlo: Ah! Flaminia! Most fortunate name!

Elisabeta: It is?

Carlo: Yes! To belong to such a lady!

Elisabeta: Oh!

Carlo: For you are a brilliant flame—

Elisabeta: A flame!

Carlo: —of brightest beauty!

Elisabeta: Ah! It burns!

Carlo: Yes, burns!

Elisabeta: It must be—quenched!

Just when it sounded as if Elisabeta must faint from excessive breathing, Silvio hoisted himself to his feet and returned to the stage. He and Carlo started shouting at each other, and the audience was shouting at both of them. Piero joined the quarrel, followed by Papà.

Oriela picked the script up off the bench and flipped through the pages, but already Piero had departed from the written lines. When it came Silvio's turn to speak, it was clear he hadn't read any of this and was making it all up on the spot.

At the end of the scene, Silvio stomped loudly off the

stage, then slumped with a quiet groan onto the bench. He coughed.

"Are you sure you're all right?" Oriela said.

Silvio coughed again. He took off his helmet, his gauntleted hands shaking.

Oriela showed him the script. "Do you know where we are?"

He shook his head without looking at it. He was wheezing hard, working to breathe.

"You're sick," Oriela said. "You should tell Carlo."

Silvio didn't look at her but stood up, wriggled his body from head to feet like a restless dog, and returned to the stage. Carlo pulled Elisabeta off stage right and into a fold of the outer curtain, where he started kissing her almost indecently. If this was their usual reaction after playing a scene like that, no wonder Carlo was in favor of having his wife on stage. Oriela returned to her viewing spot at the left edge of the backdrop in time to see Papà dodge a flying turnip. It struck his canvas house, which teetered on its supporting post.

Someone shouted, "Coward!"

She heard Papà whisper, "*Cagá*," and she realized from the chagrin in his voice that he should have let the turnip hit him. Today, here in Brescia, his Mask was no longer just an old man who happened to be Venetian. Today, Magnifico was Venice, and Venice must not be seen to duck.

A moldy eggplant came flying toward Piero, and Papà moved to block it, taking the black slime squarely on the chest. Today, Venice must protect men of the provinces. Instead of railing at Zani for annoying the Capitaine, instead of threatening to beat him for helping Elisabeta talk to Carlo—both of which he would ordinarily have done without thinking—Magnifico beseeched him with praying hands to save him from the treacherous Frenchman.

Oriela retreated to the bench, deciding it was safer there. Scenes passed. People came and went. Oriela became absorbed by the challenge of trying to match what was on the page to what was actually happening. She was startled by a crash at her feet, like someone had overturned a tinker's cart.

Silvio had collapsed, the French armor clattering onto the wagon bed. His mask fell off. Oriela put down the pages and knelt by Silvio's head, pulled off his helmet. The next moment, Piero was at Silvio's feet, unbuckling the plates that covered his shins.

"Idiot," Piero muttered, "Damn Toni and his 'ague.' And damn the French," he put the strips of metal on the bench, wincing as if they were hot, and proceeded to the cuisses. "And damn all blacksmiths and armorers."

Oriela wasn't sure what the last curse had to do with anything, but it was clear that Piero thought the armor should come off. Something was certainly making Silvio ill, glassy-eyed and struggling for breath like a landed fish. She went to work on the breastplate buckles.

Carlo arrived next and looked down at Silvio. "What's the matter with him?"

Oriela started to say, "We have to stop," but Piero broke in.

"We'll finish the play, Siór," said Piero, "I'll take the Captain." He had already started trying to fit the greaves onto his shins.

Carlo said, "But then we won't have a servant."

That's what he was worried about? The play? Piero was struggling with the metal plates, which were clearly too small for him.

Carlo sat on the bench and sighed. "What will I tell Governor Diedo?"

Oriela passed the breastplate to Piero and unbuckled the arm pieces. Silvio turned his head away from her, clearly embarrassed. "Carlo," she said, "You'll tell him that two of your players are sick now and you have to stop."

A silence on the stage went on too long. Papà and Elisabeta must have run out of lines. The crowd's mounting tension was palpable, even backstage.

Piero said, "We can't do that, Dama. Not in this city, not in the middle of this play." He had just managed to strap the shin piece onto one leg. At this rate, every costume change from Captain to Zani would take an hour. He said, "There's only one Act to go."

Oriela heard her father's voice now, a little too loud. Elisabeta took a moment too long to answer. They were making things up to fill time, clearly confused. She looked at Silvio's face. If he appeared less fish-like, it was only because he was now unconscious.

"Piero, give me your mask," Oriela said.

He handed it to her without question, probably thinking she only meant to put it away. Oriela opened the prop box and started burrowing through it. In a perfect imitation of Francesca's husky voice and mountain accent, she asked, "Don't we have an apron in here?"

"I don't think so," said Carlo. "We've never needed one. Why?"

"We need one now." She put Piero's mask over her face, then took it off again to tighten the strap. Now the eyes were too wide apart, and she had to stuff rags into the sides to make it fit. "Borrow one from someone in the audience," she said. Francesca's voice made it easier for her to give orders, even to Carlo.

"Right away, Dama," said Carlo, rising. He jumped off the back of the stage. Just before ducking under the heavy outer curtain, he said, "But your father is going to roast my liver for breakfast."

Piero, finally stuffed into the French armor, dragged his brother out of the way and propped him up in the corner on a stack of extra scenery rolls. He passed Oriela his floppy Zani hat, and she stuffed her hair inside it. She peered around the backdrop and said to Piero, "You'd better get out there. They're fetching more fruit."

Carlo returned with a green and white striped apron. Oriela leafed through the pages until she found the end of Act II, where Carlo's brief directions had been insufficient to keep Papà and Elisabeta talking. She knelt beside Silvio and wiped his clammy forehead with the apron. He was wheezing, but at least that meant he still breathed.

Piero, now as the Captain, had picked up the threads of the scene. Magnifico called, "Zani!"

"I'll be back," Oriela whispered to Silvio, "Keep breathing." She stood and hitched the sides of her skirt up into the apron strings, then lowered the mask into place and adjusted the rags. She remembered to point its nose where she was walking and noticed that it did, in fact, feel much like a dance.

When she appeared on stage at Magnifico's summons, Papà's eyes looked as though they might leap out through the holes in his mask. He recovered his wits enough to give her the orders he must have been expecting to give to Piero, or maybe to Silvio, to just about anyone in the world other than his daughter in a black mask and borrowed apron.

Papà exited. Elisabeta's back was still turned to Oriela, and Zani hadn't said anything yet. Carlo came to tell Elisabeta that he must fight a duel with the Frenchman.

"They love to duel, those Frenchies," Oriela said. Elisabeta turned with wide eyes at Oriela's voice. She paused for half a heartbeat, and then winked at Oriela before returning her attention to Carlo. The next moment, Piero's Capitaine stormed onto the stage with his sword drawn, and the men started to fight.

Carlo's directions had indicated that *le Capitaine* should pick up Elisabeta in this scene and carry her away. The maneuver should have been child's play for a big man like Piero, but it took him two tries to get her onto his shoulder, and he stumbled as he was chased off stage by Carlo and Oriela. Once behind the backdrop, Piero took off the helmet and raised his mask, panting.

"Not you too," Oriela whispered.

Piero sneezed. "It's almost over," he said, "I'll be fine. Silvio always gets it worse." But his face was red, and he was scratching his neck.

Papà was out on the stage, shouting at Carlo that his niece had been captured. The next note in the script said that Zani was supposed to carry Elisabeta home and deliver her to Magnifico and Carlo. Oriela decided that if she thought too much about it she wouldn't be able to do it, so she bent down and grabbed Elisabeta's legs without warning her.

When she straightened, la Dama was draped over her shoulder. Oriela ran heavily toward Papà and managed to get halfway there before she and Elisabeta both fell. How Elisabeta managed not to laugh was a marvel. Thus retrieved by her uncle's faithful Lombard servant and given to her Veronese lover, Elisabeta started them all singing, "*Tutti venite armati, o forti miei soldati...*" It was a popular song, and a few in the audience started to sing along.

Piero came onstage without the armor and tossed the blue cloth *bases* into the audience, which gleefully ripped the uniform to shreds. The orange-thrower even shouted, "*Bravi!*"

Governor Diedo joined them on stage to receive the purse from Carlo as planned. But with no Silvio to toss the coins, Piero picked up Oriela and carried her around the square on his shoulder. At this, the hecklers dropped their baskets and were the first to start chanting the Venetian salute, "Mar-co! Mar-co!"

"Antonio was right," Oriela said in Piero's ear as she scattered silver *lire piccole* over the cobblestones. The hated uniform had let the crowd focus its anger, and now they all felt better. People were cheering, and she was in the middle of it. If she hadn't been so worried about Silvio, she'd have thanked him for getting sick.

Her elation dropped away the moment Piero set her down behind the wagon. She wanted to go and check on Silvio, but Papà was charging at Carlo in his stained and stinking zimara, waving the Magnifico mask by its nose. It looked as though he might be about to hit Carlo with it.

"Oriela?" Papà said, "As Zani?"

"I didn't have time to ask you," said Carlo, both hands in the air. "Silvio got sick so fast—"

"Papà," Oriela began, hurrying up beside him, but Carlo put up a hand to silence her.

"A lady can hardly play the Captain..." Carlo said.

"But my daughter can play a maidservant?" said Papà. "In the piazza!?"

Piero now joined them, scratching his hands and coughing. "If it had been any other city—"

Papà pushed Piero aside. "She can get up in front of all of Brescia to play the maid—"

Oriela turned to Piero and said, "Is Silvio—" But Piero was sneezing and couldn't talk.

Papà said, "—And to insult the French." He was shouting, waving his mask around. The nose was coming apart.

"She did well," said Carlo. "Be proud. She has your talent."

"Proud?" said Papà. "She carried your wife like a flour sack!"

Oriela raised her voice now. "Does anyone know if Silvio is still alive?"

The men stopped and looked at her. She took off the apron and handed it to Carlo, gave Piero his hat and mask, and turned back to the wagon. Silvio was sitting up on the floor, leaning against the prop box. His color was starting to return, but his chest was working as if air were hard to come by. Oriela sat down next to him.

"Did you really..." he said, stopping to cough, "Carry Elisabeta like a flour sack?"

"It's what the script said to do," she said.

Silvio smiled weakly, but his eyes were warm. "*Brava,*" he said.

22 Dido

After Brescia, they veered north, back toward Lake Garda. Oriela was worried that Papà might try and leave her there, but they went on around the south end of the lake and followed the narrow peninsula out to Sirmione. The passed the castle and the town and continued along a street lined with tall pines, oaks and walnuts. Many parts of the road were dotted with the purple-black stains of fallen mulberries.

The grand gates of Villa Pevari, at the end of a long, sloping lane, seemed to be constructed as much of cypress as of stone, living green columns ranged side by side with carved, white ones. The formal garden was smaller than Donata's, and the grounds were dominated instead by terraced meadows dotted with ancient olive trees, thickets of oleander, and off to the right a tidy vineyard whose meticulous terraces carved a wide staircase along the curve of a hill surmounted by an old chapel.

The yellow, three-story house was fronted by an arcade porch, where two grooms in green and blue livery were on hand to take charge of their horses almost before they had dismounted. Here, where Elisabeta was in charge, there was no nonsense about sending the "zani" with the wagon.

Oriela and Elisabeta took a stroll before dinner. Near the water's edge, the lake floor appeared paved with polished cobblestones of every color, the sunlight turning them to large, round gems beneath the diamond ripples.

"It's wonderful here," said Oriela, "I keep expecting to meet Catullus coming around the next tree in his white toga." She had heard the legend that the Roman poet had spent his summers at Sirmione.

To their left a grove of small willows extended from the shore, the last tree appearing to float on its own several boat-lengths away. Sunny yellow leaves shook loose in a breeze that broke the surface of the lake into small waves and dusted them with the delicate slips of gold.

Elisabeta said, "When they were boys, Carlo and Toni used to play around the grotto all summer, acting out every story they'd learned from their Latin tutor: the Metamorphoses, the death of Caesar," she laughed fondly. "By the time Carlo was old enough to join a *Conpàgna delle calze*, he and Toni had gotten all their friends from the lake to re-enact the entire Aeneid."

"Antonio mentioned that," said Oriela, "What on earth is a stocking club?'

"Oh, they plan all the social gatherings in town. Carlo and Toni are part of the Alati." As if this explained it entirely, Elisabeta went on, "One time my family was out here visiting one of the Loredan cousins, and I slipped away to explore the ruins and found this crowd of boys, some *nobili,* some locals, and the oldest one—that was Carlo—called to a little peasant boy wearing a grain sack for a skirt, '*Ehi,* Mario! Here's a girl to be Dido! You can take off the dress!' Carlo was Aeneas, of course."

"Naturally," said Oriela. Carlo must take the lead part.

"I didn't know the story, so I mostly just did whatever he told me to. Mario was grateful. Anyway, after that Carlo started pestering Papà Nicolò to 'talk to the Senator about the Lesse girl.'"

"How old were you?"

"I was eight. He was thirteen."

They continued their walk, past the willows and alongside a field of water reeds with fluffy tops. Elisabeta turned inland and led Oriela up a small flight of ancient stone steps to a terraced meadow where the men were practicing a scene from Plautus' *Miles Gloriosus* which they'd been invited to perform on All Saints' Day at the old Roman theater in Verona. They had their masks on. Elisabeta sat on the top step to watch, patting the spot beside her for Oriela.

Papà called, "Palessio!"

Silvio rushed out from behind an oleander bush. "What's the matter?"

Papà: "It's been discovered!"

"What's been discovered?"

"On my roof—someone from your house has been

spying into the courtyard. He saw Ama...A...*Aat—z—ciu!*" Papà pushed his mask onto his head just in time.

Silvio broke his pose and said, "Are you all right? That's your third sneeze since the beginning of the scene."

Papà turned to face Carlo. "Why can't we practice indoors?"

Antonio said, "There aren't any ruins indoors."

Papà mopped at his nose with a handkerchief. "There aren't any leaves, either, and this place looks nothing like an amphitheater." He sneezed again and pressed a hand to his forehead.

"Let's just get through this scene," said Carlo. "Once more, from your entrance."

Palessio: I hear the neighbor's door creaking. Here comes the old man.

Perplessio: Next time you see anyone on my roof, if you don't beat him senseless, I swear by Hercules I'll tan your hide— hhi—*ZCIUU!*"

Elisabeta slapped her knees as she stood up. She strode through the middle of the scene toward her husband. "You're a perfect tyrant, *cioci.*"

Oriela went to Papà, pulling her own handkerchief out of her sleeve. "Are you catching cold?"

"It's only the leaves," he said. "They give off a miasma...oh," he took the handkerchief she was holding out. "Thank you. There are too many trees out here. I'll be fine in Verona." He turned to Carlo. "Really, I will. Let's go inside and start again."

Elisabeta said, "Not until you boys have had your suppers and rested. Carlo, you can't expect your friends to play Romans with you every minute they're here."

23 Galliard

The Galliard lesson was not going as smoothly as the Pavana. The harder Oriela tried to be graceful and ladylike with the vigorous hop-kick step called a *grue*, the more she felt like a May Day peasant. Her hair had escaped her lace cap and was falling into her eyes. The fifth time she had to pull her sleeve back up onto her shoulder she wanted to tear it off.

Her father had gone down to Desenzano with Carlo, where Giorgio would meet them and take Stelina back to the villa. The palfrey had never been on a boat, and Carlo intended to sail across from Sirmione to Lasize on the eastern shore. He said this would be a shorter way to Verona. Antonio was to supervise the lesson—if his shrinking, sheepish glances could be called supervision. He'd been acting ashamed around Silvio ever since Brescia.

After a few dozen frustrating repetitions, Oriela finally got her feet to cooperate with the opening five steps. She was about to be proud of herself, coiling her loose hair and stuffing it under her cap, until Silvio said, "That's only the most basic form of the *passaggio*, of course. No one actually does it that way."

She let the hair fall again. "What do they do?"

"Variations," he said. "In a Galliard passage, you have to go from here," he pointed to the floor at his own feet, "To here," he crossed to a spot ten paces away, "And back again in twelve beats, but you can get there almost any way you choose. For instance..." He started the segment again, but this time he rose high into the air with each *grue*, spun a full rotation for the return cadenza, and rounded off the set with a cartwheel and a backflip.

Oriela laughed, the tension disintegrating in her throat.

Silvio said, "Your turn."

She started with a long leap in the first measure, followed by a series of spins in the second, forgetting in the exuberance of the moment that she was wearing the heavy, overlong blue skirt she'd borrowed from Elisabeta. It wrapped itself around her as she twirled her way through the third measure.

"Watch out!" Silvio cried, "Your dress!" —but it was already the fourth bar, the time to leap back to her starting place beside Silvio. With a dozen yards of silk binding her legs together, she teetered forward and crashed into him, knocking them both to the ground.

Silvio caught her as they fell, taking the impact so that she landed on him instead of falling face-first onto the terrazzo floor. By the time she realized he had his arms around her, he had already rolled sideways and released her.

"I'm sorry," she said, face burning. "Are you hurt?"

"I know how to fall," he said. He propped himself onto one elbow. "Well, usually." He reddened a little. "Collapsing in a pile of scrap metal isn't my normal method."

Once she was back on her feet, skirt straightened, sleeves in place, hair re-pinned, Silvio showed her some of the less ambitious *passaggio* variations. They weren't so hard, now that she'd survived the disastrous improvisation.

Then Silvio said, "Now that you look so respectable, I'll undo all our work by showing you the Volta." Oriela had heard of the daring new dance but hadn't expected to study it. Silvio said, "You'll have to know it. The old men think it's scandalous, so naturally the young men can't get enough of it, and I suspect your father would rather be surprised by seeing you perform it well than by seeing you knock your partner down."

"As long as I'm doomed to surprise him," she said, thinking her poor father would probably prefer fewer surprises from her.

They performed the opening sequence of Galliard five-steps in turn. Oriela kissed her fingers in preparation for a hand-hold, but Silvio wrapped his left arm around the back of her waist and planted his right hand on her ribcage, just below her left breast. The stays of her bodice gave slightly with the pressure.

"I see what you mean about being surprised," she said.

He said, "It gets worse. Put your right hand on my shoulder."

"What do I do with the left?"

"Hang onto your skirt."

Silvio counted six minims, and Oriela clung to his shoulder and her skirt as he swept her around five times in a circle with himself in the center. Each three-quarter turn left them facing a new direction. When they stopped, she was wobbling a little.

"Would you believe me," he said, "If I tell you that was actually the modest version? Depending on how energetic—or how drunk—your partner is, you might find yourself airborne. Will you mind if I pick you up?"

She looked over at Antonio, who shrugged.

Silvio said, "Don't ask him. He's one of the partners most likely to toss you around."

"Then we'd better practice it," she said.

"Right." Silvio cleared his throat, lowered his eyes. "If the gentleman intends to perform this variation, he'll grab you like this," he brought her close again and moved his right hand down to her left hip, "And he'll make his leg into a chair to boost you up."

"Are you serious?"

"I'm afraid so."

He counted off, then hoisted her on his raised knee and twirled. Five times around, her bum resting on the inside of his thigh, his soft curls brushing her chin. Oh, yes. She was dizzy.

24 Monte Baldo

Silvio sat by his brother and watched the hind-quarters of the draft horses, one dark, one pale and speckled, as they picked their sullen way along the rocky, mountain tracks toward Verona. The road grew narrower at every switchback turn. The weather had taken one of those dramatic, late-autumn reversals and was now as damp and chilly as it had been stifling a week before.

They had taken a barge from Sirmione to the eastern shore and should have been in Verona hours ago. Now, as the road wound higher into the mountains and the sky darkened, it was looking like they wouldn't be on time. Carlo was complaining, certain that if they missed their date his beloved Plautus project wouldn't happen at all.

Antonio's thin nose poked out beside Silvio's feet, the rest of his head covered with a green horse blanket. "I've come to a conclusion," he said, "The sun is definitely going down."

"*Ehi!* Toni!" Elisabeta called from inside the wagon. "The blanket."

"In which case," said Antonio, releasing the blanket

to the women, "Shouldn't it be going down behind us?" His head disappeared into the wagon.

Silvio looked at Piero, since he was driving. His brother didn't answer, focused on the horses. The speckled mare kept flicking her ears as if she were hearing something disquieting, and the old, dark one (Hazelnut? Walnut? Silvio could never remember the colors of horses) raised his head and blew every few minutes.

Pantalon's black horse came up parallel to the box, on Silvio's right. The man looked pale. "These damned mountain roads keep changing direction," he said. "I told you we should have—" he broke off, coughing, "Stuck to the valley."

Carlo, riding up on the left, said, "It was foggy in the valley. At least up here there should be moonlight."

Disappointment must be turning Carlo's wits. Even above the mist, the sky had been gray and was now slowly turning a disgruntled shade of purple. There might be a dozen moons up there tonight. Comets. All the planets in conjunction. No one on this road was going to see them.

Pantalon coughed again, harder. Piero said, "Ser Carlo, you've got another one sick." Carlo didn't seem to hear, which was probably just as well. Then Piero called a sharp, "Ho!" The wagon jolted to a stop.

They had come to a fork. On the right, a narrow, grassy track, walled in by brambles, shaded by broad sycamore boughs, faded away downhill into darkness. To their left, the road opened up, the path rising into the wide, howling chill of a rocky meadow.

"The Adige is that way," Piero said, indicating the road on the left.

"Impossible," Carlo said. "That road leads back up into the mountains."

Silvio stood up on the box and looked around for the rocky tonsure of a mountain peak that ought to be somewhere to their rear, between them and what was left of the sun. He finally spied it—through the treetops on their right. "Piero," he said, "How did Monte Baldo get over there?"

"Could be any mountain," Pantalon said, "Who can tell through all these accursed trees?" He was seized by a coughing fit, wrapped his beaver-lined cloak more tightly and shivered.

"It's Baldo," Silvio said, "If we could drive backwards, we'd be at Verona in no time."

Piero groaned and gave Silvio's knee a whack with his coiled whip.

All the men started talking at once, until Carlo outshouted the rest and called, "RIGHT."

"Hup," Piero said to the team. Silvio thought it sounded more like a suggestion than a command. The beasts replied by blowing a pair of frustrated horse-sighs before getting the wagon under way again.

The forest road grew narrower and more wild as the sun finally drew the cloudy bedclothes over its head and snuffed the light. Branches reached down and scraped along the sides of the wagon as it lurched over grassy humps and stumbled through washed-out gullies. They halted long enough for Silvio to light the two lanterns. He hung one from the rear and took the other in hand, to walk ahead of the horses.

The speckled horse snorted, her hot breath ruffling Silvio's hair. It was the only warmth to be had out here. The last traces of light deserted the sky, narrowing their world to the two circles of lamplight, the dull thud of hooves on soil, faint creaks and jangles from the harnesses, the rush and rattle of dry leaves in the wind. Pantalon coughing.

Piero stopped the wagon.

"What's wrong now?" said Silvio.

"I've seen that tree."

Pantalon wheezed. "It's a tree. They all look alike."

"Not that one," Piero said. "See the canker there, like a cat's face?"

Silvio held up the lantern. He hadn't noticed the cat-faced tree, but he'd been looking at the road.

He looked at the road again. How many sets of hoof-prints should there be? "*Mèrda*," he muttered. Back at the fork, the ground had been undisturbed. Now the road ahead was pockmarked with hoofprints.

"Piero's right, Siór," he called back to Pantalon. "These are our own tracks."

"Turn around," said Carlo. The poor man sounded like he might cry.

Piero said, "How am I supposed to do that?"

"We could keep going and watch for the fork," said Silvio. What was that faint, grumbly sound? Thunder?

"We'll be out here all night," said Carlo, his miserable face briefly visible in the first flash of lightning. "In the rain."

Antonio let out a curse in Vèneto. Piero answered in Bergamàsch, and Carlo, clearly possessed by the shade of Plautus, released a stream of invective in Latin.

"Did you hear that?" The voice was Oriela's. Silvio turned around. She was leaning out the front by Piero's feet.

"Besides thunder?" Elisabeta's face, wrapped like a nun's with the horse blanket over her own blue mantle, appeared beside Oriela's. "I heard five grown men bickering like schoolboys."

"No—something else. An animal." Oriela said.

"It wouldn't surprise me," said Elisabeta, "My Carlo never does anything by half measures. If he's going to get us lost, it must be in a dark forest full of wolves."

Now Silvio heard it, something howling—no, baying —uphill and behind them.

Antonio said, "Isn't it a bit late in the day for hunting?"

Hunting. Silvio returned to Piero's side and whispered, "Do you think it's Zio...?"

Instead of answering, Piero stood up on the box and called to Carlo and Pantalon. "Sióri! Quick, tie up the horses and get into the wagon!"

Silvio handed Antonio the lantern and dashed away up the hill toward the baying, which was louder now, closer. There were definitely three hounds. Silvio could hear hooves and voices. A horn sounded. He had heard that note only twice before, and he knew what sort of unearthly hunting party would be following it.

Ser Carlo's world of human reason had never—must never—meet Mamma's world of feral gods and the secrets of wild places. Silvio hurled himself through the tangled and thorny blackness, in desperate pursuit of the very last person he wanted to see. Great-uncle Herlakin.

Rugged walnut trunks appeared inches from his nose, and he dodged these only to blunder into prickly pillars of cypress. Bare switches of young poplars lashed his face. A trailing bramble snared him, and he ripped himself free, leaving bits of his hose dangling in its claws. Then a pair of enormous paws struck him on the chest and knocked him to the ground.

"Off!" he choked out breathlessly. The hound had come out of the night so fast that Silvio hadn't had time to fall properly and had landed hard on his back in a sharp crackle of walnut shells. He managed to suck in enough air to wheeze out, "Off, Brugliera! It's me!" The big dog was wriggling with joy, its long tongue bathing his face.

"She knows it's you," a voice drawled from somewhere up above, "That's why she pounced." Uncle Herlakin's handsome, alarming face emerged from the shadows and leaned down from the back of a dark, weirdly dappled horse. "She likes you, *Cuzin*."

"*Buna sira,*" Silvio said. "Couldn't help hearing the dogs." He tried to sound nonchalant, which was difficult to do lying flat on his back with a dog the size of a pony prancing on his chest. He wasn't sure how he felt about being liked by Brugliera, the hound named for thorns, who tracked the scent of suffering. "I assume you haven't brought the Wild Hunt out here for the sole purpose of alarming my friends."

Herlakin leapt off his horse with a smile that might have appeared affable had it not been for the pair of six-point antlers sprouting from his brow. The many leaves —oak, fig, sycamore—that comprised his plate mail-like garments made a whispering sound as he moved, and a few tattered remnants of antler velvet swayed. He whistled, and Brugliera stepped off Silvio. "We always ride these hills on Samonios Eve." Herlakin said, "Why are you here?"

"Because Ser Carlo said to go right," said Silvio.

Herlakin gave a deep, throaty laugh which was echoed by a low rumble of thunder overhead. "Lost yourselves, have you?" he pulled Silvio to his feet.

Two more hounds arrived. The golden and white coat belonged to Boralisa, the tracker of love. At her side was Beladona, her coat a gray so deep it was nearly blue, the one who could smell the difference between hope and despair. All three wagged their tails at Silvio, presenting their heads to be patted. He patted them.

Herlakin said, "Where are you trying to go?"

"Verona."

Herlakin gasped. "Did you say Verona?" He shook his head, feigning alarm, and cried, "No, surely not Verona! You don't want to go there!" Dropping to a dramatic whisper, one green leather gauntlet resting on Silvio's shoulder, he said, "Beladona tells me we may have prey in Verona tonight."

Silvio ignored these histrionics. "You won't get there on this road."

Herlakin gave his antlers a smug little toss. "I know a shortcut."

"That's what my friend thought."

"Well, you're better off lost. Lost is the best place to be tonight. Verona is trouble." Herlakin paused, looked at the ground, then cocked a sly eyebrow and grinned. "Want to come along?" Beyond Herlakin's horse, cracking nut shells and blowing beasts hinted at the Hunter's unnumbered companions still concealed in the wind-tossed shadows.

"You just said it was trouble." It sounded to Silvio like the trouble was probably Herlakin himself and his wild companions.

"Not the *humans*," Herlakin said, as if Silvio had proposed inviting a flock of sheep to the Doge's palace. "You and Piero." His smile broadened. "Well, you, mainly." Herlakin pulled Silvio into a side-hug, leaning so close to his ear that one of his antler points poked Silvio's head. "Beladona expects a lot of despair. I could really use an extra pair of lips."

"No, thank you," Silvio said, feeling queasy.

The Aivàn frowned. "You're sure?" One could almost say he pouted. "Such a waste of talent."

"*Mader di Dio,*"

"Oh, well." Herlakin held the pout a moment longer, then let it drop away. "In that case, you might want to tell your friends to let the horses go."

"Let them go?"

Herlakin said, "When my ladies are questing, any horse that hears them will follow the Hunt. I can't stop them, but I can decide which way they run. I'll send Brugliera and Boralisa with you. They can lead your horses away from the Hunt to the river and catch up with us once you're all safe."

"It sounds like your plan will leave us even more lost."

Herlakin took a step back, looked Silvio in the eye and said, "I swear by Lord Pan's most beloved flute: when my hounds leave you, your friends will know where they are."

Silvio found himself believing this. "We won't get to Verona on time, will we?"

"Trust me, you don't want to." He patted Silvio's back. "When you're ready, whistle for the hounds."

"All right," Silvio sighed. "How do I explain this to Ser Carlo?"

"Explain?" Herlakin laughed as he vaulted into his silver-chased saddle. "He won't want it explained. Humans are happier with their own explanations. Let him think of one himself once you all get to the river." He whistled, and Beladona dashed away to take her place in front of Herlakin's troop.

"Wait—what about the wagon?" Silvio had to shout now as a cold gust rattled the dry leaves and Herlakin's horse started off, at the head of a column of shadows.

"No wagon!" Herlakin's voice blended with the wind. "Ride!"

Something like a hundred war horses, asses, goats and assorted other beasts thundered past as the Wild Hunt veered off through the trackless dark. Beladona's baying faded into the tumult of the growing storm.

Silvio hurried back down the hill to the wagon with Brugliera and Boralisa at his heels, imagining what the big cart horses might do in such a stampede. When the two points of lamplight came into view, he turned to the dogs and whispered, "Stay." To his surprise, they obeyed.

"Everybody out of the wagon!" Silvio cried as he burst out of the trees. "Get on the horses!"

Piero was on the back running board, about to climb inside. "Are you mad?" he said. "I just got everything tied down." Large drops of icy rain were now slapping at the wagon's cover.

Silvio grabbed his arm and whispered, "Two of the hounds are coming. The horses are going to run."

"You couldn't get rid of him?"

"What do you think?" Silvio said. Brugliera and Boralisa hadn't come closer, but they were howling.

Piero sighed. "So the wagon will be destroyed if we don't unhitch the team." He turned and put his head inside the wagon. "Change of plan," he said, "Everyone has to ride."

25 Tempest

Everyone groaned, groused, bundled into their wrappings and crawled out of the wagon into the storm. Oriela stopped at the rear hatch and looked back. Papà had settled himself into a corner among the rolls of scenery and didn't seem inclined to move. Outside, Carlo was untying his perplexed and unhappy bay mare while Piero started the process of unhitching the team.

"Papà," Oriela said gently, "Silvio said we have to—"

"Silvio said! Why should we..." He trailed off in a fit of sharp coughs, pressed his hands to the sides of his head, and curled himself further into the corner.

Oriela said, "El Moro is waiting."

"You take him," said Papà. He must be feeling wretched if he was offering her his horse. Oriela took her father's arm and pulled him, inch by inch through the wagon, out into the icy rain. His face looked ashy in the lamplight. He leaned against the front wheel and let Oriela untie El Moro. She checked the girths, readied the reins. The unseen dogs were yelping, the sound coming closer. As the hounds approached, the rain came harder, colder. The wind picked up. She could hear Piero swear as a flash of lightning startled the draft horses and Silvio cried out in alarm.

"He whistled," Papà said, "Silvio's calling those hounds."

"It's the storm, Papà," said Oriela. "The whole world is whistling. Up you go."

Once Papà was mounted, Oriela noticed that he wasn't sitting as securely as usual. His posture was hunched, his legs dangling in the stirrups. She got up behind him and settled herself against his back. Piero put out the rear lantern and mounted the chestnut draft horse while Antonio joined a complaining Silvio on the roan's back. A moment later, two of the most enormous dogs Oriela had ever seen darted into the road in front of them. Carlo reached for the front lantern, but it fell into a puddle and went out. El Moro dashed away, following the monstrous hounds off the road and down the hill through the lacerating branches and the wet, driving blackness.

Papà was coughing again, hard and breathless. His arms jerked as he tried to tug the reins now this way, now that, but he might as well have asked the Adige to flow upstream. El Moro had forgotten he had riders, forgotten that there were such things as people. The piercing wind bayed in Oriela's ears as if the storm itself were made of hounds.

There was a loud crack overhead. Away to the right, Antonio's voice punched through the rain in fierce, percussive curses. The roan's heavy hoof beats faltered very slightly and then sped up.

Papà was shivering violently. He said something that sounded like, "*Sha sovage*," and some other words Oriela couldn't hear over the bellowing tempest. He slipped a little off balance, a groan vibrating through his back as he righted himself. She tightened her arms around his ribs.

She heard Antonio shout, "Ho! Damn you!" What was it about this storm and those dogs that was turning perfectly good horses into wild things?

"...devils...army, *francexe*." Papà started to laugh, but it dissolved into another fit of coughing. He shook his head, sending streams of water off his hat and down the front of her dress. "*Le mesnie...*" He was speaking French now? He tilted heavily to the right, his back muscles rigid with his struggle to stay upright.

"Papà, hold on," Oriela shouted. He flinched as if the sound hurt his ears. After the words were out, she realized she had used the familiar verb, and it felt right. Without his cursed child, Papà would fall and be lost. And she would not let him fall.

They flew past a pine trunk as it cracked, bringing the tree down at El Moro's heels. A sudden gust from another direction carried Papà's hat away behind them, and for a brief instant his head seemed to fly off with it before slumping away sharply to the left. He ceased making sounds in any language, and this time she was sure that without the stirrups and her arms he would have fallen. Sleet stung her hands. Papà would be getting the ice pellets in his face, and there was nothing Oriela could do about it except hang on.

She shifted her weight a little further back and pulled him closer to steady them both. He was quaking like a drumhead. She felt for the armholes of his beaver-lined cloak, traced his quilted sleeves—sodden as sponges—and found his fingers locked into icy claws on the reins. She grabbed for the soaked leather, tried to communicate with El Moro, but all she could do was to keep her Papà on his back until they reached whatever destination the conspiring beasts had chosen. The air was so full of water, the darkness so complete, it felt almost like they were swimming through the night. The cold seeped through her cloak, through her riding dress, into her bones. Her father was nearly limp against her breast.

And then the baying faded into the distance, the strange dogs leaving them as mysteriously as they had arrived. El Moro slowed to a canter, to a trot, his ribs heaving, forcing Oriela to concentrate harder on keeping balance for two. Several more moments passed before she realized that the rain had stopped. She heard splashing up ahead, and then Antonio's voice.

"*Ahi!* You're in the river, you overgrown whore to a jackass."

El Moro brought them into the open on a grassy river bank. Already the clouds were breaking up. After the blind murk of the woods, the fragmented moonlight seemed like the break of dawn. Antonio rode up the riverbank, kicking hard at the roan's sides. Water streamed off her tail. Antonio was alone on her back.

"*Now* you stop," Antonio said to the horse. "Witless clod-breaker!"

Oriela said, "What happened to Silvio?"

Antonio dismounted, slapped the mare's big haunch —hard—and turned his back on her. "Knocked off by a branch," he said. The roan snorted and walked back toward the woods. Man and beast had evidently had enough of one another.

Oriela said. "I think Papà has caught a chill. He almost fell off, too." She wondered whether she'd be blaming El Moro if he had. Antonio tapped her father's leg, rousing him just enough to elicit a moan and start him wheezing.

Piero came barreling out of the trees on the big chestnut, leading the roan. He reined to a halt beside them, dismounted and said, "Is Silvio with you?"

As Antonio merely kicked the gravel, Oriela said, "Silvio fell off."

Papà was suddenly writhing in the saddle. He said, "...with the French devil...hounds."

Oriela said, "Help me," as her father tried to dive off El Moro's back. Piero caught him, which caused him to thrash harder, trying to push Piero away, even when his left foot got tangled in the stirrup and he nearly landed on his head.

Oriela dismounted as soon as Antonio freed Papà's leg, and in a moment he was leaning on her shoulder, clinging to her neck, calling her *maledeta, povera maladeta.*

Carlo and Elisabeta rode into view in the now-full moonlight from somewhere upstream. As Carlo helped his wife down from their horse, Elisabeta said, "I'm half frozen. Do you think there's any dry wood on the boat?" They all stared at her. "Just upstream, by that big rock. Didn't you see it?"

Papà was muttering something about armor and bastards. Carlo and Antonio took off to look for the boat. Then Elisabeta asked where Silvio was. Piero shook his head, and Papà said *diavol* again, but he was quiet after that.

In the brief calm, Oriela realized that three people had now asked where Silvio was, and no one had answered this question. Well, except Papà, but *with the French devil* wasn't very useful. She imagined being knocked off a horse on such a night, alone amid the howling and cracking, branches flying and falling through the darkness. That's what Antonio had been thinking about from the moment she'd heard him shout, up on the mountain. He must be sick about it. No wonder he preferred to blame the horse.

A loud whoop came from the direction of the river, jarring Oriela out of this new anxiety. Carlo stood on the deck of a two-masted river boat. He was waving his arms and pointing at the aft mast. "Look!" he cried, "St. Mark sent us a ship!"

It took some imagination to call the cargo craft a ship, but Oriela thought Carlo might be excused for a little hyperbole. When Elisabeta had said the word *boat,* Oriela had pictured maybe a half-wrecked, one-oared *sandolo*. By comparison, this broad, sturdy sailing barge was a galleon. It had a deep hold in the front and a low, round-roofed, cabin aft, with enough room on the deck between them for all four horses. A banner hung wet and limp at the top of the mast. The moonlight washed out the colors, but there was no mistaking the filigreed streamers. In its folds Oriela could just make out the shape of a lion's head and the tip of a wing. Elisabeta gave a cheer and rushed down the bank.

Antonio emerged from the cabin, bent low to fit through the hatch, and reported that there were two cots inside—the eerie suggestion of an absent crew. Carlo looped the bow line over a willow sapling at the water's edge while Antonio laid out a gangplank. Then Piero and Antonio carried Papà aboard and into the cabin, where they managed to get his sword and some of his wet clothes off, him struggling the whole time and talking about devils. Oriela wrapped him in the blankets from both beds and turned to leave, but he called to her and wouldn't lie down unless she sat beside him on the bed.

Antonio and Piero went to look for Silvio. In the gently bobbing darkness, listening to her father's wheezing breath, as feeling returned tingling to Oriela's icy fingers and toes, she thought about Silvio lost in the cold, no cabin, no blanket, and no friend to warm him. She wished someone had taught her a prayer, that God would listen to her if they had.

26 Demons

Pantalon kept thinking he ought to be able to slow El Moro. He couldn't remember why they were galloping through an impenetrable wood in a thunderstorm. He was sure it hadn't been his idea. Someone was behind him on the horse, warm against his back, squeezing his lungs. Oriela. For a moment he'd thought it was Margarita, but of course, she hadn't been in the wagon. Why had Pantalon been in a wagon? Why was he out of the wagon now? Something about dogs. He could hear dogs. Who would be out riding to hounds at night, in this weather? A madman, or a devil. There was a tale he'd heard about a devil with a hunt. How did it go? A French tale, the *Mesnie d'Herlakin*, a demon riding on stormclouds with a host of the damned.

So. Along with their uniforms and their bastards and mountains of burnt rubble, the French had left one of their devils behind. What a careless army they were. This seemed extremely funny, and he tried to tell Oriela the joke, but for some reason only bits of words were finding their way out of his mouth. But no, it wasn't funny at all, because Silvio was in league with it, had run to meet it and called the hounds. Whistled. Summoning them for what? What were they hunting for?

Of course. He shuddered, not from the cold. It seemed so clear now. The Aivani and their hellish confederates were after Oriela again. Was she one of them, after all? No, she would have let him fall and run to join them, and instead she had wrapped him in her arms, her muscles taut with the effort to keep El Moro from throwing them both, calling him *te*, clinging like an infant that has found its mother after being lost in the market. She was his own. She had to be. But the thieving Aivani had marked her and would never give up trying to take her back.

Pantalon struggled to sit up, to be alert, to turn around and hold onto his child, keep her from the hounds. He must have dozed off, though, because suddenly the rain had stopped and someone was calling for Silvio. Why Silvio? We don't want him. His teeth were chattering.

He said, "He's with that French demon!" He kicked free of the stirrups, trying to dismount, but he started to fall, coughing hard and worn out from talking. The cough made his head feel like it was going to split open. Arms caught him. He tried to look and see whose, but his eyes didn't seem to be following orders. Neither was his voice. It was laughing again. "Armor," he said, "Bastards..."

It was Piero who had grabbed him, and he was talking to someone else on another horse. Their words kept sliding around between his ears, colliding with each other, refusing to arrange themselves into speech. Except the woman from the horse, she was also looking for Silvio. He was gone, then. Would he stay away or bring the other devils back with him?

Oriela slid to the ground after him. He was having trouble standing up, so he leaned on her shoulder. "Poor *maledeta*. Why do they want you?"

Other voices were shouting, and then there was a dark shape on the water, long and flat, like a headless grebe with two great feet at its tail. Too big for a bird. Someone was making him walk toward it, climbing onto its back. Ah. A boat. The feet were the double rudder of a *rascona*, so that water must be a river. St. Mark's banner was clinging to the foremast. Safe there. What French demon would dare board a Venetian boat?

The hands were loading him onto the cargo vessel like they'd mistaken him for a sack of flour. Into the hold? No, it was a little cabin. Dark. They stood him on his feet, and he felt the water moving below the wood and sighed. It was a relief to have water under him again at last, to be down from the mountains and out of the terrible forest and on a boat.

Someone wrapped a musty-smelling blanket around him, but he kept shivering. Hands were pulling at his clothes. Cold. He tried to wriggle away from all the hands. Oriela's voice telling him to lie down, and here was a bed. Straw mattress, a bit thin. Dry, though.

Someone said, "Piero, get his sword, will you?" Of course, Piero would be in league with his strange kin. Pantalon tried to fight him, but Piero got his sword and belt, and he heard metal sliding along the boards beneath the bed. He must remember where they put it, in case the forest devils came for her again. Where was she?

"Oriela?" Why couldn't someone light a lamp in here?

"Here, Papà." Her voice was right by his ear. The hands on his shoulders were hers, too, coaxing him toward the pillow. The other hands went away. A little moonlight came in when the hatch opened and shut, and he could see Piero and Antonio leaving, and his daughter tucked a second blanket around him. It smelled worse than the first one, but it was warmer. The little bed rocked on the cradle of the river and eased his shivering. La *donxèla* Oriela was rocking with her Papà.

27 Curses

S ilvio fought his way to consciousness. Finding himself entangled in the fierce branches of a dog-rose bush, he immediately wished someone would knock him out again. Another blow to the head couldn't make any difference to the throbbing in his right temple.

Toni? he tried to say, but his mouth wasn't obeying. No matter. Antonio wasn't there. No one was. The storm had departed along with Zio Herlakin's hounds, and the forest was wrapped in wintry silence. Silvio tried to push himself upright, but his left hand wouldn't work properly, either. He slipped further into the mass of thorns, landing nose-to-bark with the jagged end of a pine bough. The smell of the sap jabbed into his sinuses like a dagger.

He tried to close his eyes and nose and return to oblivion, but a loose cane of wet rose thorns slapped his face. Doomed to remain awake, he tried to pull free of the vine's talons, systematically plucking each cane from his clothes. One thorn at a time. He kept his mind off the cuts to his fingers by damning, in turn: the rose bush (*pluck*), the broken bough (*tease*), the tree it grew on (*rip*), the speckled mare (*prize*), the mare's mother (*tug*), the iron horns of her collar (*tear*), and the English-man who invented horse collars (*suck blood from finger-tip*).

He decided to waste a malediction on Herlakin, even if the creature was already damned. It was his fault Silvio had been on a horse in the first place. Lumbering, treacherous beasts. Finger throbbing, he considered damning Antonio but decided the poor man was probably already cursing himself.

When the last prickly cane finally broke, the sudden release shot him forward like a catapult and landed him face-down in an icy stream. He added the stream to his list of things to consign to the inferno, though as he lay there he noticed that the mud was cooling the sting from the thorn scratches. Only when his fingers started to ache from the cold did he haul himself grudgingly to his reluctant feet.

A full moon was now glowing among the naked branches overhead, but its light only served to confuse the shadows on the ground. Silvio took a few careful steps in each direction until he'd determined which way was downhill, reasoning that navigable rivers were not usually found at the tops of mountains. Herlakin had said they would all find a river. A few steps further on, he tripped over a beech root and pitched forward, landed on his sore wrist, and curled his body around the fresh pain.

The chill from his wet clothes had long since sunk into his skin. He was desperately thirsty. His mouth was the only part of him that was dry. Making a mental note to damn the tree root when he came back to his senses, Silvio rolled onto his back and fell once more, gratefully, into unconsciousness.

When he next opened his eyes—well, one of them—it was forced shut again by the blast of sunrise in his face. His right eye hadn't opened. He heard voices.

His brother's: "Siór, over here!"

Antonio's: "*Ósti*, he looks terrible."

"He opened his eyes for a moment."

"I'm going to kill that nag."

Piero's firm hand was under Silvio's back, raising him to a sitting position. Silvio blinked at them. Winked, rather.

"*Danada* nag," said Silvio, "*Danado* tree." He was damning things in Bergamàsch. His mouth couldn't recall how to shape Vèneto sounds, not even for Toni.

"Can you walk?" Piero said.

Silvio didn't know. "Damned root," he said.

"Well, he can curse well enough," said Antonio, hoisting him up by the right elbow. Piero reached for his left arm, but Silvio pulled it back with a cry.

"Damned arm," Silvio said.

Somehow they got him onto his feet. With one eye shut, he had no clear notion of how far away the ground was. Piero and Antonio kept having to say, "Watch out," and, "There's a rock," and catch him as he stumbled over some treacherous mound of primrose.

At last they were out of the trees, and full daylight

attacked Silvio's one good eye from both sky and river. There was a boat. A fairly big boat, in fact. Piero and Toni pulled him aboard. The two saddle horses were tied loosely to the mast, nibbling at a pile of something green. Silvio considered asking where the boat had come from, but the question required more words than he could string together.

Oriela met them at the hatch to the cabin. "Is he all right?"

"Bump on the head," Piero said.

"*Danada* head," Silvio said, by way of a greeting.

"How's Ser Pantalon?" said Piero.

Oriela looked over her shoulder. "Sleeping," she said. "I think." She stepped back to let them inside.

The cabin was dim, its louvered shutters closed tight to keep the wind out. Pantalon was curled up on the narrow cot to their left. Oriela, moving stealthily, took one of the blankets off her father and spread it on the second cot. She left while Piero and Antonio helped Silvio out of the outermost and muddiest layers of his clothes. He settled himself with a sigh onto the thin mattress. At last, something to lie on that was neither wet nor prickly. He closed his good eye.

Piero went out to bring the draft horses aboard, although Antonio called after him, "Don't bother with the roan." Warmth and quiet settled over the cabin like a blanket. Silvio started dropping into a blissful doze.

A thump. Scraping metal on wood. The peace was shattered by a shout. Silvio rolled over and opened his eye.

"Get it out of here!" Pantalon was on his feet, wrestling with Antonio for possession of something under his bed.

Silvio sat up, groaning.

"Get what out?" Antonio said.

"That!" The old man tossed Antonio aside—how could someone that pale be so strong?—and Silvio found a drawn sword shaking in the air, much too close to his chin. He got off the bed and backed away from the steel point.

Pantalon said, "You should have left it with the devil!"

"It's only Silvio. He fell off the horse. Lie down."

Pantalon turned on Antonio, swinging the sword around the tiny room. "Get. It. Out."

"*Che casco?*" said Silvio.

"Fever," said Antonio, reaching for Pantalon's hand.

"Where is she?" Pantalon took a step closer, prodding Silvio up toward the hatch.

"Where is who?"

"Oriela, villain!" Pantalon pushed Silvio out onto the open deck, where Piero was trying to coax the nut-colored horse on board. "Where is my daughter? You took her to your French devil!"

Antonio grabbed Pantalon from behind and pinned his arms, pulling him back into the cabin. Piero abandoned the horses halfway up the gangplank and dashed across the deck, planting himself between Silvio and Pantalon.

Silvio shouted down through the hatch, "Crazy old nanny-goat. I'll take *you* to the French devil!" Piero started pushing him toward the low hold in the bow. "*Strüs!*" Silvio said, "Addle-pated son of a three-horned cow!" He dragged his blanket into the hold and flopped down on a row of grain sacks.

Piero sat on a nearby packing crate. "Oriela said he's been raving about French demons that follow hounds." He paused. "And steal children."

Realization oozed like cold mud into Silvio's pain-jumbled mind. "Oh." He lowered his voice. "I probably shouldn't have said that about taking him to the devil."

"Probably not," said Piero.

Silvio turned his face to the bulkhead, shut his eye, and mumbled, "*Danadi demòne fransés.*"

28 La Serenisima

Through the day, the boat made its way downstream to Verona without much help. Oriela was glad they weren't trying to head the other way, because Carlo's attempts to steer the rascona would have run them aground. Clearly there were some subtle differences between commanding a war galley and piloting a river barge. They passed under the old Stone Bridge at Verona about an hour after dark and were met at the torch-lit pier by four men-at-arms. Curiously, there were no other people about along the riverbank. Where were all the fruit traders, the bales of filament silk, the firewood sellers from the mountains?

The soldiers heard Papà coughing and sent for the doctor, who declared Papà's ailment to be the result of an unfriendly *influenza* of the moon on Scorpio and likely to be catching. He couldn't let them land, but he offered to bleed Silvio's badly swollen left arm. Silvio glanced at the stained iron fleam and declined. Carlo stepped onto the dock to argue with the men.

"You don't want to come ashore, anyway," one of the soldiers said. "Hell broke loose up in Piazza Erbe last night. It's a mess. Funerals all day tomorrow."

Antonio joined Carlo on the dock to argue some more. If they must sleep on board, someone should provide them with pallets and blankets. They needed provisions. Another soldier arrived and recognized the boat. He accused Carlo of stealing it from someone named Montecchi who had been murdered the night before. Carlo said they were not thieves, they were invited guests and should have been dining with Governor Loredan right now, that furthermore he had found the boat drifting, and if the soldiers didn't believe him, he'd prove it on their bodies.

Piero joined the quarrel, but he seemed more interested in what had happened to Montecchi. When the soldier described a band of mounted brigands in strange clothes, Piero ducked into the hold and spent a long time in conference with Silvio. A crowd was gathering on the dock.

Oriela left the men to their debate and went to see Papà in the cabin. She said, "We can't go ashore. Carlo's shouting at someone about it."

"Poor Carlo," said Papà. "After all this trouble, no Plautus."

Elisabeta came in to join them, shaking her head. Outside, they could hear Carlo: "...demand to see Pietro Loredan. He invited us..."

Antonio's more pragmatic conversations with people in the crowd produced a hot meal, a whole cask of wine, and a father and son from Friuli who could sail a rascona. He also sold the draft horses, sent Montecchi's widow more than enough ducats to buy the boat, and even conjured up a second-hand lute.

Once his spleen was spent, Carlo calmed down enough to arrange for food and blankets to be brought aboard, including hay for his mare and El Moro. He exacted a promise that someone from the governor's household would try to retrieve the wagon, but for now, all their scenery was gone, along with their extra clothes. Carlo seemed to mourn the masks above all, but Piero was inconsolable over the loss of his costly viol and venerable rebec.

Early next morning, now provisioned for the journey, they raised the sail and cast off with the banner of St. Mark fluttering like torch fire against the profound blue of the Autumn sky. Oriela was feverish for one night, but she recovered quickly. From her bench on the main deck, she watched farms fall away behind them almost as soon as they came into view. Gangs of harvesters in linen tunics and cross-tied leggings cut reaping patterns through the wheat fields, filled baskets with olives and tied up grape vines for the winter.

As his health improved over the next few days, her father's mood underwent a remarkable transformation. He would bring Oriela to stand with him in the bow and point out silk farms and weaving operations he controlled—or he'd tell her which of his competitors owned them and what he thought of them. He didn't quarrel with Carlo once, and he even laughed at some of Silvio's jokes. Maybe all that was needed to cheer him up was a boat.

In fact, all the Venetians were in better spirits. Carlo actually spoke of an upcoming vote in the Great Council with what sounded like eagerness. Elisabeta talked constantly about her children: how beautiful Caterina was becoming, whether Iacopuzzo would have grown taller than his mother yet, how much Nicolino hated Latin verbs. Antonio taught Piero how to play the lute, and the two of them took turns plucking out melodies.

As long as there was music, Papà proposed another dancing lesson. Unfortunately Silvio was as unsteady on water as he was agile on land. After he'd been thrown to the deck four or five times, twice landing on his injured arm, Antonio volunteered to practice the steps with Oriela while Silvio sat on a coiled rope and offered advice. In this way, Oriela acquired the basic moves of the Canario and Coranto.

A cousin of Elisabeta's had a small villa outside Zevio, and they stopped there for an hour or two to have dinner and unload the remaining horses. Papà had to give El Moro three apples before he was persuaded to stay quietly in an unknown stable while his master went away. His usual winter quarters were at a Morèr silk farm near Padua.

They sailed through the night and met the sunrise among the strange, pale desert landscape of a salt works, just before the widening river finally decanted into the crystalline glitter of the morning sea. Carlo and the sailors were very busy for a few minutes, adjusting the sails and the two rudder-paddles to turn northward up the coast.

In the sudden wind shift, Carlo momentarily lost his grip on the mizzen sheet and got himself wrapped up in the wildly flapping sail. One of the sailors caught the rope, cursing, but Carlo just laughed with delight and slapped the man on the back. Antonio scooped up a handful of saltwater and tossed it at his brother, who returned fire with a two-handed splash. Elisabeta screamed and ducked behind Oriela's bench.

"The sea makes us all a little wild," Elisabeta said, as the two noblemen methodically soaked each other. "They'll grow up again in an hour or two. Look." She nodded toward the bow, where Papà had climbed onto the small foredeck and reached down to trail a finger in the water. He pressed it to his lips.

La mara. Oriela was reminded of a strange argument she'd once had with her tutor. *Mare,* the sea, was a masculine noun in Latin and in all the Italian languages but one. In Vèneto, the sea was feminine.

"It doesn't make any sense," Oriela had complained, after Profesór Gregorio had corrected her adjective agreement for the twelfth time.

With one of his rare smiles, el Profesór had said, "It will."

Suddenly the deck lurched, and Piero and Silvio each grabbed a mast and hung on. The rascona, built more for rivers and shallows than for open sea, bounded and plunged like a rearing horse on the swells. The green spikes of the waves tossed bits of foam at Oriela's hair, and the wet salt breeze made her heart caper in her chest. Maybe she was a Venetian, after all.

Presently they were crossing the paths of several fishing boats, some heading toward land with the night's catch to take to market, others starting out for a day's work, empty nets draped like spiders' webs from the booms. Once the *rascona* was overtaken by a long, slender ship, propelled by oars that protruded from its sides like quills on a hedgehog. A galley.

Oriela was fascinated by the synchronized dance of the crew, their three rows of oars undulating like eels' fins in smooth, rapid triple meter. The effect was more like a single enormous creature swimming through the waves than like a hundred men rowing.

They all watched the oarsmen for several minutes. Even Carlo seemed mesmerized. Then Antonio said, "Why isn't she under sail?"

Papà said, "She's a new ship, probably only left the Arsenale within the past month. See the ramming prow? Just like mine. The crew's still training. Their timing is a little off."

Oriela thought they were already perfect. She said, "I think she's beautiful."

Papà's face opened into a wide, doting grin. For a moment Oriela thought he was smiling at her, but he said, "Of course she is." He was besotted with the ship.

Some hours after this, the rascona threaded its way between two sandy, brush-specked islands. As they emerged into the lagoon, the bounding surf relaxed into the easy rocking of a cradle, and Silvio ventured away from his mast to huddle, instead, against the starboard gunwale near Oriela's feet. They were following a narrow channel marked out by *bricole*, thick wooden poles bound into tripods and driven into the mud.

Oriela remembered another lesson. Profesór Gregorio had told her that if the city were attacked by sea, they had only to pull up the *bricole,* and anyone who wasn't Venetian would run aground. It gave her a curious thrill to see these memorized book-facts taking concrete form, like finding a unicorn in your stable.

More islands went by. A convent, pouring music over its high walls and across a grassy marsh...a fishing village with boats moored all in a row, nets spread in the sun...a clam bed where barefoot boys stooped to dig, tossing their treasures into their sack. Weren't they cold?

Then the rascona slid between two strange islands. The big one on the port side was covered with walled gardens. To starboard was a much smaller island with nothing on it but a church, fronted by open pavement right to the water's edge.

Papà rose to his feet and moved toward the bow. He was followed by Carlo, then Antonio, all of them standing as easily on the bobbing deck as on land. No—more easily. They inhaled the damp, salty air as if they hadn't taken a proper breath in months. There was new color to their cheeks and a fierce fire in their eyes, aquatic creatures returning at last to their habitat. Papà looked at least ten years younger. Antonio looked like an adult, which was almost as great a transformation. Had they sprouted fins and become mermen, it would hardly have surprised her.

The Friulians struck the sails and took to the oars, and Silvio slid up onto the bench by Oriela. He was looking out across the bow, a strange, almost unwilling smile playing at the corners of his mouth. Oriela followed his gaze and found a lump in her throat. There it was—astonishing, improbable, and even lovelier than she had imagined. Venice.

There was no shore at all on these central islands: just water, then city. Tight clusters of stone and brick buildings seemed to float directly on the surface of the lagoon, as if some special magic of this place made solid rock weightless. Before Oriela could get a proper look at these, she was distracted by the tallest bell tower she had ever seen. Its copper pyramid of a roof was still new and gleaming, casting a dazzling reflection into the sky. It started to chime, a penetrating note that could cut through walls, that set her bones singing. She only realized her mouth was hanging open when her father turned to look at her and laughed.

"Carlo," Papà said, "Have you ever seen anybody look at it for the first time with their mouth closed?"

Carlo shook his head and grinned back at her. "Gape like startled sheep, every one of them."

Oriela was too full of amazement to be embarrassed. Her eyes felt too small to contain all the wonders trying to squeeze their way in. A huge, pink lace castle stood at the edge of a paved piazza that ran to the water's edge. There, dozens of boats of every size and description milled around like a flock of water birds or bobbed beside colorful mooring posts. Beyond the palace she could make out a clutch of domes like eggs in a bird's nest, each topped with a little pointed bulb like a sprouting daffodil. Only when she realized that the sprouts were crosses did she figure out that it was a church. What she could see of the walls was covered with whimsically lavish shapes and colors, but then the boat had moved on.

They were in the Grand Canal. On either side, rows and rows of arched windows punctuated the fronts of —were those their *houses?*—round-topped windows, pointed windows, and exotic-looking windows with tops like onions. Windows in pairs, trios, rows of five or six, fronted by balconies, outlined with brightly painted shutters, and all of them fully glazed and sparkling like jewels in the light that danced off the soft jade face of the water.

Ripples from the wakes of hundreds of boats lapped against the walls of houses three and four stories high, their brick, stone and stucco façades marked with salt where the highest tides reached. There was a house decorated with what looked like huge, stone flowers, each petal a different color of marble. Another was covered all over with pictures of ordinary gentlemen talking to ancient gods, painted into the plaster and gilded. Others were overlaid with such delicate gothic filigree, they might have been built of bobbin lace. And clearly people lived in these fantastical palaces. Oriela now lived in one. Drying poles draped with their laundry jutted out from rooftop gardens, and smoke rose from the orchard-like rows of tall, conical chimneys. Their front steps descended into the water, boats tied up like horses at the doors.

"I can guess what you're thinking," Silvio said quietly.

If anyone had asked Oriela what she was thinking just then, she wouldn't have been able to guess it herself. "Tell me."

"You're afraid if you look away it might disappear." He moved a bit closer to her and lowered his voice: native Venetians wouldn't understand. "Or worse, you're afraid that when you look back it will have turned into something ordinary, someplace just like everywhere else."

"Yes." How had he known?

"It won't," he said. "About the only thing this place can't do is be like anywhere else."

The rascona was now fighting its way through heavy traffic. All around them swarmed canopied gondolas, low-riding sandolos and cargo and fishing boats in varieties too numerous to list, filled with baskets of fruit, fish, sacks, barrels, loads of wood, and large, closed boxes that might have contained anything from dishes to hats. Boatmen and passengers greeted each other as one might walking down a street.

One of the gondolas passed close to starboard. The round *felze* canopy was decorated with a picture of a golden staircase in a red shield, and the oarsman in the stern was dressed in red and gold to match it. Oriela was thinking a stairway was an odd coat of arms, and then she noticed the gondolier's face. It was the color of a roasted chestnut, and his hair was like the wool of a black sheep after shearing.

The man laughed when he saw her staring. She looked away, embarrassed. But the dark-faced gondolier bid the rascona's sailors *bon dì* in a voice so soft and musical that her eyes were drawn back to his remarkable visage. He smiled at her. Then the boats were beyond each other.

She whispered to Silvio, "Was he a Moor?" Silvio nodded very slightly without meeting her eyes, his mouth twitching with suppressed laughter.

The sailors managed to slide the ungainly craft neatly alongside a row of stone steps. These led up to a large door, open to the water, through which Oriela could make out a vast, empty room lit by an inner courtyard. The younger sailor tossed the painter rope over a blue and green striped post and made it fast. Before the knot was tied, Carlo and Antonio stepped nimbly out onto the stairs and turned to assist the ladies.

Papà leapt onto the dock with the agility of a man half his age and was instantly out of sight through the heavy doors. A moment later, Oriela heard his voice shouting, "Pasquela!" This made Antonio laugh. Who was Pasquela?

Elisabeta vanished into the shadows beyond the door, followed a moment later by Piero. Childish voices and a dog's barking were echoing through the empty ground floor. At one time the stately warehouse level, the *fondaco*, must have been packed with shelves and crates. The shield painted above the water door showed three green pepper berries on a blue field, but it seemed Ca' Pevari no longer imported the spices their House was named for. Like many ancient families, they had probably ascended to higher and more abstract levels of finance.

After several days on a boat, Oriela felt the solid ground shift and had to fight for balance. Letting the others go in ahead of her, she paused on the middle step to regain her footing and looked out across the Grand Canal. The tide was coming in, and the lowest step was already underwater. While she waited for the pavement to stop rocking, Oriela watched the swarms of boats that skimmed along the strange thoroughfare, leaving flat snails' paths among the sparkling ripples. The air breathed of watery things: fish, brine, seaweed, wet stone. She felt a hand on her shoulder.

Silvio leaned confidentially toward her ear and said, "I promise it won't disappear if you come inside."

29 Siren

Silvio pulled his hand away and steeled himself as Oriela turned to face him. Her smile was both bashful and merry, one friend laughing at her own folly with another. Yet the sea air and the strange light off the water were already transforming her, shining in her eyes and kindling small golden flames in her hair. He saw now that she was a part of this place after all, its beauty, its impenetrability. Once Dama Oriela went through that door, the city would not vanish, but Silvio's friend probably would.

They were alone on the stairs. He suddenly longed to hold her, as if his touch might keep her from changing, but this was like the urge he sometimes had to set his foot on the glassy surface of a canal, to walk on it like St. Peter, knowing he would sink and be lost. The kind of urge a sane man would not act on, a sensible one never think of—but you can't help thinking it, and the water is always there, whispering its mad invitation. A moment of exaltation, and then ruin. He pulled his eyes aside and turned to go in.

"Ah, *pignoli!*"

Silvio stopped and smiled at the rustic half-oath. He

had never heard a Venetian swear by pine nuts before. He looked back at Oriela. Her hem had trailed into the water, and a wave of the rising tide had lapped over the edge of the step and doused her skirt to the knee. She was struggling to lift the now-leaden cloth and mount the top stair, the skirt binding her legs, holding her back, pulling her down toward her native element. Her hand reached for him.

If he took that hand, what tangled stew of brine and weeds would he fall into? What strange fishes waited there, in the green depths of her eyes? On the other hand, he couldn't very well leave her to flounder around like a dry-lander and ruin her last dress. All the extra clothes had been lost with the wagon.

"That's just the Lagoon's way of saying *sciao*," he said as he hauled her up to the dock. "It's glad you're home."

She was laughing now, blushing, saying, "Thank you. Oh, my poor dress. What will Papà say?"

Elisabeta came out of the water door with young Nicolino clinging to her skirt and bouncing on his toes, in unison with a small yellow dog that bounced even higher. Elisabeta said, "Are you two going to stand out there all day?"

In her wake appeared Iacopuzzo, now nearly as tall as Silvio. Over the summer the fine hair on his upper lip had begun to thicken. Red-haired Caterina, nearly a young woman, peeked from the shadows in the doorway.

Elisabeta looked at Oriela's dress. "Silvio," she said, merrily severe, "Did you push her in?" She scooped up

Oriela's arm and half of her skirt and took her into the house, her children and dog clustered in her wake, all talking at once. Their voices echoed along the mosaic floor of the fondaco. Silvio followed them in.

Piero was in the courtyard, holding a baby and kissing his wife Smeraldina, the Pevaris' nanny. A new Speronelli had been born in their absence, the first one conceived after Piero married her and found her a respectable job. Every child of an age to speak was talking at once, determined to describe an entire season in one breath. Carlo sat on the courtyard stairs with his youngest, Nico Pevari on one knee and Rico Speronelli, Piero's eldest, on the other. Caterina was bending her Uncle Toni's ear about something that had offended her. Poor Antonio, the perpetual uncle. Not unlike Silvio.

Feeling suddenly disinclined to join the noisy reunion, Silvio slipped past them into the *canpièlo,* the open yard between Ca' Pevari, Ca' Morèr and the smaller house that Silvio and Piero rented from Carlo's father Nicolò. He trotted between the clumps of grass and around the well and thought about the potion he had brought from Mamma's shop and was keeping in a box under his bed: powdered lettuce milk suspended in a decoction of water lily roots. Mamma sold it sometimes to lovelorn youths and priests intent on keeping their vows. Maybe it would help Silvio remember that Oriela was a lady.

They wouldn't be seeing any more of the farm girl from Moniga now. Pantalon would hire another dancing master, dress her in his best wares, and most likely find her a *nobile* husband before Easter. If the old man was feeling particularly generous, he might hire Silvio —as the *bufon* Salvàn Mandragora—to perform at the wedding feast. Silvio saw himself composing a comical rhyme or juggling something while Oriela sat across the room with her new lord, just watching.

Watching would be all she'd be allowed to do for the rest of her days. The thought hit Silvio like a blow to the chest, pressing the air out and leaving a hollow ache in its place. Knowing it was none of his business only sharpened the pain.

The effect of the water lily medicine was limited to the corporeal symptoms of love. There was, Mamma said, no remedy for what ails the human heart. The drug could dull one's wits and was difficult to stop taking once you'd begun, which was why Silvio kept it only for emergencies. He thought of Oriela on the step, helpless as a beached siren, reaching for him, and decided this was an emergency.

His hand on the latch, Silvio was startled by the sharp, boatyard voice of Pantalon's housekeeper Pasquela. "Maìstro Salvàn!"

Many people in Venice called Silvio by his *bufon* name. It often made him wonder whether Silvio Speronelli really existed in their minds, but he tolerated it from Pasquela because he knew she meant it as respect. He turned as she barreled towards him, looking like she might knock him through the closed door with her powerful shoulders.

She said, "Am I glad to see you! I need an extra pair of hands, if you're not busy. Are you busy?"

"No," honesty forced him to say. "Why?"

"The *patró* has come home—well, of course you know that, you were with him—and he's brought a daughter, of all things—I guess you know that, too—and he wants Dama Margarita's room fixed up for her by the time they finish dinner at Ser Carlo's."

Silvio put on the mask of a smile. "At your service."

"Good," said Pasquela, "Go and help Alberto move the big boxes while I find Luca. I think he's been taking fares again. Don't tell *el patró*."

Luca, Ca' Morèr's African gondolier, wasn't supposed to use the family boat to carry paying passengers, but it was commonly known that he did it anyway when *el patró* was away. As long as he removed the *felze* canopy with the Ca' Morèr shield, Pantalon pretended not to know.

Silvio and the others worked until past Vespers shaking, hanging and beating various textile objects and toting boxes and furniture upstairs to Pasquela's room, downstairs to the already-cluttered fondaco, and into and out of the other chambers that opened off the wide portego that ran the length of the house from canal to street. They polished the round windowpanes, shivering in the last of the daylight at the open shutters. They placed new candles in wall sconces, filled and lit the lamp, and cleaned the stone hearth to start a fire. They brushed cobwebs off the ceiling beams to reveal a pattern of painted roses.

At last, Pasquela and the shop boy Luigi tied back the carefully arranged bedcurtains—borrowed, for the time being, from the big row of windows at the end of the portego—while Luca and Alberto the bookkeeper mounted a small mirror inside the bed alcove, and they all stood back to admire the transformation. Suddenly exhausted, Silvio sank onto a carved clothing chest and looked out the window. Light from other houses twinkled on the water.

The room faced onto Rio Ca' Foscari, one of the small canals that encircled the island parish of San Pantalon, but the angle of the *rio* allowed for a fairly good view of the Grand Canal. Oriela would be able to assure herself of the city's continued existence first thing every morning. Silvio thought she'd want to sit and look at it, so he went out into the portego to fetch one of the folding armchairs that were lined up along the paneled walls.

"You've met la Dama, haven't you?" Pasquela said when Silvio returned.

"Yes," Silvio said. He was looking out the window to arrange the chair for the best view.

"Do you think she'll be upset that we didn't have time to sew new curtains?"

Silvio stared at Pasquela for a moment and then collapsed into the chair, laughing as he tried to imagine Oriela being offended by used draperies. Pasquela watched him with a pinch of worry between her sturdy eyebrows.

He said, "She just saw Venice for the first time, Pasquela. The last thing she's going to notice is the age of the bedcurtains."

Luca said, "I say we've worked a miracle here. How about a reward for your diligent and hungry saints?"

Pasquela clapped her hands to her cheeks. "Of course. You've all missed your suppers. Come up to the kitchen."

30 Cardamom

Having deposited his daughter with Pasquela in the now-tidy bedchamber, Pantalon stood alone in his familiar portego and tried to get used to the idea that someone else now lived here.

Furniture had been moved. Boxes were stacked beside the big fireplace with a Turkish rug tossed over them. The quartet of windows facing the canal had lost two curtains, and a chair was missing from the wall by the credenza. And there was now a lady behind that door on his left where no one had slept for seventeen years. Not that Margarita had ever used it much. She had preferred to share his bed, as companionably as a peasant's wife. When he thought of her in the house, it was always either there or in her sunlit sitting room adjacent to his study.

He decided to help himself to a drink before retiring. Pasquela had mentioned mulled wine, so it was probable she had a pot on the fire in the kitchen upstairs. Pantalon needed a drink after Carlo's news about the old dancing master, Gonxalo. Sweet Gesù, what nerve! Not only was Caterina Pevari a noblewoman, she was still a child, not even thirteen. It sickened Pantalon that he'd been planning to hire the knave to teach

Oriela.

Now, instead, Carlo was going to ask Silvio to take over Gonxalo's position at Ca' Pevari. This would make it very awkward for Pantalon to let Silvio go, even if he had known any other dancing masters, which he didn't. Yet if a father couldn't trust his daughter to a man of Gonxalo's age, what should any of them expect from a young rogue like Silvio?

As he passed the spare room at the top of the stairs, the one he'd built for a nursery, he noticed it was stuffed with rolls of silk removed from Oriela's chamber. He peered in and sighed. Pasquela had tossed them in without plan or order. It was going to take Luigi several days to sort it all out again.

The last thing Pantalon was prepared for, upon entering his own kitchen at this time of night and in this frame of mind, was to find the table occupied by his bookkeeper, gondolier and shop boy—and Silvio!— dining on thick slices of *panséta* bacon and Pasquela's excellent white polenta.

Luca and Alberto quickly put down their bowls. Luigi jumped to his feet when his master came in, but Silvio patted the boy's arm and smiled cordially at Pantalon.

"*Buna sira,*" Silvio said, in Bergamàsch. "How is Ser Nicolò? Mad as ever?" Then, to Luigi, "Why don't you pour your master a bowl?" Luigi hurried to the great fireplace and reached down the tin ladle from its hook.

"What are you doing here?" Even Pantalon was surprised at the snarl in his own voice. Although his fever was gone, his terror in the woods hadn't quite left him, nor had the tale of the French demon. The encounter with the mad hunting party had convinced him that he was right about Viola dei Fiori and her misfit sons. They were Aivani, of the same strange tribe that had stolen his child and murdered his beloved.

This didn't necessarily mean that Viola had committed the crime herself, and he'd been prepared to bear Silvio's company as a fellow traveler, even an employee, so long as he kept some professional distance. But to see the creature making himself comfortable in Ca' Morèr, gobbling up his food and wine and (Pantalon suppressed a shudder) touching his daughter's things...?

Without blinking, Silvio said, in Bergamasco, "*Moér* Pasquela requested my help, and as I was not invited to dine at Ca' Pevari..." Silvio was obviously annoyed about something. He always used his native tongue when he was trying to pick a fight with a Venetian.

"Weren't Piero and Smeraldina expecting you?"

"No more than Alberto's wife was expecting him," Silvio said. Alberto the bookkeeper looked up at the ceiling, apparently intrigued by the arrangement of pots on the overhead hooks.

Luigi set a steaming wine bowl on the table near where Pantalon was standing and then shrank toward the door. Alberto and Luca stood up. Alberto thanked him for his hospitality, as if Pantalon had had any choice in the matter, said he hoped the lady found the chamber to her liking, and tiptoed off down the stairs with Luigi behind him.

Luca, who lived on the premises, stood in the doorway as if waiting for a cue. After a moment, he said, "I'll just go and see about…" Then he was away to his apartment over the boat room in the fondaco.

Pantalon turned what he hoped was a baleful look on Silvio, who was still seated, chewing, and who apparently had no intention of leaving while there was still food on the table. Perhaps the interview would be shortened if Pantalon put the salted pork back in the larder. He did.

Silvio popped the last bite into this mouth, following it with the end of the polenta. He chewed for a moment appreciatively, then washed it down with a gulp of the wine and complimented the bacon in Bergamasco, "*Brào pansèta.*"

Pantalon said nothing.

Silvio said, "Please don't stand on my account, Sciòr. Have a seat. Try the mulled wine. I think Pasquela must have found some cardamom. Your spice cabinet is a marvel."

"I'm sure Pasquela's much obliged for your help," Pantalon said. In Vèneto. He would not be drawn into this mockery of a conversation, nor would he sit down. "When you're finished, you can show yourself out." He turned to leave.

"Sciòr."

Pantalon halted. "What?" He rolled his eyes and made a hands-wide supplication to a sausage hanging from the ceiling beam before turning back to Silvio.

"I assume neither Alberto's nor Luca's contract includes moving furniture and hanging curtains," Silvio said. "And while Luigi might be expected to carry dozens of heavy bolts of cloth up and down the stairs for hours on end, his mother was probably thinking he'd be home before Compline."

"I'll pay them for the extra time."

"Really? What will you pay them for dashing out of here like they'd been making off with your gold instead of breaking their backs for you?"

"*They* could have stayed as long as they wished."

"Pasquela could have rounded up a *zani* to help. Oh...wait," Silvio smirked, "She did. And paid him in polenta."

Was this what was bothering the man, that his housekeeper had treated el maìstro like a *zani*? "Silvio, I'm in no mood to play whatever game this is." Pantalon picked up the bowl and sniffed. Yes, cardamom. "Say your piece and go home."

Silvio said, "In seventeen years, did it never cross your mind that your daughter might need a room in your house?" He tossed off the last of his wine as he stood. "*Buna nòcc,* Sciòr."

31 Rialto

Pasquela pulled the bodice laces snug around Oriela's waist. Her movements were more brisk than gentle, and it was strange to be dressed by someone who wasn't Francesca.

The housekeeper stood back and admired her work. "Well! Here I was, thinking you didn't look like her."

"Like who?" said Oriela. She twisted from side to side, trying to see the whole dress in the small but elaborate mirror. The dark crimson of the slashed velvet sleeves seemed to make her eyes greener. Kaleidoscopic bits of her face flashed and shifted over the intricately-cut panels of the mirror's glass frame.

"Come here," Pasquela said, leading the way through the adjoining doors into a bedroom with hangings the color of mulberry juice, trimmed in dark green. It must be Papà's. Pasquela gestured toward a portrait of a young woman wearing the crimson dress. Her hair, capped with a lace net, framed her delicate face with a fringe of curls the same color as Oriela's. Other than that, Oriela didn't think her mother's face looked at all like the one she saw in the mirror. Margarita Condulmer had an aristocratic brow and a dainty nose.

"I can't wear this," Oriela said. It would upset Papà, she was sure, to see his cursed child in her dead mother's dress.

"Nonsense," said Pasquela, "It looks lovely on you." She turned from the portrait and started to straighten Papà's bed curtains.

Oriela said, "She's wearing it right there on the wall." The first thing Papà would see every morning, the last thing at night.

Pasquela turned, a green tassel dangling from one hand. "You'll have to wear her dresses for now. You don't have anything else suitable yet. Besides, Dama Margarita left them to you in her will."

Like other *nobile* ladies, the pregnant Margarita would have been expected to decide the fate of her property should she die in childbirth. Oriela gazed at the portrait, even more unnerved as she tried to imagine this woman heavy with child, packing away her favorite things for a daughter she would never know.

Pasquela's hand was on her shoulder. "It won't be long. Your father's going to Rialto this morning to hire a dressmaker."

"Rialto?" The name of the ancient market drove Oriela's pensiveness away. "Do you think he'd let me go with him?"

The door from the portego opened, and Pasquela said, "Why don't you ask him?"

Papà halted just inside the room. "Pasquela, what...?" He froze, looking at Oriela, at the dress. "Oh."

He was silent for a moment as his face betrayed some inner agitation. Then he blinked and said, "Of course."

"Papà," said Oriela, "May I come with you to Rialto?"

He scowled at Pasquela, who hurried to pick up a black robe that was lying folded on the wardrobe chest and held it up behind him. Papà pulled his business *tóga* on over his doublet, and Pasquela brushed the sleeves. When he faced Oriela again, his composure was as flawless as his austere black gown. "I suppose so," he said, "As long as you stay in the boat."

The *felze* on the Ca' Morèr gondola was painted the same color as Papà's bed curtains and was decorated with a single, dark green mulberry leaf. Luca the gondolier was dressed in matching colors, green hose and a short mulberry jacket, with a green, feathered cap perched on his wooly head. Oriela was glad she'd seen her first Moor the day before so she wouldn't stare at Luca when he took her hand in his strong, dark one to help her into the boat.

Papà seemed to relax the moment he was aboard. He breathed deeply, leaned back in his seat and smiled at her. Luca took up his perch high on the stern and glided the boat deftly out of Rio Ca' Foscari into the morning traffic of the Grand Canal. Intrigued by his graceful handling of the craft, Oriela felt she could contentedly watch him all day, but then her father spoke.

"I'm afraid you're going to have to continue studying dance with Silvio," Papà said.

Oriela tried to pretend she was disappointed. "Why?"

"Maìstro Gonxalo won't be available. How is your Pavana?"

Not sure how to answer, she said, "It's the first thing I learned."

"Good."

Oriela waited for him to say something else, but he didn't. She craned her neck to see out from under the *felze*. Hundreds of gondolas were coming and going, dropping off or picking up their passengers and vying for tie-up space with broad, cargo-filled *caorlinas*.

Up ahead, the marching rows of elegant houses were interrupted by a large, peaked wooden bridge. A structure of chains and posts protruded above the roofs of the shops that lined its sides. Beyond the bridge, Oriela could make out a square surrounded by a market arcade. It was difficult to see much more through the crowds of black-robed gentlemen and youths from the *conpagne delle calze*, these sorted into groups according to the patterns on their colorful stockings.

On the left bank, barges filled with fruit were being unloaded. Further on, linen-clad porters carried baskets of fish from the bobbing row of docked fishing boats, supervised by men with short breeches and long beards and heckled by impertinent gulls. The baskets went into a brick building, mostly square and plain but with incongruously fancy windows.

"Is it a market day?" Oriela asked.

Papà beamed. "This is Rialto. It's always a market day."

Luca slid the boat up to the stone pier, tossed the line over a mooring post and rested his long oar. He hopped ashore and bowed as Papà disembarked and vanished into the throng of uniform black robes. In fact, Oriela realized, nearly all the people she could see —hurrying along the arcade, inspecting glassware and apricots, arguing with the bookseller—were men.

Another gondolier shouted something, and Luca backed their boat away from the pier. As they hovered about halfway to the center of the Canal, one of the fishing boats left the Pescheria and started toward the bridge. The masts were too tall, and Oriela was just wondering how it would get through when, with a jingle and a creak, the chains on the central bridge structure grew taut. The center split in two, the sections folding upward like drawbridges on twin castles.

Luca told Oriela that *el patró* would be ashore for at least an hour, and he rowed up and down either side of the Grand Canal around the bridge, showing her the fruit and fish markets and all the houses as far as Ca' D'Oro, then back under the bridge to the wine shops where he disembarked and returned to the boat with bowls for each of them.

Under the felze of the gondola next to theirs, Oriela saw another lady with wine in her hand. Their eyes met, and they raised their bowls together, both consigned to drink with their gondoliers while the menfolk conducted their arcane business ashore.

32 Brocade

Pantalon had told Luca this was a short visit, but of course there was really no such thing as a short visit to Rialto. First he stopped at his newly-built weaving workshop and picked out several bolts of silk for Oriela's dresses. The cloth would be delivered to the dressmaker's by one of the dozen or so *zani* who always loitered around the market offering to carry things. One was a brocade that was not, strictly speaking, legal for her to wear. Not yet.

As he passed along the length of the ancient arcade, he met two senators near a bookseller's stall. They were hoping to launch an expedition to the New World, and Pantalon promised to underwrite the adventure if they would introduce a bill before the Great Council permitting gentlewomen of both *nobile* and *citadìn* class to wear brocade. Sumptuary laws were changed almost biweekly and were, in any case, more observed in the breach. Pantalon wondered when the legislators would figure out that if only *nobili* were officially permitted to wear brocade, then anyone who could afford brocade could pass herself off as *nobila*.

Out in the square, a slave trader had a few Croat women for sale. Pantalon briefly considered buying a *schiavona* to look after Oriela, but none of them looked any older than she was, so instead he decided to order a black gown for Pasquela. His housekeeper would complain that she hadn't been hired to be anyone's governess, but surely Oriela would be married and gone within a year.

As usual, the dressmaker tried to tell him the new gowns would take two weeks. Many customers would have ended up promising the man a higher price to expedite the order, but Pantalon showed him a swatch of the brocade, casually mentioning "my weavers."

"Oh! Messer *Morèr*," said the dressmaker. He lowered his voice dramatically and tapped his cheek. "Just for you, one week."

When they got home, Pantalon was feeling so pleased with the world that while Luca wiped down the gondola, he decided to show Oriela around the house. They started by opening several crates in the fondaco.

"This blue piece is from China," he said, "See how the reverse side is as perfect as the front. It took my weavers five years to figure out how they do that. Do you like this green one?" he unrolled an arm's length of taffeta laced with subtle accents of gold thread.

"It's lovely." Oriela held the edge and trailed it between her fingers, letting it touch the more sensitive skin between the digits. She said, "This is one of yours, isn't it?"

Pantalon smiled at her hand. "Yes," he said, "It's ours." His daughter's face lit up. He realized he'd said *ours.* And she had used the familiar *tuo,* and he realized he was glad.

He showed her the mezzanine business office, where Alberto looked up from his ledger to bow to la Dama. At the top of the main stairs, Oriela asked about the portrait facing the door—himself, foppishly armored and ready to chase the Turks off Cyprus. He'd been much younger when his father had had it done. Pantalon thought the picture indulgent and rather embarrassing, but he kept it because Margarita had liked it.

Now Oriela seemed inclined to stare at it, so Pantalon hurried her on up the next flight, to the kitchen. He led her through, past Pasquela's room, into the roof garden that covered half of the top floor. It was a dull place in November, but Oriela quizzed him about every dormant plant—she knew them by their bare stalks better than he did—before descending by the back stairs to the portego in the *piano nobile.*

As she had seen his bedchamber in the morning, he skipped it and took her through the dining room with its carefully arranged displays of dishes—Murano glass, majolica plates, silver serving pieces—and into his study. As he listed some of the more important people who had sat by that fire, his daughter looked around the room. After a while her attention seemed fixed on the one adjoining door Pantalon still hadn't opened.

"What's in there?" Oriela asked.

Pantalon pretended not to hear. "And look, this is the seal of the Chancellery office. I do translations for them from time to time. Did I tell you how I got that sword on the wall?"

Oriela wasn't as impressed with these objects as he'd hoped. She kept stealing glances at the closed door. Pantalon realized his effort to change the subject had grown pitifully transparent.

"Your mother's sitting room," he said at last.

Oriela moved closer, touched his arm lightly and said, "Please, will you show me?"

Pantalon gazed for a moment at her red sleeve. Margarita's sleeve. He backed away, and then crossed to his walnut desk, opened a small drawer and took out a key.

Although he hadn't been in there in years, he knew Pasquela had not neglected it. The spinning wheel was polished and dusted, and every round pane in the tall, arched windows sparkled through lace curtains. Pasquela opened and closed the shutters daily so that neither the wall tapestries nor the cushions on the settee were faded.

Oriela stepped softly over to the large embroidery frame that sat below one window, the linen still secured in the hoop. Pantalon knew the picture. A grove of mulberry trees, workers in berry-stained tunics gathering baskets of leaves and carrying them to the cocoonery. Just over the wall, waves on Lake Garda.

"It's Villa Morèr," Oriela said, her voice full of wonder.

Pantalon said, "Your mother loved silk." This sounded inane. What lady doesn't love silk? "I mean —she understood it." Not just because it's pretty and costly, he wanted to say, and not even because she looked beautiful in it, which she did, but because of what silk *is*, because of its improbable source, the painstaking work of reeling and weaving it, the delicate labor of the worms that give their lives to make it. He wanted Oriela to hear all this, and yet he was reluctant to say it aloud.

After a moment, he knelt to open the exquisitely painted chest by the next wall. Margarita's green mantle was folded on top, its dear pattern of mulberry leaves beckoning his hand. When he drew it from the chest, the ethereal softness of spun cap-silk stopped his breath. He held it up for Oriela to examine.

She gathered her skirt carefully and knelt beside him, caressing the green cloth with her fingertips and the back of her hand. "It's wonderful," she said, her eyes shining.

Pantalon said, "I charmed her father with painted *organsin* from the Indies, but it was this mantle, woven just for her here in Venice, that won Margarita's heart." He still wasn't explaining it right. "I don't mean that she was the kind of woman whose love is bought by pretty things."

Oriela said, "I know what you mean, Papà." She met his eyes, and Pantalon realized that for the first time he wasn't frightened by hers.

"When you marry, it will be yours," he said.

He folded the mantle with care, wishing he could bury his face in its sublime warmth, and shut the chest as gently as one might lower a coffin lid. Swallowed, blinked. He got up to leave the room, and Oriela followed. He paused in the doorway to say, "If you want to use the spinning wheel, come see me for the key."

33 Maìstro Silvio

T hree more dancing pupils. Silvio had tried his best to look pleased when Carlo approached him with the offer. It was steady work, which couldn't be said of freelance jesting, but old Gonxalo had been dismissed under circumstances no one would talk about openly. Smeraldina said it had to do with twelve year-old Caterina. Silvio would be working under heightened scrutiny.

He did his best to look serious and professional when Carlo greeted him at the top of the courtyard stairs and walked him up another flight to the music room next to the nursery. His class was on a bench near a small *ottavino* harpsichord, lined up by age from Oriela to Nicolino. The Turkish carpet had been rolled up and tucked against a wall to reveal a polished parquet floor. Silvio suppressed a sigh when Carlo settled into a chair near the fireplace. How did one begin a dancing lesson for four people—and with an audience?

"*Bon dì*," Silvio said to the group.

"*Bon dì*, Maìstro Silvio," they all said in unison—the three children looking dutifully solemn, Oriela with a playful smirk.

"*N'ol fà!*" he mouthed at Oriela in Bergamàsch, *Don't do that!* She would make him laugh and look idiotic. He turned to the others. "What were you working on with Maìstro Gonxalo?"

The young *nobili* looked at each other. An unspoken debate passed between them, and then the oldest boy said, "The Galliard passages."

"Excellent." Silvio tried to pantomime a schoolmasterly nod while he wondered what other answers the children had considered. "Who will volunteer to demonstrate?"

Iacopo, at age fourteen the leader of the trio, stood up and took Caterina's hand. Elisabeta still called him Iacopuzzo or Puzzi, but it struck Silvio that the lad was getting a little too tall for a diminutive nickname.

Iacopo looked from Silvio to the ottavino. Gonxalo probably used the instrument to accompany his students. Piero had offered to provide accompaniment for the classes, but Silvio had declined on the grounds that it would be cheating. As Silvio didn't play the harpsichord, he'd brought along a soprano *flauto dolse*. When he pulled it out, he saw Iacopo not quite hide a sneer of adolescent disapproval. The recorder music did sound thin under the low ceiling of the upper story.

Iacopo executed the most basic sequence, ending on the exact spot he'd begun, where he stood at attention like a young soldier. Caterina's answering steps were equally accurate, and equally devoid of human expression.

"Flawless, Ser Iacopo," Silvio said. Flawless if you're made of wood.

The children giggled. "Everybody calls me Puzzi," the boy said.

"Even Maìstro Gonxalo?"

Nicolino said, "Everybody. And I'm Nico and she's Catì."

"Well," said Silvio, "We don't want Dama Oriela to feel like she's in a room full of children, so in my class you are young gentlemen and ladies." He hadn't known he was going to make this rule until it was out of his mouth. Now he'd have to stick by it. "Dama Caterina, Ser Iacopo, you may sit down. Ser Nicolino, can you show me the first variation?"

Silvio suffered through three more demonstrations of soulless, textbook proficiency from the children. It was time to shake them up. He said, "Have you worked at all on the Volta?"

He saw Caterina freeze, wide-eyed. Iacopo nodded silently, staring at Silvio with new suspicion. Of course. He should have known. The Volta would have offered Gonxalo an easy opportunity to misbehave. Someone ought to slip that rascal a few bottles of the water lily potion.

Silvio decided instead to review the Pavana, since he and Oriela would be performing it in a few days at her debut. He told the class that it could well be the most important dance of a young lady's life, at which statement Oriela looked at him like a rabbit cornered by a very large dog. But there was no point pretending the stakes were lower than they were. He gestured toward the harpsichord. "Can any of you play this thing?"

Nicolino raised his hand. "I know two Pavanas. Do you want the Paduan or the Venetian?"

"Venetian," Silvio said, "Naturally. Dama?"

When he and Oriela took their positions, her hand was shaking so much that Silvio almost couldn't hold onto it. The little ottavino played everything an octave higher than it was written, making the stately Pavana sound like a procession of *foleti*. Silvio had seen a few of that diminutive tribe once, helping Mamma in the herb garden. He was imagining pairs of pixies nodding and strutting solemnly between the rows of parsley and oregano, but he didn't dare laugh. Oriela was so stiff she could scarcely manage the most basic steps.

Silvio halted, Nicolino stopped playing, and the airy sprites blew away. He wrapped his hand fully around Oriela's and turned to face her.

"Don't worry," he said, "I'll be right beside you." He decided not to tell her that this would be their only dance together that evening. He would ask Piero to help her out. It's not cheating if your future depends on it.

With the children taking turns following their lead across the room, Silvio and Oriela drilled every detail of the dance, every foot change, every turn, every glance, over and over, until Silvio declared that Oriela would be able to dance it in her sleep.

34 Masks

There was one day left until his daughter's introduction banquet. Pantalon, writing in his cozy study, was not worried. Carlo and the Alati had the entertainment well in hand. Pasquela had retained the services of a chef she'd met at Ca' Foscari and was now recruiting *zani* as temporary waiters and footmen.

He pressed the winged lion seal into the pool of wax on a letter to the governor of Dalmatia. Oriela was attending a dance lesson at Ca' Pevari, leaving him with time and quiet to catch up on some work for the Chancellery. But he had only finished translating the first letter when Luigi came knocking.

"Ser Carlo wants to see you, Siór."

"Let him in," Pantalon said.

"No, Siór," said Luigi, "At his house. He said to tell you the new masks are ready."

"So soon?" Carlo had ordered them only a week ago, from a leatherworker named Xacomo Del Verde who had just opened up a shop in Cànpo San Pantalon.

He'd been hoping to distance himself from Carlo's hobby now that they were back in Venice. The group Carlo and Toni called the Lion's Feathers had accomplished what they'd been formed to do. Brescia would have new walls. The bastards of French rapists would have a foundling hospital. Pantalon had made his report to his confraternity and hoped it would be the end of the project. He should have known better. Carlo had been waiting for something like this since he was a boy. He wasn't going to let it die, and his father Nicolò Pevari probably wouldn't try to make him.

Pantalon dawdled in his fondaco. He stopped in the office to look over Alberto's list of the day's sales, saw off the three customers still at the dock, met the dressmaker's boat and scolded the boatman for taking so long, and then told Luca to close up the water door for the day and stayed to watch him do it. When he finally ran out of reasons to delay, Carlo was waiting in the canpièlo.

"He's here," said Carlo, as they passed through Nicolò's lushly furnished library. "The mask-maker Del Verde. I wanted you because he's a little ... peculiar."

"You know many peculiar people," said Pantalon. "Why do you need my help with this one?"

In the next room, a smaller study that Carlo shared with Antonio, Del Verde was showing a tan leather mask with an obscene-looking blush at the end of its long, aggressive snout.

"Look, Pantalon!" Antonio said, "Isn't this a perfect face for the Captain? And here," he held out a dark, red-brown piece with a sharp beak of a nose, like a carrion bird, "The Magnifico. Wonderful, isn't he? Look at the little, sneering twist by the eyes. And those eyebrows!" He turned to Del Verde. "What did you use, horsehair?"

"Goat," said Del Verde. The mask-maker's eyes were a very unusual shade of green, like oak leaves. When he looked at Pantalon, he gave the impression of looking right through him at something behind his back. His voice was curiously layered, as if he carried his own echo.

Carlo took the dark mask and said, "This will be perfect for the scene Silvio's putting together for Ca' Tron. A dialogue between a *zani* and his master. Here, try it on."

Curious, Pantalon took the new Magnifico out into the portego and held it up to his face before the big decorative mirror. It fit him perfectly, like another skin. But when he met his own eyes peering out below the goat-hair eyebrows, his knees felt strangely weak. The grotesque visage reminded him of something, he wasn't sure what, that filled him with a kind of furious anxiety. He took it off, shook himself, and returned to the study where he pushed it into Antonio's hands. "I'm not going to do a scene with anyone at Ca' Tron," he said. "Oriela and I hope to be invited as guests this year."

Carlo said, "Toni can do the scene, then," and to Del Verde, "What else have you got?" Back to Pantlon, "Didn't you say you and Oriela were going to be birds for Carnevale? This fellow does have a nice beak for a raven."

Del Verde then pulled another mask out of the lumpy bag on the desk, a short-nosed yet somehow canine face—cunning as a fox, deadly as a wolf.

"For Piero?" Pantalon said, not sure why he was certain of this. Del Verde nodded as Pantalon turned back to Carlo. "I'll think about it."

"Very nice," Carlo said of Piero's mask, "The brows are beautiful. I wouldn't trust this fellow further than Elisabeta could throw him. *Alóra*, the last one must be for Silvio. Show me."

"*Siorsì.*" Yessir. Del Verde bowed and pulled the bag off the last mask with a flourish.

There was a silence the length of a paternoster while Pantalon and the *nobili* stared. It was monstrous. All masks are, to some degree, but this—it was an aggregation of incompatible forces, simian and feline, brute cunning hitched to the most feckless innocence.

At last Carlo said, "Interesting." He passed it to Antonio, who looked at it like it might bite him before handing it off to Pantalon.

Determined to give the thing an objective appraisal, Pantalon said, "The sunken cheeks are a nice touch but, I think—maybe just a bit too obvious?" He tilted it toward the light from the tall, arched window. "It's a pity you couldn't have smoothed out this bump on the side of the forehead."

"I could have," said Del Verde.

Carlo said, "You mean it's meant to be there?"

"*Siorsì.*"

"It looks like the stump of a horn." said Pantalon.

"*Siorsì.*"

"What's he supposed to be?" said Antonio, "Half a faun or half a cuckold?"

"*Siorsì.*"

Carlo examined the mask again, probably trying to think of something kind to say. "At least the asymmetry from the—what should I call it? Wart?—is balanced by the other eyebrow being raised. I'd be lying if I said it was the best of the lot, but Silvio can probably work with it."

"Siór, I beg to differ," said the mask-maker. "I believe it is my finest work."

Carlo gave Pantalon a look, *You see? Peculiar.*

"But, of course, if you don't like it," Del Verde said, "You can have it for nothing. *Amoredèi.* In fact, I'd like to propose a bargain."

"It costs nothing to propose one," Carlo said warily.

"Well, Siór," said the mask-maker, "It seems to me your *zani* should have proper names, like all God's creatures."

"Zani is a name," said Carlo.

Del Verde ignored this. "You can call Piero's Mask whatever you think best, but it would do me great honor if Silvio's were christened with my own name. If you use my name, you can have all the masks *per amore*."

"Your name?" Carlo said. "You want me to call it Xacomo?"

"No, my real name," said the mask-maker. "One of them, anyway."

"How many do you have?" said Pantalon, thinking the man wasn't merely odd, he was probably some class of thief.

Antonio said, "What name?"

"Herlakin." He said it with a French accent.

"Ell-a-chin?" Carlo tried the strange-sounding word, missing the French *r* entirely. Pantalon had heard it, though. He thought—*a peculiar French thief*.

Antonio said, "Didn't Dante have a devil by that name? El—no, Alichino, in Tuscan?" Pantalon felt misgivings squirming in his stomach. *A peculiar French devil.*

"*Siorsì*," said Del Verde, his expression unchanged, "But he was mistaken."

"I can't give the Mask a name no Venetian can pronounce," Carlo said.

"No?" Del Verde started putting the masks back in the bag. "Then perhaps I'll take them over to Ca' Cornèr. I hear they have a few young humanists with too much time on their hands."

Carlo stopped him with a hand on his arm. "Are you trying to break your contract?"

"Those are my conditions, Siór. No charge if you use

my name, no masks if you refuse."

Pantalon said, "Under what conditions do you get paid?"

"I labor only for fame and immortality."

Pantalon took Carlo by the elbow and led him across the room, whispered, "He's a lunatic."

"Clearly," said Carlo. "What should I do?"

Antonio joined them and said, "Keep them. They're beautiful."

Pantalon said, "Never trust a man who offers something for free."

"All he wants is a name," said Antonio. "What harm could that do?"

"Fine, then. We'll humor him," Carlo said, "For now." He returned to Del Verde. "Agreed. We'll call it Alichin."

"Erlichin," said Pantalon.

"No, it was Alicheno," said Antonio.

"Right. Arlichen," said Carlo.

Del Verde said, "I'll know."

"You'll know what?" said Carlo.

"If I find you've broken your word, I'll take them all back."

"All right," Carlo raised his hands in surrender. "Alachino it is."

The mask-maker put the bag back on the desk. He bowed, said, "Thank you, Sióri. *A dapò.* Until later." And

Xacomo "Herlakin" Del Verde was through the door and gone.

35 Senator

Oriela's feet tensed and flexed under the bedclothes in time to the ottavino music still tinkling through her head. Silvio had been right about dancing in her sleep. All night her neck and shoulders had twitched in the rhythm of the choreographed glances: Toward the partner, eyes downcast; toward the onlookers; back to the partner, meeting his eyes...the arresting, golden clarity of Silvio's eyes, warm as twin suns, a heat you could float in.

The next thing she knew, sunlight was streaming into her face. Pasquela had just thrown open the shutters and re-latched the glass. Oriela's bed curtains were still swinging when the housekeeper stormed back out into the central hall.

"You there, Zani!" Pasquela's shrill street-Vèneto pierced the chamber door and filled the house. "I told you to put those chairs at *this* end of the portego! Didn't your mothers teach you your right from your left?"

The ewer beside Oriela's washbasin was already cold. How long had she slept? She went to the window and looked out at the Grand Canal, its sunlit surface barely visible for the swarming, mesmerizing mass of boats. Someone knocked.

Oriela turned reluctantly from the glittering city and found Elisabeta at the bedroom door with her hairdresser Mario. They charged in from the teeming portego and began scrubbing and brushing Oriela as if she were a horse, Mario only stepping out for a moment when Elisabeta popped a new camisa over Oriela's head.

Fine-spun white linen edged with needle lace, it was only the first of the textile marvels to be pulled out of the dressmaker's box. The delivery boat hadn't docked until nearly sundown the day before, Papà shouting at the boatman, "What did you do? Row from Rialto by way of Burano?"

It took all day to get Oriela ready for the event her father referred to as a "small gathering"—the one Silvio had called the most important dance of her life. For a small gathering, it seemed to require a lot of preparation. Papà had hired a cook and several extra servants for the day—most of whom, Oriela noticed, were speaking Bergamasco among themselves.

"Pantalon got Zan Polo to entertain during dinner," Elisabeta said while she and the hairdresser did battle with Oriela's wet hair. "He *says* it's because Silvio will be busy." She didn't sound convinced, pulling at tangled curls until Oriela's head ached. "Your Pavana is first, and then after dinner, if you did well, some gentlemen may request your father's permission to ask you to dance. Never, never refuse a dance if your father has said yes."

"What if I don't know the steps?" said Oriela. What if someone wonderful, another Carlo maybe, invited her to dance a Coranto? She had only practiced it on the boat. Or a Saltarello? Not Even Silvio had been able to think of anything kind to say about her Saltarello.

"That's why Piero is here," Elisabeta said as she secured the green velvet bodice to the enormous mulberry jacquard skirt—Oriela's debut would be in Ca' Morèr colors. Pasquela's shouting ebbed and flowed beyond the door as she insulted and terrorized the temporary help, calling every one of them Zani.

When Elisabeta looked up again, she snatched a brush from the dressing table and raised it as if to strike the hairdresser, "Mario, what is *that*?" Mario ducked as Elisabeta's arm swung—surely not on purpose—toward his head.

He said, "It's the very latest style, Dama. Wives of the Dieci are begging me to do their hair this way." He held a looking-glass for Oriela. Two small, braided knots were perched above her forehead, holding the long, loose curls off her face.

"Michela Gritti likes it, you mean," said Elisabeta, "One wife of one of the Ten."

"Ladies of the best Houses always follow Dama Michela's lead." Mario added a pin to the knot on the right.

Elisabeta stepped back to see the style from a better angle and then said, "For the love of God, Mario, she looks like a goat!"

The hairdresser sighed and started to unpin the

knots. For at least the fourth time, Elisabeta pointed out the plate of dried fruit on Oriela's dressing table and told her to eat something, lest she get too hungry and gobble her supper. Oriela didn't think she'd be able to swallow. She was more worried that she'd need a quick retreat to the privy in the middle of her Pavana.

She picked up an apricot and toyed with it. Mario was rearranging the front braids into a circlet. Elisabeta answered a knock. Oriela bit into the apricot, which was very tart, and she made a pinched face at Papà as he came in to say that Zan Polo was dressing in his study and the Cornèrs' boat had just docked. Mario attached ribbons to the two braids and arranged them to form the suggestion of a veil.

Elisabeta left to meet Carlo in the dining room. Pasquela, silent for the first time all day, came in as Mario left. She lit the lamp, as the daylight was already fading from the window. Out in the portego, frantic Bergamasco was replaced with leisurely Vèneto. The guests were arriving. Oriela felt dizzy and nibbled cautiously at a fig. A few minutes later, Pasquela opened the door to Silvio.

Oriela rose carefully, trying not to disarrange anything. Silvio wore a short tutor's cloak over a very respectable black doublet. When Oriela reached the doorway, Silvio took a step back and bowed deeply, eyes lowered like a servant's, making way for Papà, who held out his hand for hers. Oriela couldn't breathe. The fragment of fig was stuck to the roof of her mouth. Beyond the door, the portego had been transformed into a modest ballroom, sparkling with candlelight reflected off jewels in ladies' hair and on gentlemen's hats. The air whispered of elegance and expectation. Pasquela had to push Oriela out the door; her feet felt like they'd been sewn to the floor.

Papà didn't look at her as he led her toward the middle of the floor. He was smiling at the guests, twin rows of *tógas* and ball gowns and the appraising eyes of strangers. Silvio walked behind them. Piero was tucked away into the curve of a rented harpsichord near the triple window, talking to a man with a viola da gamba. The Pevari were all gathered across the room by the hooded fireplace. Oriela hoped someone friendly would look at her, but the eyes that followed her progress all belonged to the elegant strangers.

She studied the men covertly. Most looked to be nearer her father's age than her own, but there were a few that might be peers of Carlo or Antonio. One of these, in a red *tóga*, seemed to be examining her with sufficient interest that she had to avert her own eyes.

When they reached the window end of the room, Papà dropped her hand and stepped away, and Silvio came forward. He bowed again, this time as a dancer, kissed at his fingertips and held out his hand. When the music started, Oriela felt all of Silvio's easy grace flow through her hand and down her arm and fill her with courage. The dance was over sooner than she expected. Silvio led her back to her father and disappeared.

During dinner, which Oriela hardly tasted, they were entertained by a man in a tattered red scholar's gown and a Florentine hat, with laurel branches sticking out of the crown at all angles. This was the famous Zan Polo Liompardi.

He recited a long poem about visiting Hell with another comic. According to Zan Polo, a *bufon* could never get to Heaven because he never told the truth, mocked people for a living and respected no one. Fortunately, however, Zan Polo's colleagues were afforded luxurious accommodations in Hell as the devil's favorites. While Elisabeta and Carlo, seated to her left, were laughing until wine came out of Carlo's nose, Oriela was trying—and failing—to put this picture together with what Silvio had told her about the afterlife. She was deep in thought when the poem ended, so she was startled by a bright voice from across the table.

"My dear, how on earth did you manage it?"

"Manage...?" said Oriela.

The voice belonged to a lady about Oriela's age whose yellow hair showed darker roots. Its gold was the result of lemon juice and hours in a sunning hat, and it was wound into two knots over her forehead. Like goats' horns. She was surrounded by girls with the same hairdo, all their faces turned her way.

"Dama Gritti?" Oriela had known a tall blond girl among the townsfolk at Moniga with the same power over her companions. The lady stretched one brocade-draped arm across the table to pat Oriela's hand, as if they were old friends.

"No, no. *Michela*," she said with a dainty wave of her hand. "How did you manage to get Salvàn Mandragora for a dancing master? My father insisted on some hideous old coot with bad teeth. What did you say to Pantalon?"

"Nothing."

Michela leaned forward, dropping to a dramatic undertone, "I'd kill for just one dance with el Mandragora."

"It shouldn't be hard. Maìstro Silvio loves to dance," Oriela said. For some reason it nettled her that Michela kept using Silvio's *bufon* name. He hadn't even been clowning that evening. "I'll tell him to invite you."

Michela appeared to grow taller in her chair. "Alvise would never allow it. My husband," she said, "Alvise Dolfin."

The name was clearly supposed to mean something. Oriela looked at Elisabeta. What had she said about Dama Michela, the wife of... "Of course," Oriela said, "Council of Ten."

Michela's eyes widened prettily, "Really, my dear! No one knows who's in the Dieci."

Elisabeta touched Oriela's arm. "It's a state secret," she said, the twinkle in her eye at odds with her serious tone. "Like how they make these goblets."

"Glass is a state secret?" said Oriela. If it was as well-kept as the one about the membership of the Ten, they'd soon be making Murano goblets in London.

Oriela looked for Silvio when everyone returned to the portego, intending to keep her promise to Michela. Maybe Ser Alvise would make an exception for his hostess' dancing master. But Silvio was nowhere in sight, and then Oriela was pinned between Elisabeta and Papà, who had carefully positioned himself in front of the silver-laden credenza, the better to remind suitors of his House's prosperity.

As each eligible gentleman passed them, most in black *tógas*, some in red, Elisabeta whispered a short biography: "A Cornèr. Very important. He was just made a Procurator of San Marco...A *citadìn*, in the glass business, almost as rich as your father...One of the very oldest *nobili* families, with three Doges!" Was Oriela expected to remember all this?

As the evening wore on, it got more difficult for Oriela to pretend she was thrilled when one of these impressive gentlemen passed her father's inspection and invited her to dance. Two Doges in that one's family tree, five in another's. Neither of those could dance worth a pine nut. She was laboring through the opening turns and passes of a Coranto when she caught sight of Silvio near the back stairs.

Oriela kept glancing his way, as if just looking at her teacher would cause her feet to remember the intricate steps. But Silvio wasn't watching her. He was talking to Zan Polo, head forward, hands in motion. Just before the tune ended, she saw him laugh, slap Zan Polo on the back, and exit down the stairs to the fondaco. His departure made her feel briefly, irrationally that she'd been left undefended, and she had to remind herself that she had other friends in the room.

For the next dance, Papà handed her off to one Marco Tron, a man about Carlo's age, with an auburn beard, sharp cheekbones and a wide mouth. His red damask *tóga* was open in front, and when he bowed, he pulled the robe aside to show off a doublet of gold-chased velvet and a glittering, jewel-hilted sword. Oriela recognized the man who'd been watching her when she'd first come out of her room.

Elisabeta murmured, "The youngest senator in living memory! On the short list to be nominated for the next Doge."

No wonder Papà was grinning like a monkey. At least this one could dance well, and for the first time since the end of her Pavana with Silvio, Oriela was beginning to enjoy herself. And then Ser Marco leaned toward her ear and said, "So you're Pantalon Morèr's long-lost child. Raised by wolves or something, weren't you?"

There was mischief in his eyes. Friendly? Most likely. But Oriela was caught off-guard, and by the time she thought of a suitable reply, the tune had changed to the mock quarrel of a Canario.

"Nothing as interesting as that, Siór," she said at last. "I've only been out by Lago di Garda, at Villa Morèr."

"He calls it a villa, does he?" Ser Marco said, "I hear he raises silkworms there."

Oriela stamped her feet a little more emphatically. So that's what he meant about the wolves. He considered Villa Morèr a farm. She said, "They have a vineyard at Villa Lesse."

"Well, yes," said Ser Marco, "As a hobby." The Canario ended with its choreographed reconciliation, which Oriela offered somewhat grudgingly.

Ser Marco turned to make a sign to the musicians. His face in profile looked oddly familiar, and Oriela realized she'd seen one like it on an old coin. The consort struck up a Galliard rhythm…with tambourine. Ser Marco had requested a Volta. He launched into an exuberant Passage, a dozen high, foot-changing hops in six minims.

When the tambourine rolled, he said, "Let's see whether Mandragora showed you this one," and drew her into the close position for the turns.

Oriela thought he was dancing a bit nearer to her hips than was strictly necessary. By the second set of turns, he got one leg so far around her that she could no longer control her own feet and had to grip both his shoulders to keep from falling. Her skirt twirled out around them, forcing other couples to clear the center of the floor. Oriela's head was spinning, her face growing hot.

Ser Marco laughed merrily when he set her down. "That's a very pretty blush, Madamoxèla. But surely el Mandragora has spun you harder than that. Stood you on your head, too, I'd wager."

Madamoxèla—"Miss"—not *Dama*. "That's a very advanced maneuver, Siór," Oriela said, trying to play along, "We won't study it before next week."

Ser Marco reverenced his hand with a flourish. "Raised by wolves and witty, too." He grabbed her tightly for the final set of turns. His hand was on her buttocks. "You, sweet *contadina*, are exquisite."

Oriela was airborne now, her thigh jammed against Ser Marco's satin codpiece. As he lowered her, a little too slowly, back to the floor, she thought for a moment that his sword hilt was poking her, but no, the sword was on his other hip. Speechless with embarrassment, as much for his sake as her own, she escaped before the last note faded and hurried back to her father's side.

The Youngest Senator In Living Memory arrived just behind her, beaming at Papà. "My humble thanks, Siór, for bringing your enchanting daughter to la Sereni-sima. I hope you will do me the honor of calling on me at Ca' Tron. I want your advice about a trade deal with Naples." The senator actually bowed to the delighted *citadìn*, just as if he hadn't practically called Pantalon Morèr a peasant only five minutes before.

36 Volta

Silvio knew he should leave, but he was curious to see how his pupil would be received by her peers, so he went up to the kitchen and let Pasquela stuff him with surplus sardines and extraneous quails' eggs when the hired cook's back was turned. When Zan Polo finished his act, Silvio met up with his friend outside the door to Pantalon's study. The *bufon* was still in his "Dante" costume.

"Mandragora!" Zan Polo flung his arms wide. Silvio looked away to avoid having to kiss the maìstro's cheeks. Zan Polo said, "What happened? You couldn't make a living with buffoonery, you had to take up teaching?"

"Just doing old Morèr a favor," Silvio said, "You heard about Gonxalo?"

"Naturally," said Zan Polo, "The more confidential a story is, the sooner I hear it." He took off his hat and inspected it for loose branches. "Didn't surprise me, either. What does surprise me," he leaned against the door frame and smirked at Silvio, "Is that Ser Carlo thought Caterina would be safer with you." They watched the dancers for a few minutes. Zan Polo said,

"Dama Oriela danced well."

"Yes, didn't she?" said Silvio. Who was she dancing with now? Some fop with two left feet. Oriela had worked too hard to be stuck with such an oaf.

Zan Polo gave him a shrewd look. "You know," he said, "I've been meaning to talk to you about these patrons of yours. Ser Carlo has all the *conpagne delle calze* writing alleged Comedies and thinking they can do our jobs. If you don't stop him, he'll put us all out of work."

"Don't worry, Liompardi, no one can do what you do."

"That's true. I can't even do what I do. Oh, look," the *bufon* waved his leafy hat toward the center of the portego, "Your pupil's got herself a senator to dance with."

Silvio looked. Oriela's partner was no less exalted a bachelor than the great Marco Tron, and she was acquitting herself surprisingly well in the Canario. Piero must be directing his enchantment. Senator Tron, for his part, seemed to be enjoying himself immensely. The man's chest was puffed out like a courting grouse's. As this was exactly the result Silvio had been paid to produce, he should have been pleased. Instead, something about Ser Marco's grin was dripping a vague, sour dismay into his stomach.

"*Éhla*, Salvàn!" Zan Polo kicked him lightly on the shin. How long had he been staring? "Gonxalo was sacked for what you're thinking of."

Silvio turned his back on the dancers. "I'm not thinking of anything."

"Of course you're not."

"And Dama Caterina's not even thirteen." Silvio said.

"So?" said Zan Polo, "You think Gonxalo would still have a job if Dama Caterina had been eighteen?"

"No," said Silvio. Though Catì's age made the scandal juicier, the tutor's fate would have been the same. "But I'm still not thinking what you think I'm thinking."

Zan Polo raised his leafy hat in front of both their faces. "At least you're not as ugly as Gonxalo. Maybe Dama Oriela won't tell on you."

"*Fà sito!*" Silvio said, *Hold your tongue.*

"Oh, dear." Zan Polo shook his head. "Defending her honor. This is much worse than I thought."

Silvio pushed Zan Polo's hat aside. "I should go. I was supposed to leave right after the Pavana." The next tune was a Galliard. Good. Piero was making sure the consort stuck to dances Oriela had studied. "Ser Pantalon hates it when Pasquela feeds me."

"She feeds you?" said Zan Polo. "Do you think she'd feed me?"

"Probably." Even as he was trying to get away, Silvio kept one ear on the music. A tambourine. Well, Oriela would still be all right, even though she hadn't practiced the Volta since they'd gotten back to Venice.

Zan Polo slid away along the wall toward the kitchen stairs. Silvio followed as far as the fondaco door, said, "*Sciao,*" and veered off through the double doors, shutting them quietly behind him. Before he had descended two steps, the door opened and someone grabbed his sleeve. He turned back. Antonio's long silhouette beckoned him from the light of the doorway with a finger to his lips, cocking his head toward the portego.

Silvio followed him. It took a moment to find Oriela through the whirling dancers, but then he saw it. Senator Tron had her up in the air, her feet at the level of his knees and swinging wildly. Her skirt was bunched in her partner's arms, her stockings revealed halfway up the calf. Silvio glimpsed her face as it spun in and out of view, her beribboned head bobbing several inches above the man's shoulder. Her lips were clamped shut like someone trying not to scream or be sick.

Antonio whispered, "It's not your fault."

"It's not hers, either," said Silvio, "But by morning half of Venice will think it is. *Casco!*" He turned back toward the door, unable to witness more of this shipwreck, and went straight home across the canpièlo without bothering to look around him. He was sorely tempted to give Tron a sharp kick to the *culo*, maybe toss him up in the air and see how he liked it. At least it was Advent tomorrow. Maybe after four weeks without parties, the gossips would tire of discussing Dama Oriela's ankles.

Halfway up his front stairs, Silvio halted and dropped onto a step, leaning his cheek against the rough hand-rope with a sigh. It was more likely that the tale would grow in the telling. He picked idly at a patch of loose plaster while he thought about what to do.

There were subtle ways a lady could communicate

her refusal to be hoisted like a cargo basket. He should have covered those before tonight. He should have anticipated this problem. Puzzi would also need to know how to read the signals if he and his sister were ever to learn the steps. If Catì could ever be convinced to try it again, poor girl. It was all too easy to imagine what advantage Gonxalo might take, holding such a small partner clean off her feet and in his power. Silvio gagged, brushed his hands on the skirt of his new black doublet, and took the remaining stairs two at a time.

The *sala* was dark except for a dying glow from the fireplace. Silvio made for the little credenza, poured himself three fingers of grappa and added two drops of his water lily potion. *Defending her honor.* No—thinking of how Oriela had looked in that new gown—three drops. Smeraldina and the children were still at Ca' Pevari. They would probably spend the night in the nursery there, since the party had run past Rico's bedtime. Silvio went to the fireplace and prodded the coals, added a log. Not two. With any luck, he wouldn't be awake that much longer.

He dropped onto the settee facing the wall, where his new mask hung on the peg formerly occupied by his lost Zani. He gazed at it as he drank, waiting for "Alichin" to ask him a question. Masks often did. After the fourth sip, Alichin's voice inside his head was deceptively childlike.

Is Silvio in a bad temper because she danced bad or because she danced good?

"She danced well," Silvio said aloud, "But not all her partners were worthy."

Really? What's a worthy partner for a citadina with an ambitious papà?

Silvio gulped the rest of his drink, letting the harsh burn scour out a sudden ache in his throat and chest. Pantalon would certainly be thrilled to see that his daughter had attracted the attention of a man as powerful as Tron. The robes and titles hanging off Ser Marco were enough to conceal his bad manners from the eyes of most girls' fathers.

Why shouldn't Oriela snare a senator? Her mother was *nobila*. Ca' Tron would be linked to Margarita's Ca' Condulmer with the Morèr fortune in the middle—assuming an alliance was what Ser Marco had in mind. It was a little hard to believe Tron's intentions were honorable while Oriela's legs were whipping around like a rag doll's, her bronze curls flying loose in his whirlwind, the man's supercilious beard brushing the lace above her snowy bodice.

Silvio worried about Marco Tron's intentions. Silvio's are pure?

"You," he said, raising his empty glass to the Mask, "Are a devil."

37 Confession

Silvio's preparations for Christmas fell into two categories. On the one hand, he had to work up new jesting routines because Carlo would want Salvàn Mandragora in hood and bells for celebrations at Ca' Pevari. To that end, Silvio spent hours each day choreographing dances with inanimate objects and puppet dialogues with edible ones. He got a rug-beater welt on his back after Smeraldina found him in the kitchen, walking a plucked chicken across the work table like a small child.

Getting ready for Christmas Mass was more difficult. On the fourth Monday of Advent, Silvio made the trek across Dorsoduro out to San Nicolò dei Mendicoli, where Fra Tomaso di Tessera had been preaching for the past several months. He waited in the ancient porch with the beggars (the *mendicoli*, for whom the parish was named) while half a dozen of the neighborhood fishermen took their turns being absolved by the friar.

Some said the Dominican Tomaso been assigned here because Father Polo was in poor health, others that the old parish priest drank too much. Either way, Silvio was glad not to have to sail across the Lagoon to the Mestre abbey to see his confessor.

While he burned off his nervous energy by hanging from the porch rafters, the Nicolotti fisherfolk offered him terrifying and hilarious tales of misfortune at sea and mistreatment ashore, all told with the placid good humor of people who expected little better from life. When it came Silvio's turn to go inside, he flipped himself down onto the earthen floor of the porch, and he repaid each storyteller with a *soldo.* This emptied his purse of the six soldi Ser Carlo had just paid him for a week's dancing lessons, but the stories were worth putting up with a hole in his shoe for another week.

Whenever Silvio stepped into the colored-glass twilight of a church and inhaled the sharp-sweet air of incense and beeswax and damp stone, his stomach hurt. He never could shake the sense that he was trespassing, that his kind weren't quite welcome in holy precincts, at least not Christian ones. San Nicolò, however, also made him smile.

Maybe this was because it was smaller, older, and poorer than its cousins nearer to San Marco, or maybe because its decoration was so joyously random. Every century or so, if a merchant's captain had a good year, or if the fishermen or boatmen all pooled a share of their profits, something was added. A font here, a votive altar over there. One fresco painted in the Greek fashion with lean-faced saints in color-coded vestments. On the next wall, a tender family scene done in imitation of the Tuscan maìstro Giotto. Nothing matched anything else. There had been no architect planning the project and making sure its pieces blended, only the most ordinary people offering whatever they could, whenever they could.

Silvio found Fra Tomaso's bald head in the sacristy, bent over a chalice and several rags that he held on his lap. He motioned Silvio to the room's one chair. The little friar was on a low stool. He set his work aside for the opening litany, "Forgive me, father...," etc., but then he went back to polishing the worn silver.

He said, "All right, Silvio, let's take it as given that you've committed all the same minor blasphemies as usual. What's really on your mind?"

"I have a new Mask." Silvio pulled Alichin out of his shirt. "I don't trust him."

Tomaso set the chalice on the stone counter, wiped his hands on the rags. "May I?" He held the Mask in his left hand and gazed into its empty eyes for the duration of an Ave Maria, signed a cross on its brow with his thumb, and gave it back.

Silvio said, "Will that help?"

"It can't hurt."

Silvio tucked it away and said, "There's someone I think you should meet." Tomaso put his fingertips together and waited. "My neighbor Morèr has a daughter. You should go and see him and ask about her."

"Is that all?"

"It would be gossip to say more."

"All right. What else?"

"I'm still afraid to go to Mass on Christmas Eve," Silvio said, leaning forward in the chair.

"Worried about Communion?" Tomaso sighed. "Silvio, we've talked about this."

"I know," Silvio said, "But I still panic. Touching God. Putting him in my—" He tapped his lips, fingers flinching away as if they'd touched hot irons, "—in my *mouth!*"

Tomaso smiled, "It should be as terrifying for the rest of us." He started folding one of the rags as tidily as an altar linen. "We just forget to think about it."

Silvio picked up the other rag. "I keep thinking that one day God will notice what I am and—I don't know..." He folded it in thirds, then in half. "Strike me with a plague of boils or something."

"You think He's never noticed you before?"

Silvio gave the rag back to the friar and sat in silence for a moment, unable to think of another argument to justify his irrational yet gripping fear. Shouldn't the Host burst into flames on his tongue? He almost wished it would. Maybe that would take the curse off his lips, like Ezekiel's angel with the hot coal. At last he said, "Smeraldina says Gianna's doing well at the convent."

"Indeed," said Tomaso, "She's got people coming from all over Lombardy for her prayers." He stood to put the rags and chalice in a rough cupboard over the counter. "If she doesn't wind up canonized, it will only be because the Pope is a fool." Tomaso paused and turned to face Silvio. "Which, let's face it..."

Silvio grinned. "*Sì.*" Tomaso could say things like that when they were together, without fear of Inquisitors. The friar's honest opinions were sealed in a kind of reverse confessional to the *bufon*.

Even standing, Tomaso could look his seated friend in the eye. He said, "It goes to show that you never know where holiness is going to come from, even a bed in a whorehouse."

"I can't take any credit for Gianna," Silvio said. "She kissed me. I was asleep."

Tomaso's gaze deepened. "The credit is God's."

"Furthermore," said Silvio, looking away, "I was wide awake when I kissed Clarissa, and nothing good came of that."

"My son," said Tomaso, a form of address he rarely used with Silvio, "You are not in a position to know that. Like Giuseppe said to his brothers, what men intend for evil, God can intend for good."

"Men..." Silvio said, realizing that he sounded like his mother, dismissing the entire human species.

"Kneel, my son," said Tomaso. Silvio slid from the chair onto the cold floor. "And hear me. Men killed Gesù, and if that hadn't happened, you and I wouldn't be sitting here talking about forgiveness of sins, and I wouldn't be able to say what I'm about to say to you, which is *ego te absolvo.*"

Silvio diffidently mirrored the sign of the cross. It would have to do.

38 Xoca

Oriela spent the Eve of the Holy Nativity in the city, in the same way she had always spent it at Moniga: sitting alone by the fire and wondering what everyone else was doing. Papà had opened Margarita's sitting room before Luca rowed him away toward San Marco just at sunset, and Oriela brought the big tapestry frame out into the portego to work on the farm scene. She set it up by the big fireplace where the Christmas log was burning and lit several candles to see her work. Then Pasquela left, to walk across the Cànpo to the church with Papà's name.

Another hour or so later, San Pantalon's bells didn't ring for Mass because the fallen tower was still being repaired, but dozens of other *campanili* throughout the city sounded almost—but never quite—at once, a dissonant polyphony only slightly muffled by the shutters that were latched tight against the cold. There had only been one church tower within earshot of Villa Morèr back in Moniga, its declarations of time and season echoing uncontested off hillsides and fortress walls. Here, it seemed no two churches could agree on the hour.

Oriela finished off the eel pie from supper while

reading through her song for Ser Carlo's pastoral. When Papà had told her there was to be a Christmas play at Ca' Lesse tomorrow and that she would be permitted to take part, Oriela had briefly hoped the script might shed some light on the mysterious festival. The play was about shepherds, which was promising. There were usually shepherds in the songs people sang about Christmas. But this was a typical pastoral, which meant that an entire pack of wolves might carry off two lambs apiece while the useless shepherds were playing tricks on fauns, whining about nymphs and listening to a sibyl —Oriela—sing a poem Carlo had taken from Virgil.

... O fortunate Lady whose son I behold!
Sweet Child, with your birth comes the era of gold!

If the birth of Gesù had brought about a golden age, Oriela thought, it hadn't lasted. Since Virgil had been a pagan, the poem might not be about Christmas at all. Oriela wondered if the shepherds in the carols were as idle and poetical as Carlo's.

She took the dish to the washbasin and dipped her hands into the cold water to take off the crumbs, reached down to dry them on her apron, and stopped just in time to avoid staining her new lavender damask. She reached for a rag.

Coming to the city had changed one thing at least. Dama Oriela no longer wore an apron. She had nothing important to do this *Natale*. Well, she could still guard the *Sòch* log (Pasquela had called it *Xoca*).

At Moniga, the day before the festival started, Giorgio would go up into the hills with two horses and half a dozen men and bring back a piece of beech or oak the size of a fattened sow. This was to be the *Sòch Nedàl*, and it was supposed to last for twelve days.

In the early twilight, after all the children had taken a turn striking the log with smaller sticks to beat out the past year's bad fortune, Giorgio, always using juniper as tinder, set it alight. Oriela was then left to tend the fire and to sweep up the sawdust from the Sòch to add to the warming fire in the *bigatèra* (Giorgio said this would keep evil away from the worms), while everyone else went to church. According to Francesca, this made her the guardian of the year's good luck. Oriela was grateful for this illusion of responsibility, even as she grew older and saw it for a ploy.

No one had asked her to do anything about the thick ash bole now enthroned on Papà's lion-headed, bronze firedogs, but keeping an eye on it let her pretend she was still useful. She tied off the white embroidery floss and threaded her needle with orange silk for the cocoonery roof.

Once during Advent, a boy of about eight years was helping Oriela lay out cocoon twigs for a tray of *bigati* that were ready to spin. While they worked, the boy sang a bit of something the choirboys had been practicing, about a Blessed Virgin and a Holy Child. Oriela had begged him to stop. Those two phrases, *blessed virgin* and *holy child*, made her feel like she had been stung through the ears. She was a cursed virgin, an unholy child. Why had the new year's fortune and the welfare of the silkworms been left in her unlucky hands?

When she asked the boy about the pair in the song,

he'd told her she might see pictures and statues of them at a church, but there were so many images of so many people inside San Martino. Maybe if she could get inside a church while the Christians were celebrating this mother and child, she'd see which ones they were.

When the candles were down to dripping stubs, Oriela put the tapestry away and closed Mamma's room. She practiced her sibyl's song once more in her own chamber, and then tried to go to bed. She blew out the last candle and closed the bed curtains, wrapped herself in the featherbed and hurled her head onto the pillow. Blessed Virgin. Holy Child. What were all the Christians doing?

The pillow was a rock, the sheets sandpaper. She sat up, cast the blankets away and slipped out into the room, shivering in her camisa. By the light of the last embers in her fireplace, she put her gown and shoes back on, threw her cloak over her shoulders and pulled up the hood. Then, worried that someone might recognize her, she rummaged in the clothes chest and pulled out what felt like a gauzy silk kerchief, which she tied on over her face for a veil.

She could only see the floor an inch in front of her feet and felt her way along the dark portego wall, down the stairs and through the echoing damp of the fondaco. At the land-side door, she paused and listened to make sure the canpièlo was empty before she slipped through and pulled it closed. She wouldn't try the parish church. The neighbors would know her and ask questions. A cold, damp wind fluttered her cloak like the wings of a great moth as she turned away from San Pantalon and crossed the bridge over the Rio Ca'

Foscari toward Santa Margarita, the church that bore her mother's name.

39 San Marco

L ike most Venetians, Pantalon loved the Basilica di San Marco with a deep, visceral affection that cradled its architectural eccentricities in a warm embrace of national pride. He joyed in the riotous beauty of the façade with its many-colored stonework and lacy, gilded doorways.

As Pantalon crossed the grand threshold between Antonio and Elisabeta, the light of the setting sun blazed through the west window, ignited the golden mosaics that covered the walls and ceiling, and set the gilded rood screen alight. The sight never failed to stop his breath. Yet he had to admit that San Marco had, over the centuries, become a very odd-looking church.

Every time the Republic acquired a new piece of finery, they added it to the pile of offerings they'd been laying at the Evangelist's feet since his bones' arrival from Alexandria. Pantalon would never say it aloud, but he sometimes wondered whether St. Mark looked on such prizes, like the bronze horses they'd looted from Constantinople—probably the biggest fool's errand the Republic's navy had ever embarked upon—with the same mixture of bemused indulgence and disgust that appeared on Pasquela's face when the cat, with much noisy ceremony, presented her with a dead mouse.

It was still Advent for the next five hours, so the music started out subdued—meaning, at San Marco, just one choir, the organ and a few strings. More musicians would gradually join them as they labored through the offices of Vespers, Compline and Matins and, finally, the Christmas Mass. Doge Loredan and all his advisers and councilors had seats near the altar. High-ranking patricians in their black robes filled the transepts, looking like overgrown choirboys.

Carlo would be up there among them, along with his father Nicolò who was a judge on the Council of Forty. Only one *citadìn*, Grand Chancellor Stella, would be included in the Doge's company. For the less prominent *nobili* and *citadìni* standing in the nave with Pantalon, it would be a long evening, but at least he and the remaining Pevari had arrived early enough to find places near one of the heavy, square pillars.

A monk from the Frari, his brown wool habit surmounted by a fur-lined hood, climbed into the lectern for the first Scripture reading of the night. He sang it on a single note, the Latin syllables ricocheting from the domed roofs, blurring into gibberish. Lessons alternated with bits of resonating plainchant and the occasional, blissful polyphonic canticle. The words might be nearly unintelligible, but San Marco was built brilliantly for music, and the new Flemish maìstro knew how to use it.

The last periwinkle shafts of twilight from the great west window filtered down through a thick haze of frankincense from the huge, bronze thurible that hung over their heads like a fragrant storm cloud. Pantalon's mind wandered, and he found himself thinking about children. Choirboys in the clerestory, dozens of children singing about the birth of a Child. All of them baptized. How many had cried?

Matins began in darkness. First, a single voice in plainsong, then the long *Venite* canticle, elaborately set in sixteen vocal parts, during which a troop of altar boys appeared with torches and began to light candles. It took the lads until the end of Matins to light every one. After the *Te Deum*, the trumpets came out. To be precise, only their sound did. Like the other instrumentalists, the men of the elite trumpeters' guild were hidden away in the mysterious spaces above the worshippers' heads. It created the agreeable illusion that the angel Gabriel himself had opened the heavens to blow his horn for their Doge.

It was now nearing midnight, but the hundred voices singing "*Audite, principes*" in thunderous unison was certain to rouse any of the congregation who might have started to nod. It was the dramatic moment when the Serene Prince and his advisers, all kneeling for confession, were admonished to listen to the news of Christ's birth, and Venetians felt very pleased with themselves for having such a splendidly humble government.

Two groups of choirboys were tossing the Gloria back and forth across the ceiling, an antiphon of angels. Pantalon thought, *All children sound holy when they're singing.* Did the boys still scribble on the walls when the choirmaster's back was turned? Somewhere in the rafters above this very pillar, there was an obscene Latin motto Pantalon Morèr had scratched into the gold to amuse his friends. He didn't think he had been more touched by the Devil than any other nine year-old. He was willing to bet his daughter hadn't profaned any holy walls.

He supposed he was going to have to get Oriela baptized sooner or later, since he planned to have her marry someone. He just didn't know how he would explain the situation to the Patriarch.

40 Infidel

Oriela found the bridge by the way the moon-light on the water was broken into triangles by the wooden trusses. She located the first step by bruising her shin on it, felt for the hand rail, and took the stairs one at a time, bringing her right foot up to meet the left before climbing again. Like a Pavana. Either the night or the veil was darker than she'd expected.

After the bridge, there was a single crowded calle to pass through, and then she could see the light of an arched doorway. But already the bells were ringing, and the people pushing past her were all moving away from the church. Then she shrieked, because someone had grabbed her arm.

"Aha! Alichin catch you, infidel!" It was Silvio's voice but not his voice, ungrammatical and strangely shrill. "Alichin tell Serenity!" Oriela realized from its odd resonance that he was wearing a mask. He pulled her back the way she'd come.

"Silvio, let go." They came to a circle of torchlight, which she felt more than saw. She squinted up at Silvio's mask. It was leather, blunt-faced and somewhat lumpy. It must be one of the new ones.

"Oriela? God's teeth, Dama. Alichin thought you were Turkish spy." Silvio pushed the mask up onto the top of his head. "Sorry," he said. "I'm not used to this fellow yet." He patted the mask. "What are you doing, walking around alone in the middle of the night?"

"Going to Mass." She started walking again.

Silvio followed. He said, "Why the disguise? Your father's all the way across town at San Marco, and there's no one else who would mind."

How much had he figured out about her? "You don't think they can tell I'm..."

At the foot of the bridge, he took her hand and stopped her, made her look at him. "Baptized people look exactly like unbaptized people."

Oriela's thoughts whirled, a confused maelstrom of embarrassment and relief. He knew her secret, had probably figured it all out when she asked about Purgatory. She turned away, started over the bridge, and struck her already-bruised leg on the first step. She took Silvio's arm to keep from barking her other shin. When they reached the top, she paused and said, "Silvio, if I ask you a very foolish question, will you promise to give me a straight answer?"

"If I can."

"Who is baby Gesù?"

Silvio pulled his mask all the way off , looked at it as if for advice, and sighed. "Why do you ask *me* these questions?"

"Because you answer them," she said. Because he was the only person who had never laughed or turned away or told her to go ask someone else. Because he knew about her curse and had never treated her like she had one.

Silvio tucked the mask into his belt and started down the steps. "He's God, and his mother's name is Maria."

"Who was his father?"

"God."

"He's his own father?" For a few paces she tried to make sense of this. "God is a family name, so they're both God but different members of the family?"

Silvio said, "Not exactly." He stopped at the bottom of the steps and held out his hand for her. Cànpo San Pantalon was already deserted except for a few pigs huddled together against the wall of the tavern. "Fra Tomaso would explain it better."

"A monk wouldn't want to talk to me," she said.

"He talks to me," said Silvio, "Which is more remarkable than you'd think."

They turned into their calle, sheltered from the wind between the tall houses, and passed the last torch before home. Oriela had left the house hoping to understand Christmas before she returned, but she was more confused than before. She said, "What about the sibyl?"

Silvio halted just outside the canpièlo gate and turned to lean against the wall. He chuckled quietly, shaking his head. "You must think we're all crazy."

Of the thousand questions still jamming the narrow calle between her brain and her mouth, the one that leapt next into the air was the last one Oriela herself expected. "Was it hard for him?"

"What?" Silvio said. She could feel his eyes on her even in the dark between the houses.

"Was it hard for Gesù," she said, "Being part human, part something else? Looking like a man but knowing he was different?"

He stood gazing at her for a long time. Then he turned, peered around the corner and said, "I think your father's already home."

"From San Marco?"

"Luca rows fast."

She said, "I'm supposed to be asleep. I have to wait until he goes to bed."

"Pasquela will have locked the doors," he said. "But I can get you inside, if you don't mind waiting a few minutes." He tugged on the front of her veil. "You'll need to see."

Oriela lowered her hood and undid the knot, letting the scarf fall around her neck. The rush of cold air on her head made her shiver, and she unconsciously took a step closer to Silvio's warmth as she wrapped her cloak tighter. Silvio gently pulled up her hood and tucked it around her face. He stayed there, looking at her, for three misty breaths, and then he took a slow step backwards. They watched pools of candlelight moving from window to window inside Ca' Morèr.

Silvio said, "When both candles go out, come to the door." She nodded, shivering again. Silvio slipped off his cape and wrapped it around her shoulders. "Here. This will only be in my way," he said, and started for his door.

41 Rooftops

Smeraldina was sitting by the fire in the *sala*, nursing the baby Belina. She nodded at Silvio but made no comment as he crossed the room, hung up Alichin on his peg, opened the window at the other end and started to climb out. Only when he was hanging from the eaves above the window frame did she call out, "Silvio! Close that window!"

Silvio stuck his head back in, upside-down. "Sorry," he said, and pulled the window shut. There were certain advantages, he reflected as he climbed up the roof, to having a former *putàna* for a sister in-law. There was very little that shocked Smeraldina. A man climbing out of a window in the middle of the night wasn't even surprising. He paused at the chimney and looked up at the looming expanse of Ca' Pevari. He planned to walk the length of that roof and then jump down into Morèr's roof garden.

The hardest part of the journey would be getting up to Ca' Pevari's roof from his own, one story lower. The upper balcony was too far to his right, but there was a pointed, antique window frame on the nearer corner that would provide a gripping surface, and he could use the quatrefoil at the top of the arch as a ladder. Once the jump was planned, he executed it with his mind disengaged, letting his arms and legs do the thinking for him.

When he got to the far end of the roof he sat down by one of the tall, conical chimneys where it was a little warmer. He waited for Pasquela's light to go out and thought of Oriela, huddled down there in the darkness, also watching the light. Oriela and her questions. She seemed to think Silvio was a good Christian. Maybe he should have told her he hadn't been to church that night.

Despite what Fra Tomaso said, when Silvio thought of approaching the altar he lost his nerve. He'd spent the evening trying out his new Mask at a small *osteria* in Cànpo Santa Margarita, entertaining his fellow sinners with a recitation of the hand-walking scene in *The Toe of San Pazzio.* He had then made a hasty, frightened exit when one of the girls planted herself in his lap. By sheer coincidence he'd arrived at Santa Margarita church while the worshipers were coming out. After teaching her to dance, Silvio had instantly recognized Oriela's veiled form by touch, by the exact point where her head reached his chin, by the width and set of her shoulders and hips.

Was it hard for Gesù? All his life, Silvio had been told he ought to feel certain things about Christ: reverence, gratitude, even fear—but empathy had never been one of them. It felt like Oriela had picked up Silvio's wits and whirled them around in the air. This surprising lady had hazarded her reputation, her father's approval and her shins to try and get into the very place Silvio was afraid to go. He had never felt like such a coward in his life.

A gust of sharp winter breath slid in over the roof-tops, and Silvio slapped his arms to warm them. The chimney was going cold, its fire banked for the night. He flexed his arms and legs to keep them from stiffening up. At last Pasquela's light went out. Silvio rose, walked to the edge of the roof, and hopped down lightly as a squirrel into the narrow aisle between Pantalon's jasmine bushes. From there, making his way down through the warm house without a sound was child's play. In a few more minutes, he had the door unlatched.

Oriela wrapped Silvio's cape around him as she stepped inside, fastening it at his throat. So close, and so warm. She took one of his freezing hands and pressed it between her own. Then she whispered, "*Grassie,*" turned, and vanished among the shadowy crates and boxes.

42 Sibyl

Oriela found it strange to be back in her room, as if none of her nocturnal adventures had really happened. Burrowing into the cocoon of her bed once more, the cold sheets assured her that she had been absent from them for some time. She curled herself into a tight ball to get warm, expecting sleep to come more easily than on her first attempt. She ought to be exhausted.

Silvio ought to be exhausted. When she first saw his shadowy figure gliding along the Ca' Pevari roof, she wanted to ask how he'd gotten up there. But when she saw him half frozen at her back door, she found she couldn't speak. Maybe it was because he was not scaling walls for show. Maybe because it looked so easy for him, as if climbing out windows and crawling over rooftops were the most routine activities, or as if—her breath halted—as if doing it for her sake had made it effortless.

Suddenly she wasn't cold anymore. She'd longed to be the cape as she wrapped him in it, to hold him until his hands thawed, until he understood how much he had come to matter to her. This was, of course, completely inappropriate and unthinkable. So the night

continued much as it had begun, with Oriela tossing restlessly, punching her pillow, and not sleeping a
wink. And then it was morning.

At Ca' Lesse the next day, Dama Donata stuffed them
all with roast peacock while she embarrassed her husband and her son Zuan with wildly exaggerated tales
of their naval victories. Oriela was perversely grateful
for the woman's constant chatter as it saved her from
having to think of clever things to say to Marco Tron,
who had been seated on her left. Ser Marco sometimes
nudged her and rolled his eyes when Donata said something especially implausible, which let Oriela feel as if
she understood the joke even if she didn't. During one of
the rare moments when Donata stopped talking to take
a bite, Oriela asked him if he still thought she'd been
raised by wolves.

"Oh yes," he said. "But you're in good company.
Think of Romulus and Remus."

A test of her education, disguised as a compliment.
She said, "I'm not likely to found an empire, Siór." She
knew by his smile that she'd passed. Maybe it was possible to be friends with this man, as long as he wasn't
dancing.

After dinner, the meal still heavy on her stomach,
Oriela joined Elisabeta and Smeraldina in Elisabeta's
old room to dress for the play. She picked up her sibyl
costume from the bed, held it up in front of the mirror, and groaned. Some of Donata's guests, including
Ser Marco, would be watching Oriela's performance
not just to be entertained but to assess her as a com-
modity. They'd be adding up her voice, figure, diction,

and posture, subtracting the disadvantage of her birth, multiplying that by her probable dowry and calculating whether she was worth a bid.

Although Elisabeta assured her that everyone loved pastorals, Oriela frankly thought she and her friends were all going to look extremely silly. She was sure her "gown," consisting of a dozen or so pale green and golden veils draped haphazardly from her shoulders and arms, was the silliest of all. She frowned into the mirror while Smeraldina dusted her face and neck with some golden powder, certain that her voice would dry up from nerves and leave her croaking like a raven.

Elisabeta, dressed as a "nymph" in a long, white tunic tied with ribbons, managed to look dignified with bare arms and feet and a long veil sagging off the back of her head. Elisabeta could look dignified in anything.

She laid her hand on Oriela's gilded shoulder and said, "Ser Marco is in the front row." Oriela tried to smile about this news, since Elisabeta clearly meant it for encouragement, but she failed, certain Marco would laugh at her costume. She followed Elisabeta behind the arras which was serving as their backdrop. Smeraldina, in a voluminous blue mantle, waited with Belina, who was to represent Gesù.

Silvio emerged from the door across the portego in his faun costume, and Oriela covered her mouth, choked back a laugh. He was clad in a pair of goatskin breeches. In place of a shirt he wore a threadbare woolen tunic that looked as if it had been knitted using the two goat's horns that were attached by a leather band to his head.

Silvio reddened as he came toward her. "Don't remind me, please," he whispered. "I'll only get through this if I can forget what I'm wearing."

"Thank you," said Oriela.

"What for?"

"For looking even more ridiculous than I do."

"*Prego*," said Silvio, with a shy smile, a tiny bow. "But you look like an..." His eyes darted away.

"I look like what?"

"Not at all ridiculous," Silvio said. "Are you nervous?"

Oriela said, "To be nervous I'd have to think there was some hope of success."

"Just go out there looking golden and exotic, sing some Virgil and swoon over Belina. Most of them will love it because it seems antique, and the rest will have to pretend to because they don't understand it."

Carlo and Antonio were dressed in some flimsy, impractical things that these water-bound city folk had imagined a shepherd might wear. Oriela half-listened to the inane dialogue, running over her song in her mind and hoping not to miss her cue.

At last Antonio said, "With the child I've seen, a new era has arrived, just as the sibyl foretold."

Oriela swept onto the stage, letting the drapery of her costume flutter around her. The Faun dropped to his knees. Marco Tron sighed audibly, and the sibyl began to sing.

43 She-Wolf

Silvio dressed early on Twelfth Night and went over to Ca' Pevari in his green-and-purple jester's regalia to survey the rooms, noting the height of the table, the locations of chairs and candlesticks, and any other objects he might use as props. Antonio and his friends in the Conpàgna degli Alati had been busy all afternoon hanging laurel and ivy from the painted ceiling beams and from everything that protruded from anything else: bannisters, doorjambs, picture frames, finials on chair backs and credenza corners.

Silvio wore no mask with the belled collar and particolored hood. He would be there under his familiar *bufon* name, Salvàn Mandragora, a being whom he trusted completely. (Unlike Alichin. It would need several weeks' practice before he felt safe bringing that creature out in public again.) As the first guests landed at the dock, Silvio relaxed and let Salvàn take the oars for the evening; Silvio himself would only advise. His first task would be greeting the guests as they arrived in the ground-floor fondaco, which after a century and two floods still smelled faintly of pepper and cloves.

"I bid you heartily welcome, my lord!" Salvàn cried to a young gondolier who had just tied up his boat and leapt onto the dock. His voice was a bit louder and sharper than Silvio's, the better to carry across a crowded room. "Your most esteemed presence does inexpressible honor to this humble House."

The *nobili* passengers were left to disembark on their own, unacknowledged by Mandragora. The boatman pointed toward his master and mumbled something to the Fool.

"I crave your pardon, Siór," Salvàn said to the gondolier, "My ears are mutinous. Might I beg your lordship to repeat your remark?"

"That's the senator," the gondolier said more loudly, "Behind you."

"Oh!" Salvàn spun on one toe, letting the long points of his hood swing in the air. The brass bells jingled when they slapped his shoulders. He scooped up and shook the hand of an old man in a fur-lined, red robe. "*Bonaséra.* Nice to see you." The senator was laughing. Even his normally sour wife smiled. So far, so good, Silvio told Salvàn.

As he whirled back, jingling, to face the canal, the gondolier had already shipped the mooring line to glide away like a long, black swan. "My lord!" Salvàn cried after him, "Must you leave so soon? You leave us desolate by your departure, Siór!"

Ca' Pevari had two staircases from the fondaco to the living quarters on the *piano nobile* above. The wide one began inside the former warehouse and led into the portego. The other bent around inside the walls of a small courtyard and led to the dining room. Pantalon and Oriela entered the courtyard by the street door, with Pasquela behind them in a new, black governess' gown, with a hard, lace-lined hood fixed like a roof on top of her head. They would have to be led to the courtyard staircase, so Silvio approached them by way of a cartwheel across the colorful tiles of the fondaco.

Morèr was sparing no expense in dressing his daughter. Oriela's gown was the color of holly leaves. The trim on the generous sleeves and quilted bodice was cloth-of-gold, probably legally prohibited for a *citadina*. Her lace cap and short, sheer veil were golden as well, punctuated by a green bead suspended in the center of her forehead by a gold chain. The effect was enchanting, and Silvio was not going to think about it.

Coming expertly upright, Salvàn bowed extravagantly to Oriela, which made her giggle. It was, Silvio realized, the first time she had seen him in his bells. Salvàn pretended to be terrified of her father. He ducked down to hide behind Pasquela's daunting black skirt. Daughter laughed. "Governess" laughed. Father did not. Oh, well. Salvàn moved away, and Pantalon hurried his daughter up the stairs.

Salvàn turned and rushed back across the fondaco as another gondola bumped against the canal steps. The Gritti-Dolfin party was docking: ancient Alvise Dolfin, his young wife Dama Michela Gritti, and assorted female cousins. As Salvàn approached the plush gondola, Michela grabbed another girl's arm and whispered something. She held out a beseeching hand to the *bufon*, said El Mandragora *must* help her out of the boat. She positively simpered, fluttering her eyelashes at him before starting away toward the courtyard.

"Look, Ariana," Michela cried, "It's *la Lupa* Morèr!" She was pointing up the stairs at Oriela's back, which was just inside the dining room door. Silvio prayed that she hadn't heard. Michela said, "The little she-wolf who threw herself at poor Marco." She took Ariana's hand and pulled her quickly up the stairs, giggling in pursuit.

Silvio wanted to stop her somehow, but Salvàn was obliged to turn and meet the next boat, which was laden with young men in the red-and-gold striped stockings of the *Reali*. It belonged to Ca' Foscari, just across the rio.

"Lovely *tragheto*, Siór," Salvàn said to the gondolier, describing the ornate Ca' Foscari boat as one of the unadorned ferry gondolas that shuttled people across the canals for half a soldino. Salvàn then demanded a coin from each passenger and gave it to the boatman for his tragheto fare. Silvio hardly noticed whether they laughed. He was wondering what else Dama Michela was saying about "Lupa" Morèr.

44 Bufon

Oriela was amazed that anyone could keep their mind on dinner while Silvio was swooping and darting around the candlelit dining room like a particolored hoopoe bird. He hid under the table, popping out from the long cloth to sit on someone's lap and snatch some of their food. He might eat the food, or he might juggle it, talk to it, or dance it like a puppet. He carried on a long, poignant conversation with a roast suckling pig. Oriela was so fascinated that the entire third course came and went without her touching a bite.

A short way up the table, Michela Gritti and her friends kept looking at Oriela and giggling. Oriela had heard Michela on the stairs, knew the girls were laughing at her, but watching Silvio's antics made it seem like a fine thing to have other people laugh at you. She smiled boldly back at the girls and pretended to howl at the ceiling, even wishing Marco Tron were there to share the joke. Had he been invited?

In fact, she noticed that the Fool's performance had a transforming effect on the whole party. Everywhere hostility got a foothold, Silvio tripped it up and pounded it into peace with the sheer force of his lunacy. When a cross-looking, one-armed man started shouting at Michela's husband about the Spaniards, Silvio sat on the table between the two and picked up a spoon.

He told the spoon, "It was entirely your fault!" The strong Vèneto accent coming out of Silvio's mouth startled Oriela's ears, and she realized that this was the voice of the famous Salvàn Mandragora she'd been hearing about.

Silvio—Salvàn—held the spoon to his ear for a moment, saying, "The fork did it?" He held it out at arm's length. "How dare you accuse the fork! The fork defended the bowl with all its might! What's that?" He listened to the spoon again. "Well, you can't blame the fork for the knife switching sides. You know knives can't be trusted." Then he leapt lightly onto the table in front of them and began to dance the Volta with a roasted peacock.

When a little girl suddenly burst into tears, saying her brother had hit her, el Mandragora sat down at the children's table and started to weep even more loudly. This so astonished the child that she stopped crying and offered the Fool her handkerchief.

Salvàn said, "My brother calls me *diàvolo* and throws me in the fountain." He was struck in the head with an Epiphany fig cake thrown by Piero, who was also at the children's table with Smeraldina. The *pinza* cakes had not been served yet. "And he steals cakes," Salvàn said with a sniffle, taking a bite. He broke the rest and gave half to the girl, half to her brother, and then dashed away to intervene in a dispute that was brewing between Antonio and one of the youths in the red stockings.

After dinner, the evening grew duller. Oriela sat between her father and Pasquela in a chair by the wall as dances came and went. No one spoke to them. They had all seen or heard about her Volta with Marco Tron. Even watching Salvàn dance with housemaids and candlesticks was starting to bore her, but then the Fool approached them. He scooped up the hand of a *citadina* matron who was walking by.

"Dama," he said, "I beseech you not to be so cold! Would you pass by my poor friend Pantalon as if he weren't there? Can't you see he is half dead for love of you?" He then grabbed her father's hand. Papà was too startled to resist.

"Look, Ser Pantalon, I have acquired her for you," Salvàn dropped his voice to a dramatic stage-whisper, "At great risk to my own safety, I might add. Her extremely large husband was none too pleased."

He slid between Oriela and her father and gave Papà a push from behind, said, "Quick, before he escapes."

"You want to dance with me?" Oriela said. As she watched Papà and his partner move away, she noticed Antonio and another of the Alati (she could tell by their matching green stripes) arguing again with the boy from the Reali.

"No," Salvàn said, "I want to toss you in the canal." He glanced over his shoulder at Antonio but didn't move to intervene. It was Silvio's own eyes that turned back to meet hers.

The opening Pavana of the set was by now second nature for Oriela and Silvio, but when the Galliard rhythm started, Oriela saw the drummer take up his tambourine for a Volta. Unwilling to attempt that dance again in public, she dropped Silvio's hand without a reverence and started back toward Pasquela.

Silvio slid into her path. "No," he said quietly, in his own voice. "Show them."

She met his eyes, nodded. Her hand rested on his green shoulder while his purple arm reached to cradle her waist. The long tails of his hood brushed the back of her hand, and the bells on his collar rang softly through their flawlessly synchronized turns. There had never been a Volta so graceful or so irreproachable. Surely one of the gentlemen would ask her to dance now.

Silvio set her down on the last note, softly as a settling bird, and released her. Oriela's hand lingered on his shoulder, trailed reluctantly down his chest. She caught one of the bronze bells on his collar and shook it gently. She'd been wanting to do that for hours. The tone was clear and sweet.

"Thank you," she said, wishing she could hug him.

Antonio's voice sailed over the crowd. "Hat dance!"

Oriela saw Antonio's friend push the Reali youth, who was reaching for his sword. The call was echoed by several other Alati, and immediately all the ladies started racing around the room while the men retreated to line the walls. Silvio vanished into the confusion, just when a dancing master would be most useful. Their lessons hadn't included anything called a Hat

Dance.

All around her, grown women were running and squealing like little girls. One by one, each lady chose a gentleman, removed his hat and put it on her own head. Then the man took back the hat and escorted the lady onto the floor. She caught a glimpse of Papà's new brimmed, velvet cap on the veiled gray head of someone in a blue gown.

Oriela wandered through the heaving mob, looking for Pasquela or Elisabeta, someone who might explain the rules of this game to her. Was that Marco, in the red-gold cluster of Reali? When had he arrived? Should she try for his hat? She tried to move in that direction, but her way was blocked by an unseemly scuffle between three young women, all vying for the same hat. Well, not a hat, exactly. It was Silvio's hood.

Michela Gritti had the crown and was defending her prize against two other girls, each of whom had taken hold of one of the long tails and was pulling with all her might. Salvàn was standing on a chair between two candlesticks, pretending to shake with terror.

"Let go," Michela said, "If you rip it he won't dance with any of us!" She looked up at the theatrically cowering Fool. "Tell them, Maìstro!"

Oriela watched curiously for a moment. Assuming the mysterious transaction with the hat signaled invitation and acceptance, how might the game proceed if the ladies managed to destroy the hat in question?

"Be fair, Michela," one of the girls whined, "He helped you off the boat. It's my turn!"

"Why should it be your turn?" said another, "Haven't you got all the Alati crawling to your father for dances? Let me have el Mandragora for one dance."

"I had it first," Michela said, tugging on the crown.

Òro! Fine ladies these were. A she-wolf had better manners. Before she could talk herself out of it, Oriela ducked low and slipped under Michela's elbow. She popped up in the middle of the mêlée with her own head inside the hood. A moment later she was hoisted out of a screaming flurry of fists and fingernails and found herself standing on the chair beside the Fool.

"That was a perilous maneuver, Dama," he said. "I'm not sure whether it was clever or reckless." They watched the three combatants move away pouting, throwing furious looks over their shoulders at Oriela.

"Either way, I saved your bells," she said, lowering her head to let him retrieve his hood. But instead of taking it back as the other men had done, Salvàn lifted his hands away.

Oriela raised one of the hood's velvet tails from her shoulder and rang the bell. "Don't you want this back?"

He shied away, his golden eyes wide in the candlelight. "Are you determined to die tonight?" he said. "If I accept it now and dance with you, Dama Michela will tell Ser Alvise you're a Turkish spy."

She looked over at Michela, who had returned to her husband. The old man was listening sympathetically to her complaint and looking up every few moments in their direction.

"I don't understand," Oriela said, "Did Ser Alvise want his wife to dance with you?"

"He didn't want her to be outwitted by you," Silvio said, relaxing into his own voice. He gazed out over the dance floor where the ladies were lining up opposite their chosen gentlemen for a contra-dance. The music started.

"Depending on how she tells the story, Alvise Dolfin might decide to take it as a direct insult from Ca' Morèr. Insulting the Dieci is never good for business." Still facing the dancers, Silvio slid a hand toward her. "All right, they've started. You can give me the hood now, as long as you take it off your own head."

Oriela carefully lifted Silvio's unwieldy headgear off her own cap and veil and inspected the seams. The fabric was a little strained, but nothing was torn. She slid the hood into his hand, patted her own cap and asked, "Is this thing falling off?"

Silvio turned to look. "Your hair's come out a little here," he said, tapping the right side of his head. She tried to tuck the stray wisp back in place but couldn't find the pin. Her fingers seemed to be attached to someone else's hand. Silvio reached to help her. Oriela held her breath, dropped her hand. His fingers were warm on her temple.

He looked away and said, "Wait here till it ends, and then go back to your father."

"I think someone took his hat," Oriela said.

Silvio tied the hood under his chin and hopped

lightly to the floor, not meeting her eyes. He went to the dining room, and she sat down to watch the rest of the dance. After it ended, Pasquela came to sit beside her. When Papà joined them, a few men came by to request a dance with her, but Papà didn't seem impressed with any of them and gave his consent grudgingly. If Marco Tron had stopped by Ca' Pevari, he had already moved on to another, probably more important party. Silvio didn't reappear. She danced several sets with Antonio while Piero was playing. For some reason, every time Piero took a break, no one asked for her at all.

45 Sonnets

A Saltarello ended. Oriela realized she was out of breath, and her feet were getting sore. She was holding the hand of a bearded gentleman whose name she couldn't remember. He was also panting and a bit red in the face. The musicians were moving around, rearranging stands. She saw Piero tuck his new viol under one arm and head for the back stairs with a few of his companions. Someone else took his place.

Everyone seemed to have been dancing without a pause for quite a while. The room had grown stuffy from so many leaping bodies. Oriela slipped away toward the main stairs, keeping out of her father's line of sight, descended into the cool silence of the fondaco level and strolled between the columns toward the courtyard, working the cramps out of her feet.

The former warehouse was empty except for a few stone benches and a bronze Mercury hiding in the shadows, but the briny air still held faint aromas of nutmeg and peppercorn. Ripples of the incoming tide whispered gently under the closed water door and caused the boats in the adjoining room to bump together at lazy intervals. The torches were going out.

Oriela halted when she heard the voice of a tiny bronze bell. Silvio was there, on top of the well cover in the moonlit courtyard. He sat cross-legged, facing the door, his gray cape covering the particolored suit. Had he been out here since the hat dance? He must have heard her footsteps and had turned his head, the bells rolling across his back.

"Oh," he said when she came into the light. "Piero finally took a break?" He uncrossed his legs and pivoted slowly to face her.

"Yes, just now." Oriela said. She hopped up to sit beside him on the edge of the well. "Why? Did you want to talk to him? I think he was heading up to the kitchen."

"He's getting careless," Silvio said. "Someone's going to get hurt one of these nights."

Oriela couldn't make anything of this remark, and Silvio immediately resumed staring motionlessly into the shadows. His head drooped, eyes fixed on nothing. Maybe he was tired. It struck her now that Silvio had spent the last five hours in constant, mad motion, carrying the good humor of the whole gathering on his shoulders. Oriela waited for him to say something else. The chill started to penetrate the layers of her gown.

She was about to give up and go back upstairs when Carlo and Elisabeta floated out onto the balcony above them. They paused to talk, framed in the arch of the central window like saints in a triptych. Carlo took Elisabeta's hands and pressed them together between his own, then bent to kiss her fingertips one by one. Oriela couldn't hear what he said, but Elisabeta must have liked it, because she pulled him closer and tossed back her head so that his nose was very near her throat. They kissed briefly and tenderly, and then Elisabeta took his arm with flawless poise and led him back indoors. Oriela sighed as they vanished.

"What?" said Silvio. He sounded annoyed.

"They're so sweet together," she said. "You know how they met?"

"You believed that tale? Dido. Hmf," Silvio—or was it Salvàn?—said. "Do you really think it would have happened if old Nicolò and Iacopo hadn't set it up?"

"Maybe, but I still think it's charming that they're so in love."

"I'm sure it would be," he said, keeping his gaze fixed on the carving above the balcony door, "If I were convinced such a thing as love exists."

Oriela laughed uncomfortably. It should be Salvàn saying such churlish things, but the dialect was clearly Silvio's. He had said *amùr*.

He jumped off the well and started pacing. "Patrician couples have to believe they love each other. Otherwise their life would be unbearable. Most of the brides are half-grown girls, ready to swoon for the first man who touches them," he paused and looked at her, then away, "And the bridegrooms have been so long without a woman they'd put a ring on a goat if they could stick their cock in it!" He sent a sidelong glance her way, clearly expecting a gasp of polite outrage. She declined to give him one.

He paced faster, "They only have to give their sons a sonnet to recite, and behold: True Love!" He faced her and spread his arms to punctuate his conclusion. "It's how all these proud Houses keep la Serenisima serene."

Oriela studied his face closely for traces of levity and —with dismay—found none. "That was quite a speech, Maìstro," she said coolly. She hoped the title would sting him a little. "Did you practice it long?"

"Dama," he shot the honorific back at her like an obscene oath, "I make fun of people for a living. I've seen enough of these True Lovers to ape them in my sleep." He launched back into motion, manic now, the bells on his whirling hood points nearly hitting her in the face as he flung himself to his knees at the base of the wellhead. He roughly grabbed both her hands and put on a pleading, hungry look.

"Most radiant lady!" he said, his voice broken with mock emotion, "Only show me your face, and I am the most fortunate man in the world!" He loudly kissed the air a few inches from the backs of her hands. Squeezed them harder, too hard. "Your beauty shames the very face of the moon! (*kiss, kiss*) At the sight of your lips, the rose hangs her head!"

When he looked at her, suddenly Oriela thought she saw pain in his eyes. For just one moment, she allowed her imagination to be invaded by a perilous thought: *what if he were serious?* This turned out to be a terrible mistake when she realized that she hoped he was. A moment before, she'd been safely annoyed by his mockery. Now she was shattered by it.

"Gold feels itself base (*kiss, kiss*) beside your hair!"

"Stop!" she cried, "You're cruel." Her heart pounding, Oriela tore her hands sharply away from his and sprang to her feet, knocking him off the platform. He landed on his ass in a half-frozen puddle by the drain.

"Cruel, Dama?" Silvio pulled himself to his feet. "It would be cruel to let you keep walking around with a head full of nursery tales." All the manic energy seemed to have drained out of him. His shoulders sagged. "Your father will get you a husband to make his House more powerful. Don't expect any silly poetry about it."

"Silly poetry," she said, meeting his eyes and trying to fill hers with ice. "All right, Maìstro, explain this to me, in your great wisdom." She could hear her voice getting hoarse, but she couldn't control it. The ice in her eyes threatened to melt. "Where do the sonnets come from?"

He looked startled. Good.

"I'll let you know if I ever find out," he said quietly. He turned away and straightened his hood. "I'm not paid to quarrel with you when no one's looking. Back to work. Senators to insult...hags to flirt with." And then he was away up the courtyard stairs.

Oriela felt her throat tighten and her eyes burn. It wasn't Love she was defending, it was herself, and Silvio probably knew it. The man who lived by seeing through people had peered inside her heart and had found its contents laughable. And they were. Elisabeta's good luck had been a chance in a thousand. Marco Tron was no Carlo. Even if he'd have her, a *citadina*, a she-wolf. And did she want him to? There would be no more singing sibyls or borrowed aprons and masks. No more dancing with Silvio. She thought of the other *nobile* ladies she'd met, Donata, Michela—her success would be measured in her similarity to them.

She sank down onto the platform, pulled a hanky from her sleeve, leaned a shoulder against the side of the well and mopped at her eyes. Presently a new set of footsteps pulled her attention toward the stairs. Antonio was descending into the courtyard with his blue cape on one shoulder, carrying two steaming goblets.

"May I?" he said, nodding toward the step beside her. He sat without waiting for an answer. "Here," he said, handing her one of the cups. "My own recipe. I saw you out the window. You looked…thirsty."

She tried to thank him, but her tongue wouldn't obey her, so she just nodded and took a sip of the concoction, inhaling the strengthening fragrances of cinnamon bark and lemon.

Antonio said, "Never thought I'd get rid of that Falier crone. You'd think she'd have been exhausted after Piero's last set, but the old goose is unnaturally vigorous." He took a sip, then set his cup down and slid his cape across both their laps.

"Thank you, Ser Antonio."

"Toni," he said.

"What?"

"When I'm giving you punch and sharing my cape with you, I'm Toni."

"All right." She blew her nose. "Toni."

Antonio drank. "Fascinating, isn't it," he said, "The way one's feet can't help moving when Piero plays? Don't tell him this, but he could be playing at Ca' Loredan for twice what Carlo pays him, and the Doge would consider it a bargain."

Oriela let him talk, not really listening. She had the impression he wasn't expecting to be listened to. Antonio had the ability to soothe by talking.

He said, "I'm surprised your father let me dance with you so may times."

"Why?"

"I'm the designated bachelor. Once Carlo found Betì, my lot was sealed. He has the heirs, and I have the business."

"That doesn't sound fair," Oriela said. She was finding that Antonio's punch was an excellent remedy for the after-shocks of an emotional earthquake.

"I don't mind," he said. "Except that I have to dance with everyone's mother. Anyway, I saw you weren't on the floor just now and asked him again. He said, 'Certainly you may dance with her, if you can find her.' He didn't sound happy." He took another sip. His imitation of Papà's voice was uncanny. "So I decided to find you, and here you are, looking very much like someone who needs a drink. And…maybe a friend?"

Antonio might not be on Papà's list of prospective sons in-law, but he was the kindest nobleman Oriela had met so far. Why was it that the men she liked—and she still liked Silvio, even if he was in a foul mood—were the ones she couldn't marry? "Toni," she said after a moment, "What do you think about love?"

His eyebrows jumped. "What do I think about what?"

She fixed her gaze on the balcony that had started her quarrel with Silvio. "Do you think it's better," she said, "To hope for love, even if you're not likely to find it?" she stole a glance at Antonio, who was watching her with a taut expression, "Or would I be better advised to pretend there's no such thing?"

He drank pensively. She thought a trace of bitterness crossed his face, but it was quickly put aside. At last he said, "I honestly don't know." He swirled the punch in his mouth as he leaned back, staring into the darkness of the fondaco. Then he gulped it down, and this seemed to drive out all brooding. He sat up straight and said, "What do you think of the punch?"

Oriela drained her cup and handed it back to Antonio with a hopeful smile. It was really working wonders.

"I knew it would help," he said. "You look much better. Would you like another?"

"Please," she nodded. "It's very kind of you. Toni."

"Not at all. It gives me an excuse not to ask some other nasty old cat to dance." Antonio returned up the stairs. He left the cape on her knees, and she pulled it up over her chest like a blanket. The heat from the punch reached down to her toes. By the time Antonio returned, she was feeling warm and dreamy.

"Now, Messer...Toni," she said when she'd finished her second drink. Forming syllables was becoming difficult. "You said something about a dance with me?"

"I'd be obliged, if you're sure you're quite recovered."

"Absolutely."

"In that case," he said, rising and replacing the cape on his shoulder, "Will you do me the honor—" He held out his hand.

"Absolutely," she repeated with some effort, pulling herself unsteadily to her feet, "I'd be honored to do you the honor."

46 Punch

A t first, when Oriela didn't return to his side at the end of the Saltarello, Pantalon thought she must be with Elisabeta or Pasquela. He had been dancing for the last few sets himself. Gentlemen with more daughters than ducats were as eager to press their girls on him as he was to introduce Oriela to all the scions of ancient families who were avoiding him. As long as Piero Speronelli's viol was leading the tunes, Pantalon had been powerless to evade those daughters. His feet must dance, and so he must have partners. Even then, only the most unsuitable sorts of men seemed willing to partner Oriela.

He wondered why no one else seemed to notice this uncanny effect when Piero played. But perhaps it was only that Pantalon had more reason to be alert to phenomena that hinted of unnatural forces. Especially where the Speronelli brothers were concerned.

He would have stopped some time ago if he could have, not least because he had caught sight of Marco Tron during the last set. Now that the elder Speronelli had put down his bow, exhausted dancers were dropping into chairs or crowding into the dining room for a drink. Pantalon surveyed the eddying clusters of young women, expecting to spot his daughter, hoping he might even find her with Tron. She must have been dancing somewhere; everyone else was. Everyone, he now realized, except Silvio. Where was the Fool?

At last he caught sight of his housekeeper, mincing toward the dining room as if her feet hurt. She was holding her hood crookedly on top of her snowy head. Pasquela wasn't supposed to be dancing, She was supposed to be watching Oriela. It seemed the servants were no more immune to Piero's spell than the guests. Pasquela gave a parting curtsey to a liveried footman half her age.

Pantalon met her near the punch table with the grin of a prowling lynx. "Pardon the intrusion, madóna, but where is your mistress?"

Pasquela's eyes widened. Her face was red, whether from shame or exertion he couldn't tell. "Isn't she with you?" She fanned herself with her thick-knuckled hand. "Just now, I thought I saw you dancing with…"

"With Lucia Grimani in a green dress," he said, "You nearsighted old cuttlefish."

"Oh." said Pasquela. "Well, I'm not sure, then. I think she was dancing with one of the boys from the Immortali *Conpàgna.*" She grinned wickedly. "Or maybe it was Lucia Grimani in green hose. Did you ask Dama Elisabeta? Maybe she's with her."

Pantalon thrust his nose barely an inch from Pasquela's and said, "I hope you realize, madóna," he let his voice crescendo, "That your continued employment is thanks only to the fact that I'm too busy to interview replacements!" He knew this was pure bluster, but he was worried, which made him feel like quarreling with someone. No one quarrels so expertly as a Castello boatman's daughter.

"Busy, nothing." Pasquela said. "You're cheap." She met his eyes defiantly. "I'm doing you a favor, old man, and you know it. I could earn a better living if I borrowed Luca's second-best suit and rowed a *tragheto*."

Pantalon would really have liked to box her ears, but people were already looking their way, a few of them snickering. Besides, she was right. She should have had the evening off, but he'd trussed her up in this uniform and dragged her out to work a late shift as Oriela's temporary governess. Furthermore, the woman really could row a boat.

He paused for a slow breath and smiled. "Just try to find her, if you would. Tron's finally arrived."

Pasquela went off in search of her charge without further comment. Pantalon turned toward the punch bowl, where he finally failed in his night-long effort to avoid Dama Donata Mosto. He should have known his luck couldn't last all evening. That would have been more unnatural than Piero's music.

"Oh, *there* you are!" said Dama Donata, "I've been meaning to tell you what a *lovely* voice your girl has, so pure and...*unspoiled*, like—a wild poppy, yes?"

Pantalon took a gulp of the fiery potion Antonio liked to call punch. The cough it produced saved him from answering her.

Donata took advantage of his debility. "Simply

charming, her sibyl. Pity about her dancing, but you did hire that *zani,* so she does well, considering. *Fresh,* you know, like the country air. It seems almost a *pity* to—how shall I say it—to *domesticate* her. Oh! Dear *me,* are you all right?" She had (probably deliberately) mistaken Pantalon's bulging eyes for further respiratory distress.

He cleared his throat. "Perfectly," he choked, "Thank you... for your concern." He patted her arm amiably as he caught his breath. "Do try the punch." He turned away from her to find Pasquela at his elbow.

"I located your shipment," she said, "And I'm not responsible for the condition it arrives in." She stepped aside to let him see Antonio escorting—no, dragging—his daughter from the courtyard door to a chair a few feet from them. Oriela kept trying to stand back up.

Pantalon sat beside her and said, very quietly, "Where have you been?"

"With Toni," she said loudly, with a beatific smile. "He wants to dance with me." She leaned toward him and breathed grappa and cinnamon in his face.

Antonio put one hand on Pantalon's shoulder without taking the other off Oriela's. "La Dama is fatigued. I would suggest that she retire soon. It has been a long evening."

Pantalon looked from Antonio's inscrutably formal expression to his daughter's face. Her eyes were red, her cheeks blotchy, her very hair seemed to be wilting. *Fatigued* was a nicely diplomatic choice of words. He looked around them. Other guests were moving toward the stairs in twos and threes. To his unexpected relief, Marco Tron was among them.

He and Pasquela got the wobbly Oriela wrapped in her cloak and waited until Tron was rowed away with a boatload of Reali, and then they took her quietly across the canpièlo and home.

Once inside his fondaco, Pantalon turned on his daughter. "I didn't see you for three whole sets! What on earth were you doing all that time? Besides drinking Toni's punch?"

All Oriela said was, "I'm sorry, Papà." And then she was crying on his new doublet. He handed her off to Pasquela, charged up the stairs into the house, and had to content himself with slamming the door.

47 Hounds

A s soon as Silvio reached the top of the stairs, he glanced over his shoulder to make sure Oriela hadn't followed him. Then he slipped through the door and pushed it closed. Inside the dining room, he leaned heavily back against the wall and tried to start breathing again.

Piero had returned and was tuning up for another set. The thought of more dancing suddenly made Silvio extremely tired, so he edged along the wall to the nearest adjoining chamber door—Antonio's—and dropped into a chair as the door swung shut behind him, leaving him in the dark.

Silvio didn't know how much time was passing. He stared at the faint red glimmer of the banked fire, telling himself that he really ought to get back out to the portego, swearing he'd do it in a minute or two, and then repeatedly failing to move. Nothing out there seemed especially funny just now. All the folly he usually feasted on had soured and curdled, leaving him with a woozy feeling in his stomach.

Why had he bothered to quarrel with Oriela? Why had he even been talking to her? He should have taken her directly back to her father the moment he saw her wandering alone. Her reputation was in enough peril already. *Where did the* fotuti *sonnets come from?* Confound Oriela and her questions. What a child she was. He pulled off his hood and tossed it across the room, where it landed with a discordant jangle on the bed. So different from the song of the collar bell he realized he was rolling gently between his fingers, the one she had rung.

She'd learn soon enough. Some magnifico with a brain full of ducats and ambition and his heart in his codpiece would flatter Pantalon, sign some papers, and take her home. If she was lucky, he might throw a little flattery her way before getting down to the business of producing an heir. At least she was the only daughter in her house. If she'd had sisters, the odds were that she'd be packed off to a convent, where the dowries were cheaper, and where the bachelor sons might come and have their fun, because nuns were cheaper and cleaner than prostitutes. Dear God!—he used to think all this was hilarious.

He put his hand over his eyes and groaned. All he could see behind his eyelids was Oriela's face—and comparing it to the moon didn't seem so implausible, really. He could still feel the imprint of her hands in his. Letting go of them at that moment had been like tearing away his own skin. He couldn't stop himself from imagining what it might have been like to stay there, to hold her, to kiss her in earnest. Idiot. She'd be dead, of course. And the world would be infinitely poorer because the lovely, astonishing Oriela Morèr was not in it.

And she would be where, instead? Unbaptized, cursed by her father...Silvio shuddered, queasy and horrified. A single weak moment on his part could send the dearest of ladies to a Hell she in no way deserved.

No, by all the saints. Never. Not Oriela. He would destroy himself first.

Suddenly the door from the portego flew open behind him, flooding the gloomy chamber with light but not, Silvio realized, with music. The dance must be over. Antonio stumbled in, arm in arm with a small, cherub-headed *putto* of a man in Alati stripes who was laughing loudly and carrying a pitcher, the last of the punch. It was the same man the Reali boys had been harassing earlier, the one Salvàn had nearly failed to rescue from a duel he would certainly have lost. Antonio halted when he saw Silvio sitting in his chair. His friend kept on for two steps before he stumbled, splashing the aromatic potion onto the floor.

"What the devil—*ehi*," said the *putto*, "Toni. There's your Fool." He dissolved into another round of laughter while Antonio went to the fire, stirred the coals and lit a candle. "I didn't know you stored a *bufon* in your bedroom." He put the pitcher down on a painted trunk where it splashed some more. Silvio wondered if the punch would damage the picture of a knight on the lid. "What's he doing here?"

Antonio said, "I have no idea. I'd better ask him. No, Xandro," he put up a hand. His friend had staggered a few steps toward Silvio's chair. "Wait there." He turned. "Silvio?" he said gently, "What are you doing here?"

Silvio didn't know what to say, so he just looked at Antonio. His expression must have been alarmingly doleful, because Antonio turned back to his companion and said, "Good night, Xandro." Antonio poured a glass of now-cool punch and offered it to Silvio, who shook his head and started to rise. Xandro hadn't moved.

"I apologize, Siór," said Silvio. "It's your room, and I'm in the way."

Antonio waved him back down. "*Toni*, damn you," he said, pressing the glass into Silvio's hand.

The *putto* backed off and leaned against the door-jamb. "You like him better," he said.

"Go home, Xandro," said Antonio. "I'll see you at Lena's." The cherub slouched away. Silvio tried the punch. It tasted better than it smelled.

Antonio sat on the end of his bed. "So, my friend," he said, "You're the second person I've discovered tonight hiding in the dark and looking melancholic. I wonder whether there's any connection."

Silvio said, "Who was the other one?"

"Oriela." Antonio studied him for a moment. "Well?" he said at last.

Silvio pushed himself to his feet. He handed the empty glass to Antonio and said, "Toni, you're a worse gossip than Betì's mother." He turned to leave.

Antonio said, "I got you to call me Toni!"

Silvio gave a parting wave over his shoulder. "*Buna nòcc, Siór.*"

Xandro was still hanging around the dock. Silvio bid him good night so he'd see him leave. It was the least Salvàn could do for him. He wasn't surprised to hear Antonio's footsteps coming down the stairs.

There was another reason Nicolò Pevari had been so agreeable to Carlo's interest in Elisabeta. More often it was the eldest sons of the old Houses who were expected to forgo marriage and look after the business, but the younger of the Pevari was not, as the more polite gossips put it, well-suited for marriage.

Faced with the evidence, Silvio suddenly wondered whether this explained Antonio's insistence on terms of familiarity with Silvio. Il Siór would have noticed how Silvio avoided women. Maybe he thought they were the same. Maybe it was unkind to indulge the poor man by calling him Toni.

If someone who disliked Antonio were to find a credible witness and denounce him, he or the harmless Xandro could be beheaded and burned between the columns. This struck Silvio as diabolically unjust as he headed for home, thinking about his water lily medicine. How many years had Silvio gone unpunished for murder?

It would have to be five drops tonight. He was already on the second bottle, but surely Oriela would be married soon and out of his reach, and then he would only have to worry about ordinary women, those who might tease his body but could never, now would never, touch his heart because they could no more be Oriela than Padua could be Venice.

He wrapped his cape tighter and paced around the canpièlo, hoping the frosty air would slow the whirlwind in his head. The human sounds of the city were silenced for the night, and all he could hear was water. Standing on a spot of supposedly dry ground at night in

Venice, a person could feel the whole place balancing on its tiptoes, dancing with the tide.

Something caught his eye from the water's edge, and he looked down the cluttered alley between the big houses toward Rio Ca' Foscari. A square of warm lamplight pooled and rippled below Oriela's window. Even on such a cold night, she'd opened the shutters to look out at the Grand Canal in the moonlight.

"*Sì*, Dama." Silvio whispered. "It's still there."

A rat jumped off the end of the alley into the water, breaking the pool of lamplight with its small splash. The window's reflection went dark. Silvio jumped, startled by something wet on his hand.

"*Ai!*" He spun. "*Oste,* Brugliera. I thought you were a rat." The big dog lowered her speckled head for a pat. Silvio patted it.

Uncle Herlakin moved into view with the gold and white hound Boralisa just ahead of him. At first he resembled a man in an oversized hat. Then, evidently because he recognized Silvio, he dropped the clumsy *malöcc* and showed his antlers.

Silvio stepped between him and the door to Ca' Morèr. "I thought you'd left town," he said. "You've finished the masks."

"Do you like yours?" said Herlakin.

"It's perfectly hideous," said Silvio. "And Carlo can't pronounce your name." Herlakin came a few steps closer to the door Silvio was blocking. Silvio said, "What do you want here?"

"Boralisa asked to come out." The hound that tracked love was circling the canpièlo, sniffing at each door in turn before sitting down by Silvio, in front of the door to Ca'Morèr. She nuzzled his hand.

"There's no prey for you here," said Silvio. "Go back to your mountains."

Herlakin looked up and studied the windows of Pantalon's study, and then he knelt for a moment near Boralisa. Silvio shrank away from the points of his antlers, his back pressed against the lion's-head knocker.

Herlakin stood up and said, "She says I should stay nearby until at least the end of Carnevale. In case I'm needed." Then he walked away, both dogs at his heels.

Disquieted by the hounds' interest in the house, Silvio remained on guard in front of Ca' Morèr until it started snowing. In the morning he would visit the apothecary up the street for some verbena and St. John's wort. Smeraldina didn't keep these anti-Aivàn herbs in the house because they made Piero sneeze, and Silvio's own nose twitched at the thought of them. By themselves they probably wouldn't be enough to keep Herlakin away. Silvio could get some red yarn to tie them with, but what he really needed was a piece of iron. There should be a stray horseshoe nail on the ground by the Santa Margarita market. He'd burned his toes on enough of the damned things when he wasn't looking for one. If only the charm might repel Silvio himself.

When he got to his room, Silvio reached under the bed. He'd been thinking of Oriela far too much and needed a strong dose of his water lily potion. His hand fumbled through empty air with growing alarm. The medicine box was gone.

48 Nosegay

Carnevale season was always a busy time in the cloth business. Pantalon took on another shop boy, to help Luigi fetch bolts to show to clients, along with a sturdy Brescian delivery man whose name really was Gianni, and Pantalon made a point of pronouncing it with a firm, provincial *Gi*, not wanting to offend him by slipping into a Venetian *Z* and calling him a *zani*.

Today, most of the business was happening at the water side of the fondaco. A procession was planned for the Grand Canal in two weeks, and every House needed to reupholster and re-drape at least one gondola, usually along with a cargo boat or two whose oarsmen must be dressed up in livery to match the gondolieri. Luca had spent the whole day on the dock, measuring boats and offering his opinions.

"Yes, Siór, that's a fine color," Luca said, "But it won't stand up in the rain."

"Nonsense," Pantalon said, hurrying over from the ledger Alberto was showing him, "My reds are as fast as the black on Luca's face. Do you see that washing away in the rain?"

"Not the color," said Luca, "The weight. Such a thin, loose-woven satin—"

"*Charmeuse*," Pantalon said.

"Give it a French name if you like. When it's wet, it wilts and sticks to itself. Now this one over here," Luca led the customer to a bolt of sturdy, tight-woven true satin in the same color. It was almost twice the price. Pantalon left him to it, making a mental note to add a soldino to Luca's pay this week. Marco Tron had just come in from the street.

"Senator, I'm honored," Pantalon said, bowing. "Your man left with the boat some time ago. I hope," he said, uneasiness stirring in the back of his mind, "I hope everything was what you wanted."

"It's fine. Actually, I came to see you. Could we..." He nodded toward the stairs.

Pantalon glanced once more at Luca, who was about to convince Ca' Foscari's men to shell out sixty lire for a seat cushion, and motioned for Ser Marco to precede him up the stairs. When they reached the top, Pantalon noticed the man held a little bouquet of dried flowers tied with a red ribbon. It was an oddly rustic offering. Was Tron making another ill-advised joke about Oriela's upbringing?

Pantalon showed him to an armchair by the grand portego fireplace and called for Pasquela, who managed simultaneously to fill both their hands with wine glasses and to produce his daughter from wherever she'd been hiding.

Tron stood and held out the nosegay when Oriela came in.

"How pretty," Oriela said. She took her seat, studying the bundle. "Where did you find them at this time of year?"

"My garden," Ser Marco said. Pasquela filled his glass.

Pantalon tasted his wine. Pasquela had chosen an Amarone from Villa Pevari, a tasty reminder of Ca' Morèr's *nobile* friends.

Oriela sniffed the bouquet. "Verbena," she said. "A warming scent for winter. What about these little yellow ones?"

"Well, they're..." Tron said, "Yellow. Like gold. Or the sun. Which denotes..." The man was improvising, Pantalon saw. He hadn't made the bouquet. "... warmth."

The yellow flowers were St. John's wort, as Oriela surely must have known. The only reason Pantalon had ever heard for pairing it with verbena and tying it in a red ribbon was to keep the *foleti* away. But that was a superstition for peasants, like hanging rowan branches over a cradle to prevent the Aivani stealing a baby. Margarita's midwife had done that, which proved how ineffective such measures were.

Oriela examined the nosegay more closely. "What's the nail for?"

Tron looked as surprised as Oriela by the discovery, but he soldiered on. "From the True Cross," he said.

"Those must be very rare!" said Oriela. "Where did you get one?"

Pantalon was starting to feel proud of her. She was handling this bizarre conversation well, her words all ingenuousness, her tone scarcely betraying the fact that she didn't believe a word of it.

"From..." said Ser Marco. "A trader."

One could almost pity the senator. He could talk the veil off a Turk's wife, but he was out of his depth with a daughter of Ca' Morèr.

Oriela said, "What's the red ribbon for?"

"To—er—symbolize the blood of Christ?" Tron took a breath., scratched his head, and finally confessed. "It was on your door when I got here."

Pantalon asked to see the thing and examined it with growing unease. It looked like something a witch might put together. But he remembered how Silvio had gotten sick from wearing armor and handed the charm back to Oriela. Maybe the iron nail would keep at least one impertinent Aivàn at arm's length.

Marco tasted the wine and nodded approvingly. "Will you and your daughter be coming to the ball at Ca' Tron next week? I know," he said, "I didn't invite you last year, but it was my impression that you didn't care for dancing."

Pantalon realized he had failed to hide his surprise. Marco Tron had never invited him to anything before. He said, "And last year I didn't have a daughter." Ser Marco was squirming again. It was so fun to watch.

"I hope," said Pantalon, arching his eyebrows at him, "That you've been practicing your Volta."

He heard Oriela inhale sharply, a silent gasp. He waited to see that Tron had the good grace to blush before he turned to look at his daughter. She was staring back at him, her eyes wide as the Lagoon.

Still looking at Oriela, Pantalon said, "It's a pity you didn't come earlier to Ca' Pevari the night before last. My daughter could have given you a lesson." Her gaze relaxed, eyes shining.

No answer yet from the senator. Pantalon had rendered him speechless. "Yes," he said, only now turning to face Ser Marco, "We will come and dance at Ca' Tron." He stood, to let the senator understand that he was a busy man and needed to get back to work.

After Pasquela shut the door behind their visitor, Oriela grabbed Pantalon's hand. She was grinning and pulling him closer, as though she might try to kiss it. He patted her hand and disengaged his own. Being proud of her didn't mean he was ready to be doted on. He was rescued from the tender moment by Pasquela, showing in another visitor.

"Fra Tomaso from San Nicolò," she said, adding with a tiny smile, "Dei Mendicoli." Not, in other words, the highly respectable San Nicolò di Lido, where the Doge annually offered a marriage ring to the sea. The *other* San Nicolò.

The black-robed friar was so small that Pantalon didn't see him until Pasquela stepped aside. The man's dark blond tonsure barely reached the housekeeper's shoulder. A Dominican preaching at the fishermen's church, a parish noted for the poverty of its congregation, was little more than a holy vagabond and as likely as not to be some sort of heretic. What could such a fellow want with Ca' Morèr?

Fra Tomaso greeted Pantalon with a quick bow, and then turned to Oriela, who was gaping at the little man as if he were the Pope. "Please excuse my presumption, Dama, in calling on you uninvited. I am here at the recommendation of a mutual friend."

Oriela said, "You're the priest Silvio told me about, when I asked him—I mean..." She stopped as her face turned red, looked away.

Pantalon was trying to imagine when such a conversation might have happened. At a ball? During a dancing lesson? Why then would the girl be embarrassed to mention it? He realized he'd been silent too long when it was Oriela, not he, who sent Pasquela for another bottle of Amarone and showed the friar to a chair. Had Pantlon had his wits about him, he would have ordered a less costly wine for a mere friar.

Regathering his wits, Pantalon resumed his seat. "Did my daughter's dancing master happen to mention why he thought you should call on Ca' Morèr?"

"No," said the friar. He paused. "He only said that I should come to you and ask whether I could be of any service to la dama." Fra Tomaso poured himself a glass of Amarone, sipped it with an appreciative sigh, and said, "Maìstro Silvio suggested the matter might be of some urgency."

Pantalon found he was squeezing his own glass rather tighter than its delicate Murano tracery could withstand, and he set it down. Damn that *bufon* to the ninth circle for blabbing Morèr family business—and to such a person as this Tomaso. No doubt every fishmonger in Dorsoduro had now heard of the mad silk merchant's heathen child.

Tomaso said, "I was hoping you might tell me why I'm here. The maìstro was so discreet as to leave me mystified." He lifted his glass. "This is wonderful, by the way."

"Villa Pevari," Pantalon said. It was like a reflex, this urge to remind everyone who his friends were. As if a friar would care. He realized he had no idea what to say next.

"Padre," said Oriela—Pantalon had nearly forgotten she was still there, standing quietly behind his chair —"I think I know why Silvio sent you."

"You know why, but your father doesn't." The friar looked from one of them to the other. "This is interesting. Go on, my child."

Oriela stepped out from behind the chair and stood between them. "Papà," she said, "I'm tired of being *maladeta.* I want to be a Christian."

It was a wonder the friar hadn't choked on his wine. His astonishment was betrayed only by a sudden widening of his gray eyes, which seemed to make his tonsure jump back farther from his forehead. Pantalon wished his own chair would close around him like a clam's shell.

Oriela said, "I want to understand Christmas. I want to know what that sibyl was singing about and how Gesù can be his own father, what makes someone a saint, and why being one makes his toes important, and why all the lions around here have feathers."

Fra Tomaso raised one eyebrow even higher, and Pantalon couldn't tell whether the man was appalled or amused.

Pantalon said, "Oriela, leave us." He waited until the door of Margarita's sitting room was shut behind her before looking at Fra Tomaso again. It was unavoidable that he talk to some clergyman about the situation, and he hadn't yet worked up the courage to mention it to Father Mateo at San Pantalon. An itinerant preacher assigned to an undistinguished parish on the outermost edge of the city was perhaps as safe a confidant as he was likely to find. He sighed. "This will be a rather strange story."

49 Patches

The morning of Martedì Grasso, there was a sewing party in Elisabeta's sitting room. Every female from around the canpièlo was there, ladies and servants alike. Tonight was the Doge's Ball, the final, climactic night in a long season of merrymaking for those notable enough to be invited. Of course everyone in town would be celebrating somewhere or other, but Elisabeta, Oriela and Caterina—who had just turned thirteen—must each arrive at the Palazzo Ducale that evening in some one-of-a-kind marvel.

For Oriela, the excitement of this last great celebration before Lent merely marked the prelude to Ash Wednesday, the much more interesting, if somber, start to her journey toward being a normal Christian. Still, it wasn't every day you got to meet a Doge. As the women sewed, they gossiped about the Ca' Tron ball the night before.

Oriela said, "Ser Marco was much better-behaved at his own house."

She and Pasquela were finishing the endless hem on her silvery gray brocade. Its pattern was white feathers, and it would be paired with an elaborate beaked and feathered mask. This was the first year Ca' Morèr had been asked to the Doge's Ball since Margarita's death, and Papà wanted to make a grand impression. When Oriela had seen the brocade in the storeroom, it reminded her of Francesca calling her *colombina*, and she had decided to go as a dove. Papà would be a raven.

"They didn't play any Voltas," Elisabeta said. "Leo Tron disapproves."

Thundering footsteps overhead suggested Nico Pevari and Rico Speronelli were reenacting some battle in the nursery.

"At least there was no repeat of the 'sword' incident," said Pasquela. Everyone giggled except for Caterina. Oriela wondered when her private complaint to Elisabeta had become public knowledge.

"Well, you know" said Smeraldina, "Men can't help that." She tied off the end of a pink thread. "It just means he likes you. Can't be all bad, being liked by a senator." She looked up. "I wonder what those boys are up to. Here," she handed the sleeve to the young schiavona Marta, "Hold this while I go bring in the laundry."

Elisabeta licked the end of her thread and squinted at the tiny needle. "Ser Leo is hoping to be buried by your father's *scòla grande*," she said to Oriela. "He would disinherit Marco if he caught him insulting Ca' Morèr. Did you like Toni's new play?"

"He and Silvio were wonderful together." Oriela wove the needle through another short row of straight stitches. The performance with Antonio's new Captain was the first time she'd seen Silvio since Epiphany, outside of dancing lessons with the children. Even there he'd been avoiding her, making Puzzi her partner. She didn't know what she'd done to annoy him that night at Ca' Pevari, but it seemed he was still mad at her.

"Toni was frantic," Elisabeta said. She and Pasquela had just managed to get the front and back pieces of her satin bodice pinned together. "Silvio kept forgetting his lines. Smeraldina says his humors have been off for weeks. Up at all hours, hardly eats anything, almost never talks. She said he just about tossed Piero out a window over some medicine Piero threw away."

Then it wasn't only Oriela. It seemed Silvio was mad at everyone.

Pasquela said, "If I had to guess, I'd say the maìstro is in love."

Oriela felt her face flush and hoped no one would notice, keeping her eyes fixed on the needle. She knew she had no business envying whoever it was.

Smeraldina barreled back into the room with a white bundle in her hands and a face like a thunderstorm. She shoved the bundle under Marta's nose.

"What happened? Did you stir the wash cauldron with a saw?"

"Let me see." Oriela hooked her needle into the brocade and leaned over. It was Silvio's Zani tunic, and there was a three-finger hole right in the front.

"Busiest night of the year for a *bufon*," said Smeraldina, "And with the mood he's in!" She flung the tunic toward the cowering Marta. Oriela caught it. "I don't have time for this."

Elisabeta said, "Silvio ought to get his own wife."

"Can't he just wear his bells?" said Caterina.

"He's doing that scene with Ser Antonio tonight," said Smeraldina, "In the Palace courtyard!"

Oriela examined the hole. "I'll patch it," she said. "My sleeves are almost done." She turned to Elisabeta. "Where do you keep the scraps?"

An hour later, a fine rag collection was scattered on the floor around the tunic. Elisabeta's and Caterina's costumes were done, and Pasquela went home to help Papà with his wings. Oriela and Marta puzzled over what ought to have been a simple job.

Although it looked like plain linen, the tunic turned out to be knitted of an unusual wool-linen blend, designed to stay in place while he was turning somersaults and walking on his hands. There were no scraps of the same stuff in Elisabeta's bag, only cut-off ends from the colorful everyday clothes of a *nobile* household. There were also bits from the stage costumes they'd lost with the wagon, but none that matched this. It was surprising how many different shades of white there were, and the closer any two came to being the same, the worse they looked together.

Frustrated, Oriela picked up a handful of scraps from the nearest multicolored pile and tossed it into the air. The pieces fluttered down onto the tunic and landed higgledy-piggledy all over the front. In the light from the window, the chaos took on a jewel-like glow. Oriela laughed out loud and startled Marta.

"That's the best it's looked all day," Oriela said. "Here, take some of these and cut them into squares. On the bias, like this." She chose a piece from Elisabeta's dark blue gown and cut it diagonally to the grain. This would keep the woven patches from fraying and allow them to bend and stretch with the knit. "We'll put different ones all over it." She selected another piece. "Here: a heavy lump of Magnifico for his shoulder," and another, "Let's give him a kick from the Capitàn on his backside." Soon she and Marta were both giggling like children.

When they had a stack of pieces of every color, Oriela sighed, wiped her eyes and asked Marta to go and fetch the leggings from Smeraldina so they could match. Oriela waited until the girl was gone before she started pinning on the patches. She wanted a moment to collect her wits.

Whatever—whoever—was weighing on his mind, Silvio was in pain. It was unbearable to know this and be able to do nothing. She couldn't comfort him, could scarcely speak to him anymore. But she could, perhaps, wrap him in her thoughts, weave something into her stitches. Love, maybe? She closed her eyes for a moment, wishing again that she knew a prayer. Then she threaded a needle, slid her left hand inside the tunic— with a little shiver—and began to sew.

50 Lions

O riela and her father stood on the dock and watched the torch-lit Alati barge float by.

Papà raised his new, leather "raven" mask an inch and said, "What happened to his suit?" There was no need to say whose. Silvio's wearable kaleidoscope could be seen from three boats back, hanging upside-down from the boom.

"No one knows," Oriela said. "Smeraldina found it torn on the drying pole and was ready to rip the head off anyone who confessed. Francesca would have said it was the *foleti* playing tricks."

"Would she, now?" said Papà, lowering the strange mask again "How many holes did these *foleti* make?"

"Only one, but I couldn't find a matching piece, and just one patch of the wrong color looked silly."

He peered out at her from beneath the goat-hair eyebrows above his mask's eye holes, but she could almost hear his own eyebrows rising. "This way, it doesn't look silly?"

Oriela was saved from trying to explain when Luca held out his hand to help her into the gondola. He had dressed their boat for the occasion with a pair of green-draped chairs in place of the usual low seat and felze. The everyday bow and stern irons had been replaced by gleaming silver ringlets of mulberry leaves with copper berries sprouting from the stems.

Luca himself stood at his freshly-painted oar in a completely unseasonable costume. He was shielded from the early March chill only by a short, red waist-coat that hung open over his shirt and a pair of huge, baggy trousers. On his head was a turban of violently green Morèr satin. Had Papà given him the cloth, or had he borrowed it without asking? Yellow Turkish slippers with long, curled toes completed the outlandish effect.

Papà looked him up and down. "Won't you be cold?" He didn't mention the turban.

Luca said, "Not while I'm rowing, Siór." He unlooped the mooring line and cast off, steering them into the midst of the parade.

Oriela said, "Is that how people dress in Africa?"

"I don't know, Dama," Luca said, "I've never been there."

The Grand Canal sparkled, its ripples and eddies reflecting and repeating the light from hundreds of lamps and torches. Many of the boats bore musicians: trumpeters on the Doge's long, gilded Bucintoro, masked singers with lutes on gaily painted household sandoli.

Below the sharp bill of her rag-and-paste dove mask, Oriela felt like her face might split open from grinning. It would have been a fine thing just to watch the colorful parade going by, but Oriela was actually a part of this riotous splendor. It was much too soon when Luca slid them up alongside the dock at San Marco.

As she and Papà followed the noisy Alati procession between the columns and through the Palace gate, Oriela saw a small stage set up on the other side of the vast, paved courtyard. Silvio leapt onto it, followed by Antonio, both in their new masks. There was only time to hear Antonio call, "Zani, where are you?" before Papà led her away to an open ironwork portal and up a staircase, its walls and ceiling encrusted with gold-trimmed scrollwork.

At the top, they turned toward a pair of double doors so big they opened in sections and had to fold back on themselves like shutters to fit against the wall. A footman inside the ballroom announced their arrival, and Oriela looked from her father toward the most impressive-looking person she had ever seen.

El Serenisimo Lunardo Loredan greeted them with acute gray eyes and sharp, austere features that lent an unassailable dignity to the extravagant, golden robes he wore and even to the Corno, a hat with a point at the back that might well have looked funny perched above another face. Oriela reminded herself to stop staring and curtsey, just as Papà looked out into the crowd and hailed an apparently male person covered head to toe in red feathers with an enormous rooster tail planted on his hindquarters.

"Ser Ignatio! I'm delighted to see you. I trust business is good these days? Allow me to present my daughter, Oriela."

"Enchanted," the rooster-man said, politely but without warmth. "May I have the honor—?"

Her father gave her a slight push, and she found herself in the line of masked couples making their stately way around the circumference of an enormous dance floor. It was hard to remember to look at her partner during the Pavana, because there were so many other things to look at.

The walls and ceiling were covered with frescoes of saints and gods, grand processions, battles at sea, all brightly lit by hundreds of candles set in sparkling colored glass chandeliers. Between the chairs along the paneled walls were statues, mostly of solemn-looking people wearing little or no clothing. When Oriela did glance at the Rooster, the feathers on his hat bobbed and made her think of Silvio's Pavana birds, and she had to look away again to keep from laughing.

Not that the other costumes were less funny. Her next partner was a man in ermine breeches with a pair of exquisitely carved wooden horns affixed to his brow. Satyrs, Oriela thought, were supposed to be excellent dancers. Evidently the reputation was exaggerated, because this one couldn't have found his way to the beat with an astrolabe and compass.

A long sequence of partners followed. No one seemed to mind being seen with "la Lupa" while she and her partners were masked, even though several of them greeted her by name. She was sure not all of them had bothered talking to Papà, either. How many other rules were suspended in observation of the day?

Oriela was getting tired, the air inside her full-face mask growing stuffy. She was ready to find Papà and sit for a while when she found her elbow in the hand of someone whose large, tawny mask bore fangs, whiskers and a flowing lion's mane. A pair of golden wings was attached to his back. St. Mark. He held her arm as if they were old friends.

"There you are, little bird," the Lion said, leading her off the dance floor and toward a table of sweet-meats. "I was afraid you'd run off with Toni Pevari's pet jester again." The voice was Marco Tron's. Of course. He would turn a holy icon into a bad pun on his own name.

"Maìstro Salvàn is nobody's pet anything," Oriela said. "Don't you think your costume is a bit obvious, Ser Marco?" She was wondering whether Marco had been watching her at Ca' Pevari on Twelfth Night, if that was why he hadn't stayed long enough to speak to her.

Marco peered out between the teeth of his mask. "Oh, do you know who I am?" His laugh was a little too loud. How long had he been celebrating before he'd arrived at the Palace? "You're hard to miss, little bird, with Morèr peddling you around the room like one of his overpriced brocades."

"What are you talking about?"

"The ones he claims he shipped from Cathay when everyone knows they were woven in Desenzano." Clearly Marco didn't know much about the silk business.

"My father is over there," she said, "If you want to

dance with me."

"*Brava!*" Marco said, "Your prim act is improving. I nearly believed it. Did the wolves teach you that, or is it this innocent mask?"

He was pressing closer to her. Her mask was too warm, the room too crowded. She looked over her shoulder and scanned the wall to her left. There was a door to the outside loggia about ten feet away. It would be cool out there, and she could come back in by the next door along the passage.

She slid along the wall a few feet. Marco followed her, not quite steady on his feet. Maybe he was already too far into the punch bowl to dance. She pressed her hand to the latch behind her and slid through into the darkness overlooking the courtyard, where someone was singing, playing a rebec. Marco was right behind her.

Oriela raised the front of her mask, letting the air chill her face and neck. It was a silly thing to do, she realized when Marco started to caress her shoulder with one of his paw-shaped gloves. She asked him to fetch her a drink.

He said, "Certainly, Dama."

Dama? One minute "little bird," and the next "milady." Marco Tron was a confusing person to talk with when he'd been drinking.

He started to walk away but turned back to say, "I'll have to leave you for a while." He grabbed her hand and pulled it near his lips—between the Lion's teeth. "I don't know if I can bear it."

She retrieved her hand, patted his arm and said, "You're a lion and a saint. You can bear anything."

"A saint can bear anything," said Marco, "Because he knows that Heaven awaits." He peered out through the Lion's mouth. "Will my heaven be waiting?"

"Have faith, *lión mé*," she said.

Once Marco was inside, Oriela started for the next door, but first she crossed the loggia and looked out over the torch-lit courtyard, her attention drawn by a familiar melody. Silvio was perched on the edge of the stage with his *flauto*.

The *Lamento* echoed through the arcaded quadrangle, floating above the noisy revelers like a lost soul, forlorn as the wind in a ruin. Before she knew what she was doing, Oriela had replaced her mask and started down the stairs.

Piero was on the ground near the stage with his rebec, and Antonio was sprawled on his back beside Silvio, pulling on a boot, Capitàn's pugnacious, phallic snout sticking up into the air. "Look, Alichin," he said to Silvio, "It's our feathered friend!"

Piero stopped playing and looked up at Oriela. He said, "What are you doing here, Dama?"

What was she doing here? She said, "Marco was drunk."

Silvio raised his mask and handed Antonio his flauto, exchanging it for a bottle. "Who isn't?" He took a long pull from the bottle. Then he dismounted from the stage with a back somersault and brought the mask back down.

"Dove Girl not drunk yet?" Silvio said. Or rather, the strange being he had just turned into said it. "Alichin has wine." He held out the bottle to her. The colorful patches she had sewn onto his costume took on an unearthly glow in the torchlight, and the Mask's misshapen features seemed to move on their own.

Piero stepped between them. "Go back inside, Dama. Ser Pantalon must be looking for you."

"Look for Dove Girl again," said Alichin. "Dove Girl always run away from Papà." Alichin grabbed her hand and started to push through the crowd toward the stairs. "Alichin take Dove Girl back to Serenity."

Antonio followed as the crowd roared with delight. He caught up and stepped in front of them with his comically short sword drawn. "Release her, varlet," he said. Then, more quietly, "You're drunk, Silvio. I'll go with her." Alichin dropped her hand and sat on the ground, his whole body crumpling into a pout.

Antonio led her back up the grand staircase. The light from the glass chandeliers was blinding after the courtyard, and she stuck close to Antonio until she could see Papà's raven mask. He was surrounded by laughing gentlemen, one of them with a golden mane and wings and a bobbing tail. Papà looked up, and his arms flew wide to welcome his stray child. The pleasure in his eyes was at odds with the menacing effect of the black wings, spread as if soaring over a carcass.

Marco turned. "Little bird!" he said. "You see, Pantalon? I told you she'd turn up."

Oriela turned toward her father, dropping her eyes apologetically. "I'm sorry if you were worried, Papà," she said, "I'm afraid I got a little lost."

Papà raised her chin gently, black feathered gloves tickling below her ears. He looked closely through her mask at her eyes. She felt her pulse leaping up and down her throat; he must be able to feel it as well. The merriment in his eyes crystallized into something hard. *He knows I'm lying.*

What he said, however, was, "Never mind. It's a large palace."

"So, Morèr," said Marco, "Would it be too soon after our agreement for her to honor me with a dance?"

"Not at all," said Papà "As often as you wish, now."

Marco took her hand and they were off across the floor. His steps were heavy, not quite on the beat. What agreement? What had Papà meant by "now?" Marco attempted an aerial caper and lost his balance, and she had to catch him.

At last the tune ended. Oriela was relieved until Marco pulled her into an alcove between two naked statues, out of sight except to someone standing directly in front of them. He rested a hand on the top of her skirt, slid it around to the back. She pulled away, which only left her more deeply cornered in the alcove.

"Where were you really, little bird?" he asked, pressing nearer. "Shall I guess?"

"Siór," she said, "I thought you wanted to dance."

He closed the remaining gap between them and pressed his other hand to her hip, pinning one of her arms against his chest. "I don't think you got lost," he said. "I think you were dancing with your *bufon* tutor." His hand slid down to her buttocks so that somehow the more she wriggled the more securely she was held. "Weren't you, *colonbina*?" His face was very close to her throat, the Lion's teeth nearly engulfing her head. "But I forgive you, my pigeon."

"Not pigeon," she said. "Only my nurse calls me that."

"No?" He bent over her trapped hand, pouring his hot, stale-wine breath down the front of her dress onto the exposed tops of her breasts. "Maybe you'd prefer—Dove Girl?"

How could he have heard that? He raised her mask off her face and leaned forward to kiss her, trapping her face in his Lion's jaws.

"Scoundrel!" Antonio's voice, trumpeting from inside his Mask, came from just behind Marco's wings. "Unhand the lady at once." El Capitàn laid a gauntlet on Marco's shoulder, the other resting on the hilt of his sword. Antonio seemed completely transformed.

Marco turned and cried out with pretended terror. Then he turned his back on Antonio, laughing. "Nothing to be afraid of, Dove Girl. It's only that cowardly Capitàn Pevari."

El Capitàn didn't move. "Let her go, or I will be forced to draw!"

Marco said, "Well played, Toni. I almost thought you were serious." He took a step closer to Antonio and ran a finger tenderly, almost flirtatiously, along the lower edge of the Capitàn mask, and then raised it by its nose. "How fortunate for dear little Xandro that you weren't." He patted Antonio's bare cheek and slid past him out of the alcove and away.

Antonio pulled his mask all the way off, and Oriela saw that he was pale. In his own voice, he said, "I can't believe I just called your future husband a scoundrel."

"My what?" She instantly forgot to be worried about Antonio.

"The other man with your father just now was Leo Tron, Marco's father." He shook his head. "I don't know what came over me. I've been ready to throw a glove at anyone I meet ever since I put on this mask."

"Marco was behaving like a scoundrel," she said, taking Antonio's hand, "Someone should tell him when he's doing that."

51 Alichin

A lichin, whatever he was, was running loose in the Piazza San Marco. After Oriela's visit, Silvio fled the courtyard, driven forward by a burning restlessness, equal parts rage and exhilaration. He couldn't tell how much of either was coming from inside himself and how much from Alichin.

Since Piero had found his medicine and chucked it out the window, Silvio couldn't sleep, couldn't sit still, and couldn't stop thinking about Oriela. The most lurid scenes flashed unbidden through his mind. He abandoned his short jackets for the black doublet, hoping its longer skirt would prevent his unruly thoughts making themselves plain on his codpiece. Dancing with her was out of the question. He could hardly bear to look at her.

Maybe the water lily potion had been weakening the Mask's power, or maybe it was these ridiculous patches, but tonight Alichin was impossible to control. Silvio let his feet go where they pleased, tired of arguing with the creature, of arguing with himself, tired of always saying no. He watched as if from outside himself as his body, transformed by Oriela's whimsical mending and Alichin's deformed visage, cut a swath of mischief through the forest of revelers like a deranged monkey.

At the Campanile's new porch, a man and woman were seated on the low wall, embracing with amorous abandon. Alichin flung himself onto the woman's lap, reclined with his head on one of her generous breasts and propped up his feet on her companion's shoulder. He wrapped his legs around the woman's waist so as not to fall off and hung upside down, trying to look at the copper roof of the Campanile. "Not there," said Alichin.

He sat up and looked down the front of the woman's bodice. "Not there."

"What's not there?" the man said.

Alichin said, "Don't know. What Alichin looking for?" His legs released the woman's waist and he flipped off of her lap onto the pavement. She was gazing at him hungrily, as if her companion were invisible. Silvio wondered why. His clothes were literally rags, and his mask was anything but pretty. It seemed this Alichin held some power greater than the sum of his ragtag parts.

Alichin said, "Oh. Forgot. Looking for Dove Girl."

The man said, "I'll get rid of him." He started to rise.

The woman pulled him back, saying, "Leave him be, *cioci*. He's not doing any harm." She was still looking at the rag-man, but she wrapped her arms around her lover and kissed him with renewed passion.

Interesting. Alichin didn't react with jealousy but tipped his hat to the man. Silvio thought that if anything the Mask creature felt a sense of accomplishment as it bowed its farewell and turned away to find some-one else whose night it might disrupt.

He wandered toward the basilica. Under the entry arch with the picture of the Evangelist Mark's corpse arriving in Venice, a small crowd had collected around a man ladling out cupfuls of liquor from a large clay jar.

The sharp, sweet, wild aroma stirred something primeval in both Silvio and Alichin, something unbearably nostalgic. The tender end of the bough from a very particular Alpine conifer would be curled at the bottom of the schnapps jar like the tail of a contented fox, creating a magical tincture unknown outside his home mountains.

Alichin dashed over to join the group. Luca was sitting cross-legged on the doorstep, his green turban glowing like poison in the torchlight. Since Silvio didn't have a cup, Alichin removed one of his shoes and held it out.

The man with the jar said, "*Ehi*! Luca! Can't you find this poor, ragged peasant a cup?"

"Maìstro Salvàn!" Luca cried, rising to his feet. He said, "*Dai,* Xulio. That poor, ragged peasant is my es-teemed neighbor, el Mandragora. Give him your cup. You can drink from the shoe." He picked up a cup from the step, filled it, and passed it to Silvio.

"*A Alichin piassése.*" The elixir in the jar had driven every word of Vèneto out of the Mask's addled brain.

"What the devil's he talking about?" said Xulio.

Luca said, "Only Allah knows," in his most impressively Moorish basso voice, "Perhaps he has been possessed by a djinn." He turned to Silvio. "What happened to your clothes, Maìstro?"

Alichin said, "*Colombina-Pöt gh'à cucit.*" Dove Girl sewed it. He examined each jewel-covered arm, hugged himself, his wonderful colors cut and mended by Oriela's hands, his body at once caressed and wounded by her deft fingers plying the needle against his skin. *Find her*, said Alichin, *must find Dove Girl, pretty Dove Girl with feathers so soft.* Silvio dropped onto the step with a groan.

Luca sat beside him. "Maìstro? Are you all right?"

To Silvio's immeasurable humiliation, Alichin dropped his head onto Luca's shoulder and started to cry. "Want Dove Girl," he said.

"*Cagá*," Luca said under his breath. "Definitely a djinn."

A boy darted over from the palace porch and tapped Luca's arm to say that el Siór wanted his boat. Luca pulled Silvio to his feet, and they started walking toward the row of docks along the *bacino.* Near the water's edge, Luca paused to look up and down the row for the Ca' Morèr gondola.

They were between the two great columns, the place that served Venice for both a city gate and a place of execution. One column was for poor, replaced Saint Theodore, his spear buried in the head of the crocodile that had once secured his place as the city's patron. The other pillar was for the Lion of Saint Mark.

The spot between them was so accursed that

witches gathered its dust to cast black spells. Silvio had always superstitiously avoided standing there, but Alichin wanted to show him something. He looked up and noticed that from this vantage point, all he could see of the Lion was its tail. He heard Alichin in his head. *Lion's ass. Last thing you see before they kill you.*

52 Dove Girl

When Silvio dropped his gaze, he caught sight of a different lion—Marco Tron's glittering wings. He was headed for the quay, starched tail bobbing alongside the black tailfeathers on Pantalon's robe, and beyond the gold wings Silvio could just see the flowing silver-white of Oriela's skirt train.

Before Silvio could summon the will to stop him, Alichin abandoned Luca and dashed off through the crowd to rescue Dove Girl. *Lion man will eat. Cats eat birds.* He crept up behind the trio with a hugely exaggerated tiptoe. Crouching to elbow height, Alichin pushed his head between Marco's and Oriela's arms.

Oriela screamed, startled. "Silvio!"

"What the!—oh. It's you," said Marco. "What do you want?"

Alichin walked a few paces between them, his butt sticking out like the back of a donkey. Then he ducked a bit lower, hoisted Oriela by her hips and balanced her on his shoulder. Pantalon shouted as Alichin turned and ran back toward the Palace with his prize.

People were pouring out of the courtyard now, all moving toward the quayside. Marco and Pantalon pursued him, but Alichin ran in a zigzag against the flow and soon lost them. He emerged on the other side of the thickest crowd and made for the Palace portico.

Dove Girl was flying. Oriela had leaned her body forward and spread her arms, so her sleeve-wings fluttered, brushing Silvio's neck. She extended her legs behind them, whooping with delight. Alichin carried her to the corner of the porch, and when they were under the arcade, he stopped behind a pillar. He twirled her around to face him and slowly brought her feet toward the earth.

When her breast was even with his face, she folded her wings around his head, embracing him. Her bird mask slipped off her face and dropped to the ground. Her lips caught on the wart on Alichin's brow as she descended, and she kissed it. Silvio gasped as Oriela's unmasked cheek caressed Alichin's hollow, leather one and then dropped to Silvio's naked jawline, her breath tickling his chin.

And Silvio watched with a cold, sick horror as Alichin did the one thing Silvio had sworn never, under any influence of wine or madness, ever to do. His mouth met hers, her soft lips pulling eagerly at his as he melted into her.

Across the Piazza, the two bronze men atop the Orologio began to beat out midnight on their bell. Bells tend to disrupt Aivàn influences, and the sound broke the spell of the Mask. Alichin was gone, yet still it took Silvio until the third chime to pull his lips away from hers, because for those moments, those two strokes of a bell, he had felt human and been happy.

Then Oriela's face sank to his neck and her body went slack. Silvio felt her weight sag in his arms. A hard ball of pain and dread shot downward like a cannonball from his throat to his groin. He wanted to tear the leather devil off his face, but he didn't dare let go of Oriela. He clung to her, kept her on her feet, madly thinking that as long as she remained vertical everything might still be all right.

Six, rang the bronze giants, first one swinging his hammer, and then the other. *Seven*. Oriela hadn't fallen yet, but neither had she moved.

Eight.

Silvio's mind was clear while the bell tolled. Would Alichin return when it stopped?

Luca's green turban emerged from the crowd. He was running toward them. "God's eyeballs, Silvio! Now I know you're possessed."

Nine.

"Luca, take my mask off," Silvio said.

"Why? So you don't have to let go of my master's daughter?"

Ten.

"Please. Quickly! I—I think she fainted." It was the only possibility Silvio could bear to speak aloud. One can recover from a faint.

Eleven.

Luca stepped behind Silvio and loosened the buckle. The winter breeze off the water swept across Silvio's bare nose and forehead as the twelfth stroke throbbed in the air and faded. His face felt raw, almost skinless in the cold.

Oriela let out a soft sigh, and Silvio could feel her weight shifting. Was she going down? He was about to ask Luca to help when he realized that she was standing on her own, her head snuggled against his throat, one hand stroking the patches on his back.

He let go of her and backed away, realized he was trembling, and sat down on a stone bench against the palace wall to stare at her. Luca was trying to give him back his mask. He pushed it away.

"Silvio?" Oriela said, scowling.

He realized this was probably not the sort of reaction most women expect after a man kisses them. He wanted to say something, at least to look at her, but he couldn't move.

Luca set the Alichin mask on the bench and picked up Oriela's feathered beak from where it had fallen. He said, "Dama, your father is frantic. You'd best come to the boat before he finds you here."

She raised a hand to silence Luca, not taking her eyes off Silvio. "What's wrong with you?" she said, "You've been kissed, not beaten." She sounded cross, but she came and sat beside him.

He must have looked as sick as he felt, because the bitterness dropped from her voice and she laid a hand softly on his. "Silvio, say something."

Silvio was trying to figure out what he could say. *This Mask makes me do mad things,* perhaps? Or maybe, *Your lips are fresh water to a man lost at sea?* Or how about, *Why aren't you dead?*

"So this is why Morèr promised such a generous dowry." Marco Tron had arrived in the portico and was peering down at them through the snarling teeth of his Lion mask.

"Siór," said Luca, stepping between Marco and Oriela, "The maìstro has taken ill." The beak of Oriela's mask poked out from under his arm. It looked like he'd just strangled a swan.

Marco said, "If that man is ill, I'm an alleycat." He pushed Luca, and the dove mask hit the pavement, the beak cracked, feathers drifting loose in the shifting air.

Silvio was on his feet now, not so much to defend Luca—the gondolier could probably have tossed the senator into the water one-handed—as to stop him from getting in trouble on Silvio's account. Oriela was at Marco's side now, grabbing at his arm, but he shook her off and reached for his sword.

Silvio had only a moment to wonder why a gentleman of Marco's standing would draw his weapon on a *bufon* before another blade jutted into their midst, with Antonio's arm attached to it. He was still wearing his Capitàn mask, but the sword was real.

"Run, Silvio," said Antonio.

Silvio said, "It's all right, Toni. Ser Marco owes me a

bloody nose."

Antonio assumed a fighting stance, and Marco's sword was out. Silvio tried to step between them, heedless of the sharp steel flashing inches from his face. Luca pulled him back, and Silvio kicked him, trying to get free, sending Oriela's mask under the men's trampling feet.

"Stop! All of you!" Oriela pushed her way in and gathered the pieces of her mask. "*Ostia*! Has everyone taken leave of their wits tonight? Marco, Toni, put those things away. Silvio, go home. Come, Luca, my father is waiting." She turned her back on them and hurried away toward the dock with Marco and Luca in her wake like a pair of ducklings.

Silvio gazed after her, lost in admiration, as she was swallowed by the crowd.

Antonio said, "She always manages to surprise you, doesn't she?"

"*Sì*," said Silvio, an ache forming in the back of his throat at the magnitude of this understatement. He bent to pick up a loose feather. He wouldn't take such a risk again. Anyway, it sounded like Ca' Morèr and Ca' Tron had come to an arrangement. But how had she survived his curse? Was Pantalon right about her soul being tainted by Mamma's kind? Would it be different if she were baptized? Could the power be controlled like Piero's? Silvio realized there was one person in the city who might have answers.

"Have a drink with me?" said Antonio. He was holding out Silvio's mask.

"No." Silvio fought the impulse to flinch as he took the damned thing back and tucked it into his belt. "Thank you. No. I have to see someone."

53 Herlakin's Choice

Silvio started out walking down the Piazza but soon found himself running, weaving between the bands of revelers who were meandering toward the *bacino* or toward the streets, none of them in any hurry to go home, whatever the clock might demand. Even if the Piazza was starting to empty, the streets leading toward Rialto were nearly impassable.

Silvio pressed and dodged his way toward the bridge past well-dressed drunks leaning on each other and singing, glittering courtesans hoisted on the shoulders of calze youths, tattered whores waving their bare breasts at him and shouting curses at his back, muttering *permesso* to a pair of monks who, it turned out, were physically inseparable in an act of buggery.

He'd finally managed to cross the bridge when he stumbled over a large dog that darted out from behind the dwarf statue known as the Gobbo. Brugliera wagged her tail at him, and he looked up. Uncle Herlakin was sitting on the platform atop the hunchback-shaped pillar swinging his feet, as if proudly announcing to the world that he was a rascal. This being Carnevale, no one paid any mind to the antlers. Boralisa was seated at the hunchback's side, looking like a statue herself in the flickering torchlight. She was staring at Silvio the way a normal dog might stare at a goose.

"So they finally whipped you through the market," Silvio said. "About time." Common miscreants were often sentenced to be whipped through Rialto, their torment to end when they reached the Gobbo.

"You were looking for me," said Herlakin. "So I decided to look for you."

"And naturally you thought the Gobbo was the most likely place to find me." Silvio was trying to sound waggish, but he realized that if Luca were to tell Pantalon what Alichin had been up to with Dove Girl, Silvio might well find himself embracing the Gobbo after a sound beating...if not between the columns, gazing up at the Lion's ass.

"*Zio*," he said, "Is it possible to ask you a serious question?"

Herlakin hopped down from the Gobbo. "Ask."

Silvio hesitated, stroking the top of Boralisa's golden head. "There's a lady," he began.

"I hardly thought this was about a horse, cousin," said Herlakin. They started to follow Brugliera along the street. "The silk merchant's daughter, am I right? Let me guess. You want to kiss her."

Silvio gathered courage with a deep breath and said, "I already did." He started to walk a little faster, as if he could get away from his own deeds. "Well, at any rate, Alichin did."

"I'm sorry to hear it," said Herlakin, "But why confess

to me? If you feel her blood is on your hands, wouldn't a priest be more help?"

"No, no—this is the strange part. She swooned a little, I think, but now she seems perfectly healthy."

Herlakin halted, whirled to face Silvio. His antlers knocked a hanging shop sign off its hooks. "Is she!" The ancient Aivàn looked astonished. Silvio hadn't been sure this was possible. "Well, that's good news, then! What are you worried about?"

"I'm confused." Silvio started walking again, too agitated to talk in one place. "I don't know what to do next. Has this ever happened to you?"

"No, but I'm not half human. What do you *want* to do next?" They turned the corner at San Zane. Herlakin draped one arm over Silvio's shoulders. Two old friends walking home after a party. "What is your wish?" Silvio wanted to pull away, but he found he couldn't. The Hunter's touch would pull the truth out of him, whether he wanted to say it or not.

"I wish I could kiss her again," he said. Then, "And I wish I could be with her forever, which would be impossible even if the first wish didn't kill her."

"Probably," Herlakin sighed. "I can't say for sure. The only way to find out is to try it again."

They came into Cànpo San Silvestro, and Silvio slid out of his uncle's embrace and glared at him. He quickened his pace, cutting away across the Cànpo toward San Polo.

Herlakin, trotting to keep up, said, "Look at it this

way. If you kiss her again and nothing happens, maybe you get your second wish as well. If you kiss her again and she dies, at least you get one wish."

Silvio halted, turned to stare at the Aivàn.

"What?" said Herlakin. His antlers silhouetted against the moon made a jarring contrast with the casual merriment in his voice. Silvio crossed himself and turned away.

"Wait. Silvio." Had Herlakin ever called Silvio by his name before? The Hunter was now following his human kinsman like a dog at its master's heels. "Let me understand this. You would rather spend your life in this miserable loneliness—and don't try to tell me you're not miserable; Brugliera can smell it all over you —you would give up a chance at happiness rather than risk any harm coming to this girl."

Cànpo San Polo was nearly deserted, the revelers' torches doused. A pair of lovers were embracing on the church steps, wrapped in each other's cloaks. Silvio hurried past them toward the bridge at San Stin.

Herlakin caught Silvio by the elbow and stopped him, made him turn around. "Is that what you're saying?"

"Absolutely," said Silvio.

Herlakin said, "You love her."

"Yes."

"Then let her choose."

Silvio stared, confused.

"You have the wrong idea about me, Silvio. You think I'm an assassin. I'm not. I never take anyone by stealth. I always give my prey a choice."

Silvio didn't think this advice would help. "A choice between death and captivity. How generous."

"A choice between staying with me and taking their chances on what comes after. Or they can leave. My companions are bound to me by choice. Maybe the wormkeeper's daughter will choose you."

Not likely, when her other choice was a senator— and the love of her father. Silvio turned to walk away.

Herlakin said, "Maybe, if she hadn't already chosen you, she'd be dead."

When Silvio turned around to answer, to argue, Herlakin was gone. He snaked his way down the narrow streets toward Cànpo San Pantalon with the great golden hound at his heels. Boralisa smelled love. But even if Oriela survived a second or third kiss, which was by no means certain, what future would she be choosing if she chose him? And how could he even speak to her to ask? Pantalon was not likely to let Silvio in the house after Alichin's behavior.

Silvio came to the canpièlo gate where Oriela had waited for him on Christmas Eve, when he'd gone in over the roof. There was lantern light moving in the fondaco at Ca' Morèr, the thud of an oar being laid inside a boat. Silvio moved into the shadows, stroked the hound's golden head, and waited for the light to go out .

Instead, light poured into the canpièlo from his left.

A small, curly-headed silhouette burst out of Ca' Pevari with a tall one behind it. Boralisa turned to look, ears cocked.

Xandro turned in the middle of the yard and hissed, "You're a swine, Toni Pevari." The *putto* was very drunk. "You're a swine, and Marco Tron is the doge boar of the republic of swine!"

Boralisa followed him across the yard until he stormed out the gate. Then she returned to Silvio's side, wagging her tail at Antonio.

Antonio came to stand by Silvio and said quietly, "I gave him up for Lent." The weight of this admission hung in the cold air for a moment. Antonio looked at Boralisa. "*Ehi*, I know that dog."

"Republic of swine?" said Silvio.

"Tron will denounce Xandro to the Signori di Notte if I interfere between him and Oriela." Antonio looked at Silvio. "And since I find you standing in the canpièlo staring at my neighbor's window with that look on your face, I think I'm probably about to interfere."

Silvio didn't waste time asking what Xandro would be accused of or why the threat held more weight than one against Antonio himself. He only said, "Interfere how?"

"Come with me." Antonio moved off toward Ca' Pevari.

Then Silvio said, "Why, Toni?" No more games about calling him *Siòr*, Silvio decided. A man who tells you his most dangerous secret and then helps you break into a lady's bedchamber deserves to be addressed as a friend.

"Because she loves you," Antonio said, stopping but not turning around. After a pause, he added, "And because watching you suffer is bad for my health."

Silvio followed him into the house. Antonio said, "I'll create a distraction with the small boat, and you can go in over the roof while Pantalon is looking at me." When they got to Antonio's room, he handed Silvio a length of black cloth. "You're not very surreptitious in those patches."

"Your *tóga*?" Silvio had to hold the collar over his head to keep it from dragging on the floor. "How am I supposed to leap off a roof in this?"

"You've done it before."

"Not onto that tiny balcony. I doubt even Zan Polo could do it."

"Zan Polo is only human."

"Toni, what do you think I am?"

"I don't know. A monkey. An angel. You're something different." Antonio collected a battered-looking Spanish *chitarra* from the corner and headed for the door.

"Can you play that thing?" Silvio asked. He had only ever seen Antonio with a lute.

Antonio said over his shoulder, "Not really, but it won't matter."

Once out the window and up on the roof, Silvio moved slowly in a crouch, keeping the *tóga* wrapped around him as best he could without tripping on it. In the shadow of the chimney he waited until Antonio's boat reached the corner between the Grand Canal and the rio. This took some time, as the man was rowing it himself and had only the most rudimentary notion of how it should be done. When he tried to turn the corner, Silvio had the urge to jump into the water and push, but at last Toni managed to aim the sandolo's prow toward Ca' Morer.

Silvio slid down the roof to the eaves and perched there, ready to spring like a cat, studying the narrow bit of balcony—really more like a windowsill with a railing—in front of Oriela's shuttered window. When Antonio struck the first rush of chords (in a terrible imitation of the Spanish style), Silvio jumped.

54 Poor Marco

"**L**uca told me Ser Antonio drew his sword on Ser Marco." Pasquela slid the other sleeve off of Oriela's bodice and folded it on top of the skirt in the trunk. "He didn't say why."

"I think Marco was going to punch Silvio."

"What for?"

"I'm not sure. I don't think Marco saw Silvio kiss me." Oriela wriggled herself free as soon as Pasquela loosened the bodice laces. It had been a long night.

"Silvio did what?" Pasquela turned around with the bodice still in her hand. "Poor Marco. And after his father went practically hat in hand to yours." Oriela started with her hair, letting curls fall free one by one. "Not that your father was hard to persuade. I wonder if anyone will report that dowry."

Oriela stopped pulling pins from her hair. "Report it?"

Pasquela said, "Everyone knows it's over the legal limit, but it won't matter unless someone makes an official complaint. You see," she said, taking charge of the hairpins, "There are no real secrets in Venice. Only official ones."

"Everyone knows I'm promised to Marco?" said Oriela.

"They knew that before Marco knew it. But…Silvio kissed you?"

"I'm not sure he wanted to," said Oriela. She leaned forward while Pasquela brushed her hair. "He was acting strangely."

"He was acting strangely all night, from what I hear."

"Not like that. He asked Luca to take his mask off, and he wasn't—what's it's name?—Alichin anymore." She waited while Pasquela put down the brush and started plaiting the long braid down her back. "He was just Silvio, and he looked…" Her eyes fell shut for a moment, and she saw Silvio's face, stunned, staggered. Her first thought had been that Silvio had suddenly realized, like a sot waking up beside an ugly whore, that he had kissed a woman he found repulsive. But that made no sense. He had looked terrified. Of what? He wasn't afraid of Marco. At another time of year he might have had cause to fear the legal authorities, seducing a *nobile*'s betrothed, but it was Carnevale, when people routinely do far madder things without fear.

"He looked like what, Dama?"

"Like someone had already punched him."

"Did he say anything?"

"No, he wouldn't talk to me. And then Marco showed up."

Pasquela put the brush down and shook her head. "Poor Silvio."

"Why poor Silvio? A minute ago it was poor Marco."

"Well, poor both of them." Pasquela turned to leave. "Good night, Dama."

Oriela pulled the warming pan from the bed and slid between the sheets. Her toes were still cold, so she laid her dressing gown across the foot of the bed. Then she snuffed the candle and drew the curtains. She told herself to be reasonable. Marco wasn't so bad, as long as he didn't drink too much. He was clearly taken with her, the way he drew her close, greedily, between those lion's teeth as if to eat her up. How could she hope to do better than a senator? It would make Papà so happy. Wasn't this the best possible fate?

Curling into the warm spot and squeezing her pillow, she found herself imagining it was Silvio and pondering his strange kiss. She had felt his hunger, she was certain, and it was not at all like Marco's. She had felt flooded with something at once comforting and feral, a wild serenity that made her head spin and her skin sing. It was still singing, every pore craving his touch the way dry earth craves a storm. She felt herself hiding again in the warmth between his shoulder and his chin, unwilling to move, scarcely to breathe, and when she breathed the air was all Silvio, scented with new leather and old linen and fir trees. Why had he smelled and tasted like trees?

It was becoming clear that the life she wanted didn't live in a palazzo. Not that she had a choice now. The deal was struck; Marco's father would come by to sign the papers tomorrow. Come Easter, she'd be a Christian and a wife. Marco would clip her wings and keep her in a cage to sing only for him. But now part of her soul would always be in that shadowy portico, in Silvio's arms, where she could fly.

A noise outside disrupted her confused thoughts. Singing? Oriela pulled on her dressing gown before venturing outside the bed's enclosure, but the room was already growing chilly. Since she was about to open a window, she reached for the warm something that was folded on top of her clothes chest. Only when she was wrapped in it did she feel the spun silk and realize it was her mother's mantle. Papà must have put it there in celebration of her betrothal.

Unwilling to follow where that thought would lead, she drew the chair aside and turned the window latch. Somewhere else in the house, Pasquela was laughing. With the window open, she could hear the song through the shutters.

"*Chi passa per sta strada e non sospiro, Beato s'e.*"

Antonio was singing at full voice, accompanying himself on a badly-tuned *chitarra*.

A banging of shutters, and Papà's voice: "Toni, why are you serenading my housekeeper?"

Pasquela's laughter echoed off the wall of Ca' Foscari and down the canal. Oriela started to fold her shutters open, but the right one wouldn't budge. Someone was out there, pressed flat against the wood on the narrow balcony. A moment later Silvio slipped around to the inside of the shutter, a finger to his lips. Outside, Antonio's song begged the beloved to come to her window lest the singer fall dead in the street.

Grabbing Silvio's hand, Oriela pulled him inside and led him on tiptoe across the portego to Mamma's sitting room, the room farthest from the canal and the windows. She went to the fireplace and brushed off the coals, added tinder and fresh wood, and then closed the door. Silvio was standing in the middle of the room, looking stupefied. She could see now that he was still wearing his patched costume underneath some darker garment that hung to the floor.

She motioned him to the fireside chair and said, "I assume you're here to tell me what's going on."

He said, "I'm not sure where to start." Instead of the chair, he sat on the footstool in front of it. "I don't know if you'll believe me."

She said, "I will if it's the truth."

He looked at the struggling fire. Ignoring the iron poker, he took a stick from the kindling basket and prodded the coals. "My mother is Aivana. A *fata* of the Flora tribe."

Oriela had an alarming sensation as if her liver were freezing. "No wonder Papà doesn't like her. He believes they stole me." What did this have to do with tonight?

Silvio glanced her way. He looked slightly amused, just for that moment. "Rescued, if you ask them."

"Then they also killed my mother?"

"No, she was dead when Auntie got there. You were

crying..." He looked away, serious again. "The *fate* are fairly harmless, but it seems they can pass along un-expected characteristics from their male ancestors should they bear sons with a human. Piero's dancing charm..." He looked down, and Oriela was suddenly very conscious of her bare feet.

"And you?"

Silvio pulled the mask from his belt. "I take after her uncle who kills people with his kiss. He made this." His eyes crinkled a little, "Your father calls him the French demon." He paused, took a breath, put the mask away. "I found out when Clarissa died."

Clarissa. Where had Oriela heard the name? She re-called Antonio's voice: *Which of you was Clarissa's sweetheart.* She said, "Your friend, the one with the—pipes."

Silvio's head hung so low it looked like he would fall off the stool. Oriela raised his face with her hand, felt the late-night chin stubble rasp her palm.

"It was Martedì Grasso then, too," he said, leaning into her hand, eyes shut.

"So when you thought I'd fainted," Oriela said. Silvio pried her hand from his face and squeezed it.

"You didn't move. I thought..." He took her other hand, crouching at her feet as he had in the courtyard at Ca' Pevari, when he'd made fun of love. So she hadn't been imagining it—the pain behind the mockery. This time as he squeezed her two hands, his gaze was full of such fierce tenderness she could hardly breathe.

"Your Mask," she said, the moment replaying in her mind—*Luca, please!*

He said, "He didn't make me do anything I didn't already want to do. If I had hurt you..."

The shame and self-reproach in his voice was palpable. Oriela slid from the chair and wrapped her arms around his shoulders, pulling him closer, stroking a patch of velvet below his neck as if to calm the cloth. She kissed his forehead and heard him gasp, felt his back stiffen even as he pressed his rough cheek to hers, kissed the air beside her face like an old friend, and slid his hands around her waist under the mantle. When she kissed the corner of his mouth, she tasted tears.

She whispered, "The only way you can hurt me now is to let Marco have me."

"Then I won't," he said with barely enough air to make a sound, and his mouth closed on hers, flooding her senses again with the wild sweetness of his soul. If this was what had killed Clarissa, she had died happy.

In that moment of heady silence, a slight shuffling in the portego made Oriela look to the door. Light was shifting in the crack below it.

"Someone's coming," she whispered, and they scrambled to their feet as the door opened.

55 Cheap Linen

Pantalon had been too excited to go to bed and was in his study working on the marriage contract when Antonio started singing. Now he left the papers on the desk and went out to the portego. He stepped out onto the central balcony for a better view of whatever Antonio was up to. That boy never had been able to let Carnevale end.

"*...e non sospiro, beato s'e...*" Antonio was on a boat in the middle of the small canal, singing in the light of a stern lantern. He had apparently rowed the sandolo himself. Shutters slammed open above him from Pasquela's room.

Antonio called, "Pasquela, my sweet shrimp, my Venus in a clam shell!" Something splashed into the water a foot or so off his bow. Down below, the boat room door opened a crack.

Pantalon leaned out and said, "Luca, capsize this drunken idiot for me, please."

A top-floor shutter creaked open at Ca' Foscari, then another. Lights appeared in windows up and down the Rio. Pantalon glanced out to the left, toward Oriela's window. Was she really sleeping through this? A larger splash made Antonio fall down in the boat.

"Well thrown, madóna!" said Luca. Someone at Ca' Foscari clapped.

Pantalon bent over the balcony and twisted around to look up. "Pasquela, I hope those aren't my roof tiles."

"No, Sióir," said Pasquela, "Only your potted plants."

"God's teeth, woman! Not the jasmine!"

Antonio called from the bottom of the boat, "She bedecks me with flowers!"

Pantalon wondered again why Oriela hadn't seemed to notice anything. Still leaning out over the water, he looked at her window again. One shutter hung half-folded in the middle of the tiny balcony, neither closed nor fastened open to the frame.

So she had looked out. And then come back inside without latching the shutter. What was inside the house that was more interesting than Pasquela throwing flowerpots at Antonio in the middle of the Rio?

Pantalon went back inside and heard hushed voices coming from Margarita's sitting room. Had Elisabeta come over to gossip? At this hour? He lit candles in the portego sconces as he passed them, leaving his own on the credenza where the glass and silver would multiply its light. One voice, he now heard, was a man's. Who else would Oriela want to talk to in the middle of the night?

He opened the sitting room door just as his mind was hitting upon the terrible answer. And still he wouldn't believe it of her, not until he saw the creature standing there in the dim firelight, his ridiculous patches dark against the white tunic. An Aivàn, in Margarita's room. The costume was half-concealed by something long and dark that Pantalon recognized, with some confusion, as a tóga. It hung loosely from Silvio's shoulders and covered his hands to the fingertips.

Oriela was standing just behind him with Margarita's mantle draped loosely from her elbows. Had Silvio been—touching it? Beneath it she wore only a dressing gown over her camisa. Her feet were bare.

Pantalon wished he'd thought to grab a sword from over the portego fireplace. For a moment, rage and panic vied for control of his mind, and then he was at war. He had been in enough battles, both at sea and in the corridors of the Palazzo Ducale, to be able to keep his head in the face of this intrusion. He looked his opponent up and down and said coolly, "I don't sell cheap linen."

"Siór?" Silvio looked confused. A good start.

"I find you in my house, tripping over Antonio's tóga," here he permitted himself a small, sour laugh, "And I can only assume you're here to replace that catastrophe you're wearing." He pulled a twig from the fire to light the candles by the embroidery frame.

"This catastrophe?" Silvio gestured toward his colorful legs and looked at Oriela. In Bergamasco he said, "I wouldn't replace it for the world."

"I refuse to imagine any other reason for your presence here, with my daughter, in her mother's sewing room."

As he lit the last two candles, Pantalon watched Oriela from the corner of his eye while he said to Silvio, "Have you heard our good news? My daughter is going to marry a senator. Just after Easter. We'll be having a modest gathering this Sunday to celebrate the betrothal." He noticed Oriela pulling the mantle back onto her shoulders, wrapping it tighter.

Pantalon blew out the twig. "Oh!" he said as if startled by the insight, "That's why you're here. Yes, I'll hire you for the festivities at my house. Of course I can't make any promises about Ca' Tron. Ser Marco may have reason to be displeased with your work." He turned to toss the twig into the fire. "By the way, I don't plan to make an official complaint about that little stunt in the Piazzetta. It was Carnevale, after all. However, I am a little concerned that Luca wouldn't tell me what you and Oriela were doing before Marco caught up with you," He smiled benevolently in his daughter's direction. "I wonder whether it has anything to do with why you are here now."

Silvio said, "La Dama and I were talking, Siór." The words came out just a little too quickly. A half-truth, maybe.

"Talking about what?"

A moment of hesitation, of calculation, before Silvio said, "She expressed to me that she is unhappy with this match and would prefer another suitor."

A useful word, *expressed*. There are so many ways one might do it. "Another suitor? Did she *express* who that might be?" He stared hard at Oriela as he said this, waited. "Who, Silvio—Ser Antonio? The Doge?" When his gaze finally returned to Silvio, he filled it with the bland mockery that always had a withering effect on politicians. "You?"

"Yes, him." said Oriela, stepping into the light at last.

Pantalon avoided her gaze, letting the moment lengthen, making her stand there and watch him warily, and said to Silvio, "The idiot for hire? She can pull better suitors than you out of the lagoon in a fish-net."

"That's true, Siór," said Silvio. "But might I suggest we allow the lady to choose a fish she prefers?"

Unbelievable. The boy had balls of bronze, he'd give him that. In the tone he'd employed to demand surrender from Turkish captains, Pantalon said, "You are not going to hinder my daughter's happiness." The menace in his voice would have sent a more sensible man running.

The Fool stood his ground. "I give you my word, Scior," Silvio said, again using his own language, "I will never allow anything to do that." The creature's voice was mild, but there was something in those freakish yellow eyes that gave Pantalon a chill and made him wish he had stopped for a sword after all.

"Next I suppose you'll be telling me you love her," Pantalon said, refusing to take his eyes off Silvio. There were no weapons in Margarita's room, only thread and cloth, needles and . . . scissors. Iron shears, a freshly sharpened pair Oriela had left out on the sewing table, half-buried under a swatch of dove gray satin. He had been annoyed earlier when she forgot to put them away.

Silvio said, "I don't think anyone with a heart of flesh could know Oriela and not love her, Sióv."

"And what's your heart made of, Silvio the Mandrake, son of Viola dei Fiori?" Pantalon lowered his voice. "Do your kind even have hearts?"

Silvio went pale. "My kind, Sióv?"

Pantalon didn't look at the sewing table, but he moved closer to it as he said, "Can you bleed at all?" He slid his other hand under the satin and tucked the shears into his palm.

Oriela was looking at his closed hand. "Papà," she whispered, stepping slowly between him and Silvio. "What are you...?"

Pantalon moved her aside, almost gently, and pointed the open shears at Silvio. "A nosegay with a nail in it. Pasquela put it on there, didn't she? To keep you away."

"Actually—" Silvio said, but Pantalon didn't let him finish. Using the open points of the blades, he started to prod Silvio out to the portego.

"I know what you are. You, your brother, your mother. What do the Aivani have against Ca' Morèr? Why must you keep trying to steal my child?" He snipped the thread holding one of the patches, and it pulled away from Silvio's tunic, dangling like a leaf.

"No one's stealing me, Papà." Oriela was grabbing at his arm, trying to get the shears.

"*Maladeta!*" This time he pushed her away hard. She stumbled over a chair and into the credenza, knocking three goblets to the floor with a musical crash. "The evil that took the innocence from your soul still pursues you, and this devil is a part of it."

"There's no devil here, Papà."

Pantalon jabbed the shears at Silvio's chest, cutting away part of another patch, then another, shredding Oriela's work as he pressed the ragged creature toward the open balcony.

Pantalon heard Pasquela's footsteps on the kitchen stairs. Oriela was calling for help, slowed by the broken glass at her feet. He had to get Silvio out of the house before his housekeeper came to the devil's defense. Lunging forward, he grabbed Silvio's tunic and parted the blades. He pushed him against the doorframe and squeezed the shears closed on both layers of cloth, slicing into Silvio's skin.

"*Ai!*" Silvio looked down at the two patches of dark red spreading across the linen.

Oriela screamed and tugged on the back of his zimara. He shrugged it off as Pasquela, rushing into the fight with no clear idea what was happening, pulled Oriela away and held her, trying to quiet la dama, giving Pantalon time to get rid of his unwanted guest. He drove Silvio through the open doorway onto the balcony with a slashing blow that bent the shears against Silvio's collarbone and cut a gash in his shoulder. He was surprised at how easy it was to maneuver the agile *bufon* onto the railing and hoist him up and over. The iron must be weakening him already.

Antonio's stern lantern was disappearing around the corner toward the Ca' Pevari water door, and the neighbors had closed their windows and doused their lights.

"I'm curious," Pantalon murmured in Silvio's ear, "Can a forest devil swim?"

Silvio clung to the rail with one hand for a moment, said, "Oriela, *t'amó*," and then Pantalon sliced the backs of his knuckles and watched him fall.

"Have you lost all of your wits, old man?" Pasquela swatted the top of his head as he turned back into the portego. Oriela squeezed past them both and onto the balcony, calling Silvio's name, then Luca's, Antonio's, and Silvio's again. She was leaning far out over the balustrade, wailing and shouting. Pantalon noticed red smudges on the stone where she stepped. This time when windows opened along the canal, they emitted angry shouts.

Pasquela pulled her back inside saying, "Hush, Dama. Luca will fish him out." She closed and latched the tall shutters and then the glass door.

"Pasquela," he said, "Go make sure Luca doesn't let him back up here."

"But the glass," said Pasquela, holding onto her mistress.

Pantalon took his daughter's arm and said, "Sweep it later." He waited until Pasquela had retreated, protesting, down the stairs, and then said, "Enough of this nonsense. In the morning we'll go to church together, just like you said you wanted. Think how splendid you'll feel with that cross of ashes on your face when Ser Marco comes to call."

"Papà, I can't marry Marco."

"You're not thinking clearly, Oriela. That devil has you under some kind of enchantment—"

"Silvio is not a devil. He was baptized." Oriela stepped away from him, her eyes hard with fury. "At least *his* father thought his soul was worth saving."

"You can water an acorn all you want, but it will never grow into an olive tree."

She turned toward her chamber door, heedless of the glass on the floor. He caught her with her hand on the latch.

"How can you stand there, in her mantle, and defend that Aivàn assassin? Are you determined to break my heart?" He intended this as a rhetorical tactic and only after he said it realized that he meant it.

"Silvio didn't kill Margarita." She took a step toward him until her face was inches from his, and her voice turned brittle. "No one killed her, Papà. No evil spirits. No sorcery, no plots. Mamma just died!"

When his hand struck his daughter's face, Pantalon was at least as surprised as she was. He retreated and leaned on the credenza, kicking aside the costly shards. Was it mad of them, his countrymen, to place such value on things that could break so easily? He felt suddenly very old. When his eyes caught his passing face in the big silver platter, he was more than half expecting to see the horrible Magnifico mask with its goat-hair eyebrows, was dismayed that it was only his own face. Had he actually just done that, stabbed an unarmed Fool and tossed him into the frigid water to die?

"Of course," Oriela said with a chilling calm. "What was I thinking?" Tears rolled quietly over the angry red mark on her cheekbone, but her icy gaze never wavered. "It's not the Aivani you despise. It's me. The only wicked thing that ever entered your house was me."

She went into her room and slammed the door, leaving a red toeprint on the threshold. He moved to follow her but found Pasquela blocking his way.

56 White Magnet

Silvio thrashed in the icy water. Someone was prodding him with a piece of wood.

"Take the oar, Maìstro!" Luca was on the lowest stair of the boat room doorway, standing up to his knees in the Rio, bent over the thing he was holding.

"The oar!"

Silvio grabbed at the wood with his bleeding hand —he'd forgotten it was hurt, couldn't feel anything but the cold—and it slipped, and he reached with the other, and finally felt himself drawn through the water toward the dock.

Antonio was shouting somewhere, and Luca said, "Stay in the boat, Siòr. I have him." A pair of big, dark hands plucked Silvio into air that seemed even colder than the water, Luca muttering, "...does he think, I want to spend all night pulling fools out of canals?"

Silvio tried to walk beside Luca into the boat room, but he couldn't figure out where his feet were. Luca half-dragged him inside and wrapped him in an old blanket.

The Morèr gondola had been stripped of her Carnevale finery and now bobbed naked beside her heavier, cargo-bearing colleague, drowsing under a canvas cover that was pulled halfway along her sleek length. Upstairs was not so quiet. Hearing Pantalon's voice raging overhead, Silvio tried to pull away. He stumbled and found Pasquela suddenly on his other side, helping him up.

"Oriela...?" His teeth rattled together, making it hard to say anything more. He coughed tightly.

Pasquela said, "I'll look after her, Maìstro. Luca, take him home."

Silvio thought he was arguing with Pasquela about this, but the next thing he was aware of was a sharp pain in his shoulder and Piero's voice.

"...bit of it broken off in there, can you see?"

Antonio's: "Almost got it..."

Silvio opened his eyes—they had been closed? For how long?—and found he was in Piero's bed, propped on what must be every pillow in the house. His wet clothes were off, and he was covered in blankets except for the shoulder, but he still felt like the frigid saltwater had replaced the blood in his veins and he'd never be warm again. A bandage already held a poultice to the cut on his chest, and Smeraldina was wrapping his hand while Piero and Antonio poked and mopped at his shoulder. What had been going on at Ca' Morèr while he was lying here useless?

"Toni—" Speaking caused Silvio to start coughing again. "Is Oriela...?"

Antonio said grimly, "Luca won't let him hit her again."

"Again!" When Silvio pictured Morèr striking the daughter who had tried so hard to win his trust, he felt an ache worse than any damage the shears had done.

Antonio said, "Should I fetch the barber?"

"No," Piero said, "Get Del Verde."

Antonio said, "The maskmaker?"

"Unless you know a good alchemist who's awake at this hour."

Antonio shrugged and said, "I'll get him."

Smeraldina tied off the bandage on his hand while Silvio cursed his own stupidity. He'd only made things worse by confronting Pantalon. And what if Oriela were safe for now? Ser Marco would come in the afternoon, and they'd bully her until she signed the contract, and then Marco would be free to take her, and Silvio had promised not to let that happen, but how was he supposed to rescue her (steal her?) before morning?

As if to answer, there were voices in the sala.

Antonio was saying, "...any idea how much trouble you got me into with that thing?"

Brugliera came in, leapt onto the bed and started licking Silvio's shoulder. Next came Herlakin—with his antlers showing!—followed by Antonio and a woman who looked for a moment like Pasquela. Then the *malöcc* dropped away and Oriela was staring at the bed, her hand to her mouth. The gesture drew attention to the growing bruise on her cheek.

Silvio said, "You rescued yourself."

"He helped," said Oriela, indicating Herlakin, "And the other dog, the gray one. But look at you!" She came and sat on the edge of the bed.

Silvio touched her face. "I'm sorry."

She laid her head carefully on his good shoulder.

Antonio said, "This rascal says he's your cousin."

Silvio grimaced. "Something like that."

"Didn't I say you were something different? Oh, here." He tossed a purse onto the bed. "Your wages from the Alati."

Silvio weighed the bag. "This must be twice what we agreed to." And it would be Antonio's own money. The *conpagna* never paid this promptly.

"You were twice as entertaining as we expected," Antonio said with a grin.

Piero said, indicating Brugliera's tongue, "Is that your cure?"

Herlakin shrugged, "It might be hers. But here's what you wanted. Powdered white magnet. Sprinkle the bandage with it, and the effects of the shard will clear out in a day or so." He spoke of the rare alchemical crystal the way Smeraldina might mention oregano. To the hound he said, *"Permesso,"* and she moved aside. Herlakin was threading a curved silver needle.

Oriela straightened and said, "Luca will met us at the end of the calle by Ca' Pevari, as soon as you're dressed.

I don't think anyone will recognize the boat—it looks like a traghetto—but we need to be away before Papà wakes up."

Silvio couldn't think of anything to say to this, so he kissed her—for the first time without fear. He heard Antonio say, "Bravo." Herlakin and Piero were doing something uncomfortable to his shoulder, but Silvio wasn't paying attention. Oriela was with him; there was no such thing as pain.

57 Terraferma

Papà would sleep till dawn. Oriela had heard the great dog Beladona padding through the house, spreading drowsiness, just before she found herself wide awake, looking up at a stranger who stood with his back to her dying fire, his antlers making shadows like winter trees on the opposite wall. She had't been alarmed, which only now seemed odd. She'd said, "You must be Viola's uncle."

She'd dressed in the cold room without embarrassment, and the Aivàn handed her Mamma's mantle.

"I can't take this now," she'd said.

"No? I hear you've found a husband."

She'd started to say, *Not the one Papà wanted,* but she realized before the words were formed that Margarita hadn't left this choice in the hands of her beloved. A *nobila*'s possessions were hers to give, and she had given them to her unseen child. As Oriela wrapped herself in the warm silk, she'd thought—or maybe said—"He'll miss it."

"He misses her. Having her cloak all this time hasn't changed that." The reply might have come from her mouth, from her mind, or from the Aivàn. Viola's uncle was a strange person to talk to.

She wrapped it now around the two of them, herself and Silvio, huddled in the boat. Luca had filled the hull with cushions and attached an unmarked felze to shield his passengers from casual view. Boralisa snoozed in the bow. Viola's uncle had assured Luca that the dog's presence would make the gondola—a distinctive shape even unadorned—resemble a small fishing boat. Silvio's wheezing quieted at last, and he buried his face in her neck and kissed her throat.

Oriela held him and stroked his hair. Ash Wednesday was dawning. She was supposed to have spent the day repenting, shedding her lifelong curse. It was perhaps the only thing she regretted about leaving.

Yet she was renouncing her old life, the one where she believed the touch of Silvio's people had cursed her. Curses lived in lies and pride and the desire to be well thought-of, in the life she had thought she wanted. In Marco's palazzo. Fear lived there, cheek by jowl with the murderous rage she had seen on her father's face as he sliced into his helpless opponent's hand, watched him fall, and walked away as if he had tossed out a chamberpot. Tears rose behind her eyes. Papà! He had so very nearly loved her.

The water glowed deep blue in the early predawn when Silvio finally fell asleep. There was no other boat traffic yet. The only sounds were Silvio's soft breath and the steady swirling of Luca's oar, the water echoing the cadence of Venetian voices, the lagoon whispering. Was it calling her back or saying farewell?

She looked over her shoulder, past Luca's feet at the long-shadowed city, at the deadly beauty of its reaching towers, its watching windows. The rising sun cleared the rooftops, and she turned to look out over the bow. Dawn struck the distant mountains of the *terraferma*, and their boat was bathed in light.

Author's Note

The non-English words in this book are not mis-spelled Italian. They are either Veneto or Bergamasco, regional dialects that once held the status of independent languages, just as the regions of Italy were not one country but many independent city-states.

The term *aivàn* is from Ludovico Pizzati's English/Venet dictionary and is translated as "mythical forest dweller," which leaves wide room for interpretation. I have chosen to use it as an umbrella term for all the non-human folk who have populated Europe's wild places since before the time of Aeneas, whether fauns, nymphs, minor gods, Befana (a.k.a. Gulfara), or faeries large or small.

Herlakin, the leader of the Wild Hunt, is one of the more ancient of these beings. The similarity between his French name (in England he's known as Herne) and the name of the Commedia dell'Arte's most famous and enduring Mask has been noted by many theatre historians. By the mid-1500s this Mask will be known as Arlecchino and eventually, in other countries, Harlequin.

Interested readers can now search online for more information about this fascinating theatrical genre and its impact on the history of stage and film in Western society. My characters are only working on the earliest formative stages of its development, and their performances are not yet fully Commedia dell'Arte, but the Masks they're using will find their way into the full flowering of the form.

While on the subject of Commedia dell'Arte, I want to thank some of the expert performers who have offered guidance on the background and spirit of Arlecchino, especially Fabrizio Paladin, Cristina Coltelli, and Ian Thal.

Further gratitude goes to the members of the Souhegan Fiction Writers: Sue Spingler, Josanna Thompson, J. Michael Robertson and Kathleen Ferrari O'Connor; to my professors and classmates at Southern New Hampshire University's MFA program and especially my faculty mentor Ben Nugent; to Mark Ferraro-Hauck for giving me my start in Commedia dell'Arte as Pantalone all those years ago; and to my parents and my son Patrick for their continual support.

Made in the USA
Middletown, DE
29 October 2020

22921040R00229